PENGUIN

LAYLI AND

NEZAMI GANJAVI (1141–1209) is considered the greatest romantic epic poet in Persian literature. A Sunni Muslim born to a Persian father and a Kurdish mother, he lived most of his life in his hometown of Ganjeh, in present-day Azerbaijan. He was married three times; all three of his wives predeceased him, and, rarely for a Persian poet of his time, he wrote with apparently heartfelt and surprisingly personal eloquence about his affection for them and his sorrow at losing them. His introduction of an element of mysticism into his romance narratives is an innovation that was followed by most of his many imitators.

DICK DAVIS is the foremost English-speaking scholar of medieval Persian poetry in the West and "our finest translator of Persian poetry" (*The Times Literary Supplement*). A fellow of the Royal Society of Literature and an emeritus professor of Persian at Ohio State University, he has published more than twenty books, including *Love in Another Language: Collected Poems and Selected Translations*. His other translations from Persian include *The Conference of the Birds*; *Vis and Ramin*; *The Mirror of My Heart: A Thousand Years of Persian Poetry by Women*; *Faces of Love: Hafez and the Poets of Shiraz*; and *Shahnameh: The Persian Book of Kings*, one of *The Washington Post*'s ten best books of 2006. Davis lives in Columbus, Ohio.

NEZAMI GANJAVI

LAYLI AND MAJNUN

Translated with an Introduction and Notes by
DICK DAVIS

PENGUIN BOOKS

PENGUIN BOOKS

An imprint of Penguin Random House LLC
penguinrandomhouse.com

First published in the United States of America by Mage Publishers 2020
Published in Penguin Books 2021

LIBRARY OF CONGRESS CATALOGING-IN-PUBLICATION DATA
Names: Nizāmī Ganjavī, 1140 or 1141–1202 or 1203, author. | Davis, Dick, 1945– translator.
Title: Laylī and Majnun / Nezami Ganjavi ;
translated with an introduction and notes by Dick Davis.
Other titles: Laylī va Majnūn. English.
Description: First. | New York : Penguin Books, 2021. | Series: Penguin classics |
Translated from Persian into English.
Identifiers: LCCN 2020041422 (print) | LCCN 2020041423 (ebook) |
ISBN 9780143133995 (paperback) | ISBN 9780525505778 (ebook)
Subjects: LCSH: Nizāmī Ganjavī, 1140 or 1141–1202 or 1203—Translations into English.
Classification: LCC PK6501.L33 D53 2021 (print) |
LCC PK6501.L33 (ebook) | DDC 891/.5511—dc23
LC record available at https://lccn.loc.gov/2020041422
LC ebook record available at https://lccn.loc.gov/2020041423

Printed in the United States of America

Set in Minion Pro with Requiem Display

This translation is dedicated to Asghar Seyed-Ghorab,
with my gratitude for his infectious enthusiasm for
Nezami's poetry

Contents

INTRODUCTION

The earliest Persian romances, like those in a number of other cultures, are hybrid affairs in which their authors' mores and sensibilities are blended with something that has originated in a remote time or place, or both. They have notable affinities, for example, with Greek prose romances written in the early years of the Common Era* and their plots never take place in the here-and-now of their medieval authors' lives. Although they present themselves as accounts of things that have actually happened somewhere at some usually unspecified time in the past, they always retain an aura of fantasy and make-believe. In a way they are dream narratives, filled with delicious and exciting situations, characters, and details that could almost never be present in such an unambiguously attractive form in the world of their medieval authors and audiences. We can see this dream-hybridity clearly in the three earliest Persian verse romances that have come down to us: *Varqeh and Golshah*, by the late tenth- to early eleventh-century poet Ayyuqi, was in origin an Arab story, *Orwa wa Afra*; Ayyuqi's contemporary Onsori (*c.*961–*c.*1039), based his verse romance, *Vameq and Ozra*, of which only a few pages have survived, on the Greek story

---

* For more on this, see Dick Davis, *Panthea's Children: Hellenistic Novels and Medieval Persian Romances* (New York: Bibliotheca Persica, 2002).

Metiochus and Parthenope (of which, also, only a few pages survive);* and Ayyuqi and Onsori's slightly later contemporary Gorgani based his romance, *Vis and Ramin*, which was written in the 1050s, on a pre-Islamic Persian story which he thought was Sasanian (the Sasanians ruled Iran from 224 CE to 651 CE) but which scholarship has shown to have originated in the era of the Sasanians' predecessors, the Parthians—that is, around the time of Christ, give or take a century or two. It's not unfair to the earlier authors to say that there is a noticeable jump in literary sophistication between Ayyuqi and Onsori's narratives on the one hand and Gorgani's on the other (a major reason for this is probably that Gorgani lived in a post-Ferdowsi period, and it was Ferdowsi in his epic poem the *Shahnameh* ("The Book of Kings")—completed in 1010—who can be said to have taught Persian poets how to write coherent and compelling narrative verse).

None of these authors invented the stories they tell in their romances, and in fact they would not and could not have done so as they considered them to be in some sense at least "history." The qualities that define romances—the idealized and apparently hopeless love affairs, their equally idealized and hopeless heroes and heroines whose separation and seemingly endless trials form the basis of the plot, the presence of someone in authority who has a legal right to demand the heroine's virginity but never exercises this right (a figure that goes back to the prototypical Western romance, the Persian tale of Panthea, Abradatus, and King Cyrus, as

---

* See Tomas Hägg and Bo Utas, *The Virgin and Her Lover: Fragments of an Ancient Greek Novel and a Persian Epic Poem* (Leiden: Brill, 2003).

told in Xenophon's *Cyropaedia*)—would not stand in the way of such a perception. The tales took place in other countries (and this was true even if their origin was in pre-Islamic Iran, reflecting the words of L. P. Hartley: "The past is a foreign country: they do things differently there,"* for in the tenth and eleventh centuries Persian literary nostalgia for pre-Islamic—pre-seventh century—Iran had recreated it as an almost fabulous country of the mind where almost fabulous things had once commonly occurred), and who is to say what may or may not have happened in such exotic places?

Like Ayyuqi's *Varqeh and Golshah*, *Layli and Majnun*† was in origin an Arab story (purportedly about lovers who had lived in the seventh century CE), and we know that it had been current in Iran before Nezami composed his version of the tale, because a number of Persian poets who preceded Nezami (Rudaki, Rabe'eh, Manuchehri, and Gorgani) mentioned its lovers in their poetry; it's clear from these pre-Nezami references that the fabled pair were already known for the characteristics which Nezami was later to ascribe to them—that is, Layli's incomparable beauty and long-suffering

---

* The famous opening sentence of L. P. Hartley's novel *The Go-Between*, first published in 1953.

† The name Layli is better known in the West as Layla, which is how it is pronounced in Arabic, and is of course Arabic in origin. However, in Persian it looks as though it could be pronounced "Layli," and we know that Nezami did in fact pronounce it in this way because he often rhymes on the name's last syllable, always treating it as the "ee" sound, as in "sweet" or "free." This pronunciation is now standard in Persian, which is why I have kept "Layli" in this translation. Names of course often change in pronunciation as they migrate from one language to another (as, for example, in the English pronunciation of the French place name Paris or of the Italian forename Beatrice).

patience, and Majnun's love-madness that led to his forsaking human society to live among wild animals.

Nezami, whose birth name was Ilyas Ebn Yusuf, became famous as a major poet within his own lifetime, and his reputation has never been seriously challenged since his death. Given his fame, it seems somewhat strange that relatively little is known about his life; probably the main reasons for this are firstly that he was not a poet who was affiliated with a specific court for a long period of time, though this seems to have been Nezami's own choice rather than a failure to find a suitable position, and it was court poets who tended to be memorialized; and secondly that he lived his whole life in what was then a relatively provincial part of the Persian-speaking world, away from the main centers of literary activity, which makes his recognition as an important poet in his own lifetime all the more remarkable.

He was born in Ganjeh (hence his second name "Ganjavi") around 1141 in what is now independent Azerbaijan and he died around 1209, having almost never left the immediate area of his birth. Born to a Kurdish mother, he was orphaned at an early age and brought up by an uncle. He married three times. His first wife, who was probably named Afaq (though the meaning of the line in Nezami's verse in which she seems to be referred to has been disputed), was said to have been a slave-girl presented to him by a king who admired his poetry. Instead of keeping her as a concubine, as would have been expected, he married her; she was the mother of his son Mohammad, whom he mentions with obvious affection a number of times in his poetry, and she died while still relatively young. His other two wives also predeceased him; his

poems include laments for their deaths, and at one point he bemoans the fact that for a while the completion of each of his narrative poems coincided with the death of one of his wives. The affection and regret Nezami displays in these passages is not a conventional trope of the period in which he lived (and could even have been derided as signs of weakness or effeminacy), which means that there is no reason not to take his expressions of grief at face value; this together with the tenderness he shows toward his heroines (particularly Shirin, in *Khosrow and Shirin*, and Layli in *Layli and Majnun*) has earned him the reputation of being a poet who was, for his time, preternaturally affectionate, considerate, and respectful toward women. His geographical isolation seems to have entailed his isolation from most of his fellow poets, and the only poet with whom we know he was in touch was Khaqani, another inhabitant of Azerbaijan who was patronized by some of the same local princes who patronized Nezami. Khaqani (*c.*1120–*c.*1199) was mainly a panegyrist whose verse displays much of the didactic seriousness, complicated rhetoric, and occasional obscurity that we find in Nezami's own poetry (and in a similar fashion to Nezami, Khaqani also wrote an affecting memorial poem on the death of his wife).[*]

---

[*] Nezami and Khaqani's intellectual closeness is also indicated by the fact that Khaqani too seems to have been fascinated by pre-Islamic Iran: his most famous poem uses the ruins of Iran's pre-Islamic capital, Ctesiphon (outside Baghdad, and largely despoiled and dismantled so that its stones could be reused in the construction of Baghdad's buildings), as the basis for a profound and moving meditation on the passing of empires and dynasties; it seems obvious in this poem that Khaqani is not merely going through the expected ritual requirements of the genre but is saying something of real import to himself.

Most of what we know about Nezami is gleaned from his own prologues and epilogues to his narrative poems, and out of these rather scant materials, together with his impression of the poet's character from his writings in general, the British scholar of Persian literature E. G. Browne (1862–1926) wrote a striking character portrait of the poet. Browne praises Nezami for decidedly Victorian virtues, almost as if he were relieved to have finally found a Persian poet whose personal life he could praise unreservedly in terms that his largely middle- and upper-class British audience could appreciate. (Browne was always on the lookout for ways to persuade his readers—who, as citizens of the British Empire in its heyday, were likely to assume any number of automatic and unwarranted prejudices about anyone not British, particularly anyone Moslem or Asian, or both—that there was much to admire in Persian/Iranian civilization). Nevertheless the little that we know about Nezami does support Browne's characterization, or at least nothing we know about the poet contradicts it:

> And if his genius has few rivals amongst the poets of
> Persia, his character has even fewer. He was genuinely
> pious, yet singularly devoid of fanaticism and
> intolerance; self-respecting and independent, yet gentle
> and unostentatious; a loving father and husband, and
> a rigorous abstainer from the wine which in spite of its
> unlawfulness served too many of the poets (especially
> the mystical poets) of Persia as a source of spurious
> inspiration. In a word he may justly be described as
> combining lofty genius and blameless character in a

degree unequalled by any other Persian poet whose
life has been the subject of careful and critical study.[*]

Although we don't know much about his life as a whole,
Nezami tells us quite a lot about the circumstances of his
composition of *Layli and Majnun*. He writes that after his first
romance, *Khosrow and Shirin*, had been greeted with acclaim,
a local king, Shirvanshah Akhsetan, suggested to him that he
put into Persian verse a version of the Arab story *Layli and
Majnun*. Now the "foreign country" that Nezami had visited
for *Khosrow and Shirin* was pre-Islamic Iran as mediated by
Ferdowsi's epic the *Shahnameh*, a poem that celebrated Iran's
pre-Islamic civilizations at great length, and the *Shahnameh*
was also to be the source of the romances Nezami would write
after *Layli and Majnun*. Given such a focus on pre-Islamic
Iran, an Arab story would seem to be of limited appeal to him,
despite the precedent set by Ayyuqi almost a century before
in his rewriting of an Arab story (*Orwa wa Afra*) as a Persian
romance (*Varqeh and Golshah*).[†] Nezami dithered; one doesn't

---

[*] E. G. Browne, *A Literary History of Persia*, in 4 vols. (Cambridge: Cambridge
University Press, 1969), 2:403.

[†] Some Iranian commentators on the poem—for example, Abdol Hossein
Zarrinkub, in *Pir-e ganjeh dar jostoju-ye nakoja-abad* ("The Sage of Ganjeh and
His Search for the Unknown Region") (Tehran: Maharat Publishing House,
1372/1993), 111–33—have gone so far as to depict Nezami's *Layli and
Majnun* as a covert condemnation of Arab customs and culture, implying
that Nezami looks down on Layli's people for living in tents rather than in
cities, and characterizing Layli's father as a "typical" cruel Arab patriarch,
with the implication that the kinder father of Majnun is somehow "typical" of
Persian values. But both fathers are presented as Arabs, so that one could
just as easily say that Nezami sees Majnun's father as the "typical" kind Arab
patriarch. It is true that Nezami often "Persianizes" the story, but this would be
expected of a Persian poet retelling a non-Persian narrative, and hence nothing
pejorative or condemnatory of non-Persian customs need be read into it.

want to offend a king; on the other hand, he clearly did not find the story especially attractive. And then, he writes, his son Mohammad sat beside him "like my shadow," and kissed his father's feet, and said, "When you wrote *Khosrow and Shirin* / You made people's hearts rejoice / You should write *Layli and Majnun* / So that it can be the partner-jewel [of *Khosrow and Shirin*]." Mohammad goes on to say that now that such a splendid king as Shirvanshah has made this request, his father should not hesitate but get on with the task. And so Nezami agrees to write the poem.[*]

When this exchange took place, Mohammad was only fourteen years old, and it seems a little strange that Nezami should take his son's advice on such a serious matter. Nezami also tells us that he wrote the poem very quickly (in four months, which as the poem is about 4,500 couplets long, means that he wrote at the rate of over thirty-five couplets a day nonstop for 120 days—a quite astonishing feat given the unfailingly high finish of the poem's rhetoric).[†] Both these statements, that he wrote the poem on the advice of his fourteen-year-old son and that he completed it in four months (that is, in a hurry), look like ways of subtly evading responsibility for the poem, as if he is saying, "It wasn't my choice to do this, and if you don't like it, well I wrote it very quickly." Nevertheless, as the first (or at least first surviving) verse narrative version of the Islamic world's most famous

---

[*] *Layli o Majnun*, ed. Behruz Sarvatiyan (Tehran: Tus Publishing House, 1363/1984), 49–50, lines 40–49.
[†] Ibid., 52, line 91.

love story, *Layli and Majnun* has over the centuries proved to be by far Nezami's most popular work, and has achieved the same status as the archetypal love narrative in the Islamic world that Shakespeare's *Romeo and Juliet* has gained in the West. And although the two works are very different in many ways, they share a number of similarities—the frequently lush and extravagant rhetoric of the language, the doomed nature of the lovers' relationship played out against a background of familial enmity and strife, and the violent emotions that tear a society apart and leave mourners and desolation in their wake.

Layli and Majnun's enduring popularity has had one unfortunate effect: it has survived in many different manuscripts and, as is often the case with repeatedly copied works, there are major discrepancies between the manuscripts, even those generally deemed to be "good." No manuscripts have survived that were written within two hundred years of the poet's death, so there was obviously plenty of time for widely differing versions of the poem to become current. Many lines and some whole episodes that certain but not all editors feel are genuine are missing from particular manuscripts, and printed editions of the poem often differ from one another quite radically.*

---

* For this translation I have relied mainly on the version edited by Behruz Sarvatiyan and cited above. One great advantage of Sarvatiyan's edition is his extensive commentary, which is extremely useful in elucidating many of the poem's more obscure passages.

In a number of senses, Nezami is an intensely literary poet. His chosen pen-name, Nezami, immediately alerts us to this: the literal meaning of the word, *nezam*, from which it derives is "order," in the sense of a correct arrangement, and one of its subsidiary meanings is "ordered" language, that is, verse, so that the name "Nezami" can be taken as meaning, among other things, "a poet," or even "the poet." Evidently poetry was not something he took up lightly, as he is effectively saying that for him it defines his identity, it makes him who he is, and perhaps one factor that persuaded him to write the poem is that its main male character is a poet, someone with whom Nezami could presumably identify, at least in part, and whose "poems" as they appear in the narrative Nezami, as the author, would have the opportunity to write. This literariness is also apparent in the way that he is preternaturally aware of his three main predecessors in the field of Persian narrative poetry, and it is clear that he attempts both to incorporate their example into his own work, and to go beyond them. The predecessors in question, all of whom completed their major works in the eleventh century, are Ferdowsi (*c*.940–1020), the author of Iran's major epic poem (the *Shahnameh*); Gorgani, the author of the first major verse romance in Persian (*Vis and Ramin*); and Sanai (1080–*c*.1131), who wrote the first important collection of anecdotes linked together to form a mystical-didactic poem (*Hadiqat al-Haqiqat*, "The Garden of the Truth"). It is broadly true to say that Ferdowsi and Gorgani used their poetic skills to tell the stories that were for them the reason that they wrote poetry at all,[*] whereas Nezami used

---

[*] In Western terms we can say that they are written in accord with Cato's

the stories he told as vehicles to display his truly prodigious poetic skills, and also as a quasi-didactic medium. This is not at all meant as dismissive of Nezami, who by any standard is a major Persian poet, but it does indicate differences of emphasis and purpose when we compare his practice with that of Ferdowsi or Gorgani; for them the story was paramount, and therefore clarity of meaning was also paramount. It's not an exaggeration to say that clarity of meaning often seems to come quite low on Nezami's scale of criteria as to how a poem should be written.

Nezami wrote five long narrative poems of which *Layli and Majnun* is the third; his first, *Makhzan al-Asrar* ("The Treasury of Secrets"), is a collection of mystical anecdotes that is clearly modeled on Sanai's *Hadiqat al-Haqiqat* (as is his propensity for moralizing, something he does in all his narrative poems), while the other four, including *Layli and Majnun*, are all romances. Three of these (*Khosrow and Shirin*, *The Seven Portraits*, and a version of the Alexander romance) draw their inspiration from material in Ferdowsi's *Shahnameh*, while Gorgani's romance, *Vis and Ramin*, is the main stylistic source for all four, though what was probably Nezami's last poem, on Alexander the Great, is a romance in the broader sense of the word when applied to medieval narratives, and not a love story. Nezami's treatment of Alexander is instructive: he divides this final poem into two halves, the

injunction, "Rem tene, verba sequentur" ("Grasp [that is, concentrate on] your subject, the words will follow"). It seems significant in this respect that both wrote one major poem that was to have far-reaching effects on subsequent Persian poetry, *and as far as we know, virtually nothing else*, as if they saw the telling of this one story as the single central focus of their life's artistic work.

first depicting Alexander as history has done—that is, as a conqueror of much of the then known world; the second as an ethically oriented proto-Sufi* who travels the world in search of knowledge and gnostic insight. The didacticism inherent in such an undertaking echoes that of Nezami's first long narrative poem, the *Makhzan al-Asrar*, and the three intervening love stories are also, more quietly but nevertheless palpably, imbued with this ethical/mystical quality; unlike the romances written by Nezami's predecessors, they are concerned as much with ethical and spiritual admonition as with hedonism and the search for an elusive this-worldly soul-mate.

The presence of *Vis and Ramin* as Nezami's model is most noticeable in his first romance, *Khosrow and Shirin*, which is in the same meter as Gorgani's poem and includes episodes imitated from it wholesale, but it is also present in *Layli and Majnun* (in, for example, a long astrological description of the night sky, and passages of reproach by one of the lovers comparing his or her situation to that of the addressee and couched in an "I-am-this/you-are-that" form, as well as in a

---

* A Sufi is a practitioner of Sufism, a mystical interpretation of Islam that has taken a number of different forms in different places at different times, but generally involves some kind of at least mental (and often physical) retirement from the secular world, as well as a codified system of spiritual growth whose ultimate aim is union with the divine. Much of Persian poetry is pervaded with Sufi ideas, and a great deal of medieval Persian verse that looks to the uninitiated like secular love poetry can be, and was often meant to be, interpreted allegorically as Sufi in orientation. Nezami's romances are particularly important in this regard as they are major examples of a transition from wholly secular love stories in verse, to verse romances that can be interpreted in Sufi terms while still retaining enough narrative realism to be (more or less) plausible as secular narratives.

number of stylistic mannerisms). What is perhaps especially interesting is that Nezami often incorporates material that he has found in Gorgani's work into his narratives even though this considerably stretches the reader's credulity, suggesting that literary precedence is finally more important to him than narrative verisimilitude. In *Khosrow and Shirin*, for example, following Gorgani, he includes a paraclausithyron (a lover vainly begging for admittance to his beloved's residence) that takes place in a long and violent snowstorm. This seems plausible in Gorgani's case as, in his *Vis and Ramin*, the episode occurs in Marv in Central Asia where Gorgani may well have believed that such snowstorms were likely, but seems improbable in Khuzestan and Kermanshah where *Khosrow and Shirin* is set; Khuzestan virtually never has snow, and even Kermanshah, where snow falls in the mountains, has a milder climate than Marv, making the kind of raging storm Nezami has adapted from Gorgani's model an unlikely occurrence.

More glaring instances of the uneasy fit between material adopted from Gorgani and utilized in Nezami's work are present in *Layli and Majnun*. In general these derive from the fact that *Layli and Majnun* is in origin an Arab story that takes place in an Arab setting, although at various points Nezami treats it as if it were a poem about the Persian nobility taking place in an aristocratic or even royal Persian milieu. Numerous examples of this could be adduced, but two should suffice to illustrate the nature of the discrepancy. The description of the wedding gifts presented by Ebn Salam to Layli's family would be appropriate in a royal Persian romance such as Gorgani's, but seem too lavish, costly, elaborate, and aris-

tocratic for a marriage between pre-Islamic Bedouin tribes in what are described as desert regions of Arabia. Even more telling is the fact that Layli's family live in tents, as is appropriate given the tale's pre-Islamic Arab origin, and as Nezami reminds us from time to time, but then Layli is also described as going up onto the roof of her dwelling, which at such moments is clearly conceived of as a Persian palace, in order to see if she can glimpse her beloved, or if not him someone to take a note to him, just as Gorgani's Vis had done in *Vis and Ramin*. At such moments we have to forget that she lives in a tent, and view her as being like Gorgani's Vis—that is, as a princess whose home is a solid structure with a roof that can be walked on. One thing that Nezami does not take from Gorgani is the way in which the earlier poet placed his poem's heroine (Vis) front and center in his narrative, leaving the hero (Ramin) to occupy a relatively secondary role; Nezami's romances are concerned primarily with a male hero who is supported, complemented, even educated by a heroine (or, in *The Seven Portraits*, heroines) whose role is nevertheless distinctly subordinate to that of the male protagonist. In this foregrounding of the male of the pair, Nezami was followed by virtually all his many imitators.*

Because of the many poets who took Nezami as a model, he is considered to be the greatest of romance writers in Persian, which has led to a corresponding under-evaluation

---

* Zabihollah Safa lists some of Nezami's imitators in the genre of romance: confining the list to major figures, it still includes a considerable number of poets—Amir Khosrow, Dehlavi, Khaju, Jami, Hatefi, Qasemi, Vahshi, Urfi, Maktabi, Fayzi-ye Fayazi, Ashraf Maraghi, and Azar Bikdeli. See *Tarikh-e adabiyat dar iran* ("The History of Literature in Iran") vol. 2 (Tehran: Ferdows, 1336/1967), 809.

of his own model, Gorgani. Perhaps the main reasons for this are firstly that Gorgani's one romance is entirely worldly and carnal, containing no hint of Sufism whatsoever, and secondly that it includes material drawn from its pre-Islamic sources (for example, a brother–sister marriage) that an Islamic audience might well find offensive; it is perhaps also relevant that Gorgani seems to be much more interested in his heroine than in his hero, a bias that, as we have seen, Nezami emphatically "corrects." In introducing a didactic, spiritual, and implicitly Islamic, or at least Sufi, dimension into the romance narrative, Nezami redefines the genre, making Gorgani appear to be merely a precursor who hadn't yet worked out how a romance "should" be written. Interestingly enough, although Nezami acknowledges both Ferdowsi and Sanai as models and predecessors, he does not mention Gorgani, despite his major stylistic and thematic debts to him, which suggests that he may have felt that Gorgani had wasted his talents on unworthy (carnal—not didactic, not spiritual) subject matter that he, Nezami, did not wish to be associated with.* Nezami is very much a "how to live, what to do" sort of poet.† There is something non-

---

* Although Nezami doesn't mention Gorgani by name, in his *Khosrow and Shirin* he has his determinedly chaste heroine, Shirin, refer to Gorgani's adulterous heroine, Vis, with opprobrium as having "an evil reputation," one that she herself will be at pains to avoid. Nezami, *Khosrow o Shirin*, ed. Behruz Sarvatiyan (Tehran: Tus Publishing House, 1366/1987), 493, line 74. Later, the supposed immorality of *Vis and Ramin* became proverbial, and the fourteenth-century satirist Obayd-e Zakani wrote in his *Resaleh-ye sad pand* ("One Hundred Maxims"), "Don't expect chastity from a man who smokes hashish and drinks wine, or from a lady who has read *Vis and Ramin.*" *Kolliyat-e Obayd-e Zakani*, ed. Parviz Atabaki (Tehran: 1343/1964), 207.
† "How is it that you live, and what is it you do?" The speaker's question to

judgmental, unbuttoned, almost casual about Gorgani's moral posture, at least as it appears in his poem, when we compare him to Nezami; on the other hand we can say that, for all his tenderness and empathy toward his heroes and (especially) his heroines, there is something quite prim and proper, potentially even censorious, about Nezami, at least as he appears in his poems, when we compare him to Gorgani. E. G. Browne's rather Victorian Nezami, with all the pluses and minuses this implies, often seems about right.

As well as in his consciousness of his poetic predecessors, Nezami's preoccupation with poetry as a source for his verse is also apparent in a number of his figures of speech. For example, when he is describing the young Layli's extraordinary beauty, he concludes by saying that she is "The best line in a poem praising youth" (p. 5); Majnun's isolation from Layli "is like a line of verse without a rhyme" (p. 33); and when Layli is separated from Majnun her glances are "Sadder than are a thousand sad romances" (p. 103). The poems Majnun composes are also songs (the association of music with verse, any kind of verse, was strong in the medieval world, but strongest when it came to lyric verse, as the word "lyric" tells us), and when he is in despair he says of himself that he is "a tuneless song" (p. 184); describing his relationship with Layli he says, "And we're so mixed and mingled we belong / Together like two voices in one song, /

---

the old leech-gatherer in Wordsworth's poem "Resolution and Independence" of 1802.

And if we're ripped apart the song will be / A tuneless chaos, a cacophony" (p. 230).

Not only poetry is present as a vehicle for Nezami's figures of speech, but also poetry's physical manifestations, books and pages in books. A dying warrior is described as a "book [that] had no more pages left" (p. 74); when Majnun's father senses that he will die soon, he says "My page is written now" (p. 117); "Majnun's days were a black page" (p. 245) is how Nezami describes his hero in despair; and when Majnun leaves Layli, the poet uses the same metaphor: "He'd torn himself away, as if to tear / A page from one with which it made a pair, / While Layli was the facing page . . ." (p. 231). Words themselves, even letters of the alphabet, both as they appear and as they sound, are used in a similar way: a messenger describes Layli to Majnun by comparing her different features to the shapes of different letters (p. 147); Majnun says that he and Layli are "two letters that . . . make a single sound" and a little later they are "a single letter / Repeated, making one sound" (p. 230).

Nezami's relentless "literariness" is most apparent in the deliberate complexity of his rhetoric, which, to use a wholly anachronistic term, can perhaps best be described as "mannerist."* Persian literature's major historian Zabihollah

---

* Certainly it displays many of the characteristics ascribed to Mannerism in John Shearman's authoritative discussion of this Late Renaissance style in European art: Nezami's poem unfolds as a "refinement of and abstraction from nature," it is "conceived of in the spirit of virtuoso performance," and its poet would clearly agree with the notion that "complexity, prolixity and . . . caprice are beautiful . . . that virtuosity is something to be cultivated and exhibited, that art should be demonstrably artificial." See *Mannerism* (London: Penguin, 1967), 18, 81, 186.

Safa praises Nezami's style in terms that are both extravagant and appropriate, since it really does involve an extraordinary and almost incomparable display of literary skill, but he also adds:

> A fault some have found in his language is that sometimes—either in order to find new meanings and material when he becomes wrapped up in obscure imaginative flights of fancy, or when in order to create new locutions he manipulates and plays with language to an extravagant extent—it becomes difficult for the reader to understand a considerable number of his lines. It is also the case that, following the fashion of his time, Nezami uses many Arabic words not in common use in Persian, as well as a great deal of material and vocabulary taken from philosophy and other intellectual fields . . . the result is that many of his lines have received extensive commentary, and can only be understood with the help of such commentary.[*]

And we might add that, despite such assiduous explorations of possible meanings, Nezami's commentators quite often end a wide-ranging discussion of a line by tersely stating that the line's meaning remains unclear. Some popular editions of his poetry simply miss out the more opaque lines and passages, and as the plots proceed at an extremely leisurely pace, it is usually possible to do this with little or no loss of the overall sense.

The Italian writer Italo Calvino has described Nezami's poetry as follows:

---

[*] Safa, *Tarikh-e adabiyat dar iran*, 2:808.

The decorations of this verbal tapestry are so luxuriant that any parallels we might find in Western literature (beyond the analogies of medieval thematics and the wealth of fantasy in Renaissance works by Shakespeare and Ariosto) would naturally be with the works of heaviest baroque; but even Marino's *Adonis* and Basile's *Pentameron* are works of laconic sobriety compared to the proliferation of metaphors which encrust Nezami's tale and germinate a hint of narrative in every single image . . . Nezami . . . paints a visionary world full of erotic tension and trepidation which is both sublimated and enriched with psychological chiaroscuro . . . the unbridled licentiousness of the figurative language is an appropriate style for the upheavals of youthful inexperience.[*]

As Calvino indicates, Nezami avails himself of every possible figure of speech; metaphors and similes come thick and fast, very often in a manner that is typical of a great deal of medieval Persian poetry in that only the vehicle of a conventional comparison will be given ("narcissi" for eyes, for example, or "rubies" for lips, or "a cypress" for a beautiful young person of either sex, with no mention of actual eyes, lips, or a person in the text); he delights in puns, as well as in anaphora and grammatical parallelism between lines. Wherever possible he uses gorgeous and often unfamiliar language. In the preface to his translation of the *Odyssey*, T. E. Lawrence describes his approach as a translator: "Wherever choice offered between a poor and a rich word richness had it, to raise the color";[†] this

---

[*] Italo Calvino, quoted from "Nezami's Seven Princesses," in *Why Read the Classics?*, trans. Martin McLaughlin (New York: Vintage Books, 2000), 50–51, 52.
[†] T. E. Lawrence, *The Odyssey of Homer* (New York: Galaxy/Oxford University Press, 1956), first page (unnumbered).

was deliberately coat-trailing when Lawrence wrote it in the 1930s, but Nezami would have seen the remark as simply what a poet does. Given the intentional richness of his poetry, it is not surprising that he utilizes a number of rhetorical devices that are relatively rare in English; for example, he will often use, in the words of Dryden complaining about Ovid, "a dozen more . . . expressions poured on the Neck of one another and signifying all the same thing."* Here "the same thing" is the news that Majnun wishes to hear, that Layli is at last free of her unwanted husband:

> Tell me I'll see my longed-for ruby shine
> Freed from the darkness of her stony mine,
> Tell me the pale moon will break free at last
> From the fell dragon that has held her fast,
> Tell me that the officious bee has flown
> And left the lovely honey all alone,
> Tell me the garden's nasty owner's gone
> And that the hideous crows there have moved on,
> That nightingales replace them, that the rose
> Is cleansed of dust and wears her loveliest clothes,
> Tell me the blackguard's forfeited his head
> And that the treasure's guardian snake is dead,
> Tell me the castle jailer's dreadful fall
> Has left him dying by the castle wall . . . (p. 161)

---

* John Dryden, Preface to "Fables, Ancient and Modern," in *Of Dramatic Poesy and Other Critical Essays*, ed. George Watson (London: J. M. Dent, 1962), 2:279.

Occasionally Nezami will do the opposite and use a single metaphorical vehicle to stand in for a number of different referents mentioned in close proximity:

> *When jewelry made of pearls adorned the night,*
> *Making the darkness glitter with their light,*
> *Layli, the loveliest pearl, wept copious seas*
> *Of pearls as numerous as the Pleiades . . .* (p. 218)

In the first line "pearls" means "stars," in the third line "pearl" means "virgin," and in the fourth line "pearls" means "tears."

Or Nezami will set up a metaphor and then apparently subvert or rewrite it with an unexpected twist:

> *And when the scented curls of darkness lay*
> *Upon the pallid forehead of the day*
> *That like a Georgian girl shone palely white*
> *Till daylight was a curl cut off by night . . .* (p. 69)

The basic metaphor is clear—the day is like the forehead of a pale-skinned Georgian girl whose black curls resemble the encroaching night; but then suddenly it is day, not night, that is like a single curl—one that night cuts off. The metaphor as a whole means "night fell," but within it the curls are the night and then one curl is the snipped-off day.

Or Nezami can mention something, and when he has finished with whatever it is in its literal sense, he will use it to generate similes and metaphors for a few lines. This happens

when Majnun converses with a raven that then flies off and leaves him:

> *The startled raven flew from tree to tree;*
> *Majnun spread wings of all he had to say—*
> *The raven spread its wings and flew away . . .*
> *Night like a raven's sable wing descended,*
> *Bats woke up from their sleep, and day was ended;*
> *You'd say the stars were lamps that lit the skies,*
> *Or that they shone like ravens' glittering eyes.*
> *Majnun was like a lamp that gives no light*
> *As raven-darkness blotted out his sight . . . (p. 91)*

And after a few lines in which the raven is not mentioned, when Majnun sets off the next morning Nezami unexpectedly wrings one more, farewell simile from the trope:

> *Majnun flew like a raven here and there*
> *Or like a moth that flutters through the air . . . (p. 92)*

Calvino describes Shakespeare's work as possibly analogous to Nezami's, and for the anglophone reader certain of Shakespeare's rhetorical strategies provide parallels that can perhaps give an inkling of the nature of Nezami's language and the various ways that he deploys it. Some passages of *Layli and Majnun*, particularly near the poem's opening, are very similar to Shakespeare in one of his early styles, as exhibited in *Venus and Adonis*, for instance, or in some of Berowne's speeches in *Love Labor's Lost*—a style that delights in elaborate figures of speech to flesh out consciously decorative accounts of romantic and erotic encounters and their attendant joys and woes. When Nezami employs the flights of fancy and outré expressions that Safa remarks upon, his rhetoric can be like that of Shakespeare in some of his so-called problem plays, when metaphor and syntax are so jammed up against each other that paraphrasable meaning can momentarily seem at a discount while extreme mental struggle, frustration, or puzzlement is being presented. Toward the end of his poem—for example, in Layli's speech when she dies in her mother's arms—Nezami's language can have the stately, melancholy elevation and nobility that Shakespeare sometimes gives to those of his characters who are despairing victims of circumstance, a nobility that is more than a little self-conscious on both the speaker's and the author's part, but which is none the less moving, and perhaps even more so, for that (as, for example, Constance's speech in *King John* that begins, "Grief fills the room up of my absent child, / Lies in his bed, walks up and down with me" [III.iv.93–4], or Richard's in *Richard II* that begins: "For God's sake let us sit upon the ground / And tell sad stories of the death of kings" [III.ii.155–6]).

The question of Nezami's realism or lack of realism is not a simple one. As noted above, Calvino remarks on how "the unbridled licentiousness of the figurative language is an appropriate style for the upheavals of youthful inexperience," which is certainly a kind of realism, and Nezami can also use startlingly realistic metaphors, as for example when he comments on how Layli's "husband's watchful jealousy was spread / Like broken glass wherever she might tread" (p. 177). (The Persian here actually reads "like a broken diamond," but commentators gloss "broken diamond" as a metaphor for

broken glass, indicating that Nezami is using a metaphor within a metaphor—something he often does.) Yet much of the poem evades realism. At its center is the love between Layli and Majnun, but only one love scene is described as actually, really, happening; this is the last scene in which Layli and Majnun meet, when what has been for much of the poem the lovers' consummation devoutly to be wished—that is, their physical union—is passed up as irrelevant. The other love scenes, if this is what we are to call them, are all imagined, usually by Majnun; they are fantasies, would-be encounters, not records of real events. We might say that there are two exceptions to this relative absence of "real" love scenes: the description of Layli and Majnun as children in school together near the opening of the poem; and Zayd's vision of them, at the end of the poem, together in heaven after their deaths. That is, one happens before puberty, and the other after the lovers have transcended their bodies and left them behind as earthly dross. Neither scene involves sexuality, and the love between Layli and Majnun is presented as in some crucial sense bodiless. Given Nezami's predilection for ambiguity and multiple meanings, this suggests that their love is to be interpreted in a non-corporeal, spiritual, mystical fashion.

Is the poem, in fact, a Sufi poem, or at least a poem written so that it can be interpreted in Sufi terms? This is indeed how it has tended to be read in the Middle East, but not everyone agrees, and though some commentators, such as Asghar Seyed-Ghorab,* emphatically claim the poem as Sufi in orien-

---

* See Asghar Seyed-Ghorab, *Layli and Majnun: Love, Madness and Mystic Longing* (Leiden: Brill, 2003), passim.

tation, others, including Jan Rypka, the author of a highly respected, single-volume *History of Iranian Literature*, just as emphatically deny this: "The whole conception is entirely psychological without any trace of Sufism."* What is noticeable is that although the poem does not begin with any particular references to Sufism or Sufi beliefs, as it progresses such references become more and more numerous until by the poem's closing pages they are everywhere. When finally it is legally and practicably possible for Layli and Majnun to be together physically, carnally, they seem indifferent to the possibility and don't make any use of it; as far as the reader can tell, both die without having had any sexual experience at all. If we are to interpret the poem as being primarily about a "real," physical, bodily love affair, the lovers' behavior at this point is inexplicable. And Layli's dying words, which she asks her mother to convey to Majnun, are surely crucially significant:

> *Look at how wrong you were to think of you,*
> *Your self, so that this "you" was all you knew!*
> *So that for all your shrewdness you became*
> *Mad in yourself, your life, and in your name!* (p. 237)

Layli's dying admonition expresses a fundamental Sufi tenet, that in order to reach spiritual truth the self must be suppressed, destroyed, and transcended. Majnun's single dying phrase is also significant, as it is not the expected apostrophe, "O Layli" or "O my love," but "O friend . . ." (p. 251). This

---

* Jan Rypka, in *The Cambridge History of Iran*, vol. 5: *The Saljuq and Mongol Periods*, ed. J. A. Boyle (Cambridge: Cambridge University Press, 1968), 581.

could of course be taken as referring to Layli, but the Persian word Majnun uses here for "friend" is one of the commonest Sufi words for God, and it is likely that Nezami wishes us to take this as the primary meaning, even as Layli is also being invoked as a different kind of friend, as the "illusory" (human) love that leads to "real" (divine) love. The poem seems to present a gradual volatilization of reality, so that little by little the spiritual gradually replaces the physical; what begins with two children delightedly playing at love becomes a process of denial and askesis, a continual stripping away of the mundane and the physical in favor of the extraordinary, the asocial, and the spiritual. The poem's literariness, its unremitting artifice, can be seen as a metaphorical analogy for this; for Nezami, rhetoric rescues reality from the quotidian and transforms it into something "rich and strange," both beautiful and artificial, purging it of coarse contingency. In his verse we can say that literary artifice functions as a kind of purification of gross subject matter, one that is analogous to the spiritual purification his poems' protagonists undertake. I alluded above to the way that Shakespeare's example may help the anglophone reader come closer to what Nezami is doing in his poem, and a remark by the Shakespearian critic Marjorie Garber seems apposite here; she says that in his late play *Cymbeline*, a romance in a different but not wholly different sense from that in which *Layli and Majnun* is a romance, Shakespeare turns "away from mimesis, from the direct imitation of a human action, toward epiphany and transcendence,"* and this is

---

* Marjorie Garber, *Shakespeare After All* (New York: Anchor Books, 2005), 816.

perhaps the most useful way to understand the realism/lack of realism continuum that we find in *Layli and Majnun*.

Writing about the epic poet Ferdowsi, Shahrokh Meskoob contrasts Ferdowsi's poetry, which takes place in the real world, with that of the mystical poet Attar, in which "the real world is a 'sea of metaphor' and has no truth to it. Truth cannot be found in awareness and sobriety but in dreams."[*] Farid ud-Din Attar (*c.*1145–*c.*1221) and Nezami were contemporaries living at opposite ends of Iran (Nezami in the west, Attar in the east), and although one wrote romances and the other mystical/Sufi narratives, Meskoob's characterization of Attar's work is also relevant to the way that, as *Layli and Majnun* proceeds, Nezami spiritualizes quotidian reality, which finally for him, as for Attar, "has no truth to it." Attar's most famous poem is his *Manteq al-Tayr* ("The Conference of the Birds"), which describes a mystical journey taken by a flock of birds toward the vale of "poverty and nothingness,"[†] beyond which lie both their transfigured selves and ineffable divine Truth. The journey that Nezami's Layli and Majnun undertake is also a gradual stripping away of all that makes up worldly society—family, wealth, reputation, friends, home—toward the "poverty and nothingness" of lonely death, but just as the poverty and nothingness encountered by Attar's thirty birds leads to their union with the divine, so Layli's and Majnun's journey is the prelude to their union in

---

* Shahrokh Meskoob, *Armeghan-e Mur* ("The Ant's Gift") (Tehran: Nashr-e ney Publishing House, 1384/2005), 238.
† Farid ud-Din Attar, *Manteq al-Tayr*, ed. Seyed Sadeq Gowharin (Tehran: Bongah-e tarjomeh o nashr-e ketab, 1342/1963), 180, line 3232.

heaven, as seen by Zayd. Perhaps not coincidentally, when Attar's birds see the vision of Truth and ask its meaning, they are answered "without tongue,"[*] that is, silently; and when Zayd asks the meaning of the vision he sees (Layli and Majnun together in heaven), he is answered "with a mute tongue,"[†] that is, also silently. Two great contemporary poets who were perhaps quite unknown to each other bring their poems to a close in heaven, the vision of which is described in and by silence, as if both acknowledge that ultimate truth is ineffable, or at least beyond audible language, and so beyond poetry, no matter how ravishing, complex, startling, or marvelous that poetry may be.

DICK DAVIS

---

[*] Ibid., 235, line 4244.

[†] *Layli o Majnun*, ed. Sarvatiyan, 349, line 30.

LAYLI AND MAJNUN

THE BEGINNING OF THE STORY

Hear what the teller of this history said
By stringing speech's pearls on verse's thread.[1]

There lived an Arab king, whose excellence
Increased his splendid realm's magnificence;
Lord of the Amir tribe,[2] his virtues nourished
His prosperous country, which grew great and
    flourished.
The sweet breeze of his fame made Arab lands
More fragrant than the wine cup in his hands—
A lord of virtues, chivalry's copestone,
For worth—in all the world—he stood alone,
An Arab king, successful beyond measure,
Wealthy as Korah,[3] rich with endless treasure,
Attentive to the poor, and to his friends
A generous host whose kindness never ends,
As though Good Fortune were the soul within
His nature, like a pith beneath the skin.

But he was childless still, for all his fame,
And like a candle when it has no flame.
More needy than a shell for pearls, or than
A husk without its seeds, this desperate man

Longed for a son, for Fate to let him see
A fruitful branch spring from the royal tree,
Hoping that when the cypress seed was sown
Another cypress would have quickly grown,
So that a pheasant in the meadows would
Perceive a new tree where the old had stood,
And once that tree's allotted life had passed
He'd shelter in the shade the new tree cast.
A man survives if in the world somewhere
His memory lives within his son and heir.
And to this end he gave in charity
Money to mendicants perpetually,
Giving out gold to gain the moon; but though
He sowed the seed he saw no seedling grow.
He sought and did not find, for all his pains,
And rode straight on, and would not tug his reins
And stop or turn aside, and still it seemed
He'd never find the son of whom he dreamed.
(And if you seek like this in vain, accept
That this is not an outcome to regret,
Whatever good or bad is brought by Fate—
Look, and you'll see that it's appropriate:
That pearl you thought you wanted, look once more
And see that it's not worth your struggling for.
Many desires don't see the light of day
And men are lucky that they stay this way!
Men dash this way and that, all unaware
Of what is best for them and why or where;
The clues to how Fate works are hard to see—
Many a lock when looked at is a key.
Poor wretched man! A breath of wind's enough
To scatter all his dust—a tiny puff!

Be strong within this pit of little worth,
Consign to earth whatever comes from earth.)
But still he longed, like rubies in a mine
That vainly long for light to make them shine,
And since his longing had been so intense,
God gave a son to him, in recompense—
A child whose rosy body blushed as though
It shared a pomegranate's ruddy glow,
A shining jewel that made earth's sullen night
As radiant as the dawn's resplendent light.
When he beheld the son he'd hungered for,
The father opened wide his treasury door,
And as a rose sheds petals, in his joy
He gave out gold in honor of the boy.

He ordered that a wet-nurse take his son
And rear him with her milk to make him strong;
Time like another wet-nurse kindly smiled
And nourished with her strength the growing child;
Each time his lovely lips and milk united
Prayers were both written for him and recited,
And when they gave him food they also gave him
Their hearts that would do anything to save him,
And carefully they dabbed a dark blue dye[4]
Upon his cheeks, to thwart the evil eye.
When milk had touched his tulip lips, they grew
Like jasmine petals with their milky hue;
You'd say his milk was mixed with honeycomb
Or that his cradle was the full moon's home—
That moon in two weeks was as beautiful
As is the heavens' moon when she is full;

Qais was the name they gave the royal child
And faith's rites kept him pure and undefiled,
Growing in grace until a year had passed
And his perfection was now unsurpassed.
Love fashioned him, and love's bright jewel now shone
With greater luster from this royal son.

His happy second year, and third, were spent
In gardens of sweet kindness and content.
At seven, ringlets clustered round his face
Like tulips held in violets' dark embrace,[5]
From seven to ten his beauty and renown
Became the common gossip of the town,
From those who glimpsed his face astonished sighs
And prayers arose like winds into the skies,
A face that filled his father's soul with joy;
He knew the time had come to send the boy
To school, and so he chose a master, one
Who'd day and night take pains to teach his son.
Soon others, drawn there by his reputation,
Came to the same school for their education;
With hope and fear the children did their best
To learn their lessons and to pass each test—
Among these clever boys, a few girls shared
Their classroom, and the lessons they prepared.[6]
From different clans and tribes, from far and wide,
In school they were together, side by side—
And Qais's lips were rubies spilling pearls,
Reading his lessons with the boys and girls.

*

And from another clan, a different shell,
An unpierced pearl was in his class as well,
A young girl, nobly born, intelligent,
A girl as pure as she was elegant,
As splendid as the moon, as slender as
The comely shape a cypress sapling has.
Her playful little glances were like darts
That pierced not one but many thousand hearts,
Her doe-like eyes each moment seemed to slay
A world each time they looked and looked away,
Her face an Arab moon, and yet a Turk
In stealing hearts and suchlike handiwork.[7]
The hair upon her head was dark as night,
Her pretty face a garden of delight—
Her face framed by her hair appeared as though
A shining torch were flourished by a crow;
A tiny mouth of such sweet elegance,
A sugar grain whose savor was intense—
Her mouth was just like sugar, you might say,
If sugar routed armies in this way.
She seemed to be a charm against disaster,[8]
Worthy to join the pupils and their master;
She seemed life's hidden beauty, and in truth
The best line in a poem praising youth.
Her forehead's beads of sweat, her fragrant hair
Were all the necklaces she chose to wear,
Her mother's milk accounted for her eyes
And blushing cheeks, not make-up's specious lies;
Her tumbling curls, her little mole were all
The jewels she needed to be beautiful;
Her lovely hair was dark as night; her name
Was Layli,[9] and she set all hearts aflame.

And seeing her, Qais gave his heart away
(For love it seemed a paltry price to pay),
And Layli too loved Qais as he loved her,
In both their breasts young love began to stir.
Love gave them its new wine, which worked within
These two so innocent of guile and sin
(The first time that we're drunk's the worst of all,
No fall hurts like the first time that we fall);
Once they had smelled love's roses, come what may,
They were together all day, every day.
Qais gave his soul up for her beauty's sake,
He stole her heart, his soul was hers to take;
She saw his face and gave her heart, but knew
She must still act as chaste girls have to do.
Their friends were busy studying, while they
Were busy with the words true lovers say;
Their friends were making speeches, they delighted
In other words than those their friends recited;
Their friends debated grammar, their debates
Concerned the noble feelings love creates;
Their friends read learnèd pages, while they sighed
Unstintingly, since love was now their guide—
They only saw each other, unaware
Of all their many friends assembled there.

LAYLI AND MAJNUN FALL IN LOVE WITH EACH OTHER

As beautiful as Joseph to men's eyes
Each dawn the sun lit up the eastern skies,
Like a ripe orange, lovely to behold,
Turning the heavens from basil's green to gold;[10]
Layli sat with her chin propped on her fist
So beautiful that no one could resist
Her loveliness, and like Zuleikha's maids
Who cut their careless hands with sharpened blades,[11]
Those seeing Layli's beauty felt such thirst
They were like pomegranates fit to burst.
When Qais caught sight of her, his face turned sallow
As if it shared the dawn skies' golden yellow;[12]
Their mingled scents were sweet, as though no care
Or sorrow could survive when they were there,
But even so their mingled, bitter cries
Proclaimed their sadness to the morning skies.
Love came; its sword did not discriminate
But cleared the house, and left it to its fate—
It took their hearts, and gave them grief, and made
Them anxious, and bewildered, and afraid.
Their promised hearts became the subject of
Gossip that spread the rumor of their love;

The veil was torn apart, their tale was heard
On every side, repeated word for word,
From mouth to mouth the secret story flew,
What one man knew, another quickly knew.
The lovers were discreet, and tried in vain
To keep clandestine what was all too plain—
Although the musk deer's navel dries, the scent
Of musk stays richly strong and redolent;[13]
The wind that bears a lover's scent removes
The veil from all the loveliness he loves.
With feigned indifference they tried hard to hide
The naked passion that they felt inside,
And when did feigned indifference work? Can clay
Obscure the sun, or make it go away?
When longing eyes tell tales, how can there be
A story that stays veiled in secrecy?
And when a thousand curls have chained a lover,
There can be no escape, the struggle's over;
The theft has happened; if a lover's wise
He knows it happened right before his eyes.

Now he was smitten, lovesick, wholly caught
Within the tightening collar love had wrought—
He loved her beauty with such fervor, Qais
Could find no rest or peace in any place—
He only talked of her, which made him more
Impatient and distracted than before;
His heart and senses tumbled down pell-mell,
The sack ripped open and the donkey fell;[14]
And those who had not fallen as he had
Called him "Majnun," which means, "A man who's mad,"

While he with helpless cries give witness to
The fact that what they said of him was true.
Like barking dogs that drive away a fawn
To keep it from a newly growing lawn,
They cruelly teased Majnun, and hid the bright
New moon[15] his longing searched for from his sight.
Cut off from him now, Layli secretly
Wept pearl-like tears for him continuously;
Deprived of Layli's face, Majnun's tears dropped
In copious flowing floods that never stopped.
He wandered through the streets and market place
With anguish in his heart, tears on his face,
Singing sad lovers' songs whose melodies
And words delineate love's miseries,
And men yelled, as they teased and laughed at him,
"Majnun! Majnun!" before and after him.
While he, for his part, simply let things go,
Sunk as he was so deep in crazy woe,
As if he led an ass that slipped its reins
And let it wander off across the plains.
His heart was like a pomegranate split
In two, and he'd kept only half of it;
He tried so hard to hide his heart's desire
But who can hide a heart when it's on fire?
It was as if his heart's blood rose around him
Until it rose above his head and drowned him.
He grieved for her who could relieve his grief
And in whose absence grief found no relief;
He was a candle, useless in the day,
At night unsleeping as it burns away.
It was himself to whom he gave such pain,
For whom he searched for anodynes in vain—

He tore his soul out in the search, and beat
His head against the thresholds at men's feet.
As each dawn broke he scrambled to make haste,
To run barefoot into the desert waste.

Apart, these lovers had to be content
With seeking out each other's wafted scent—
He'd leave his house and make his way each night
To Layli's street, and wait there out of sight,
And in the dark he'd kiss her door[16] and then
Reluctantly he'd go back home again;
His coming was the north wind, but his leaving
Was like an endless age that's spent in grieving,
In coming he'd a thousand wings to speed him,
Returning home thorns sprang up to impede him,
He went like water flowing, but coming back
A hundred obstacles obscured his track,
And even when he walked with blistered feet
He felt he rode a horse to Layli's street.
With wind behind him and a pit ahead,
He went back home to torture, tears, and dread—
If Fortune waited at his beck and call
He never would have gone back home at all.

A DESCRIPTION OF MAJNUN'S LOVE

Majnun was lord of those dawn wakes from sleep,
The leader of the troop of those who weep,
The hidden guide along love's way, the chain
Of captives in love's perilous domain,
Music of mourners and the merchant of
Grief's exclamations and the cries of love,
Drummer whose iron drum's a warlike threat,
Chaste monk within the convent of regret,
An unseen sorcerer controlling devils,
A juggler of desire's rebellious evils,
A Kay Khosrow[17] who has no crown or throne,
Consoler of poor thousands left alone,
A lord who sends ant-armies to attack,
Whose throne's the saddle on an ass's back,
Straw shield against temptation, sentinel
Who safeguards an abandoned citadel . . .

Majnun the brokenhearted, this vast sea
Whose waves and breakers tumbled ceaselessly,
Had two or three companions who'd been taught
Like him the truth of all the pains love brought,
And with these friends each morning he would go
To Layli's street to wander to and fro.

Apart from "Layli" he paid no attention
To any other word his friends might mention—
A friend who brought up other topics near him
Remained unanswered, Majnun didn't hear him.
It was to Najd this lover's steps were guided,
The mountainside where Layli's tribe resided,
Since it was only there he hoped to find
Peace from the fire of love that filled his mind.
As drunks do, he would clap his hands, and then
He'd stumble and fall down and stand again;
He sang a love song, though he hardly knew
In his distraction where he was or who;
His eyelashes were wet with tears as he
Sang to dawn's breeze his lovesick melody:
"O breeze of dawn, arise and go to where
You play among the curls of Layli's hair
And say, 'The one who's sent you lays his head
Upon the dusty thoroughfare you tread.
He sends to you the gentle morning breeze
And tells the dust of all his agonies—
Send him a breeze from where you are, and give
Some dust from there to him, that he may live,
Since one who does not tremble for you must
Be worth no more than is the wind-blown dust—
To die of grief's the best a man could do
If he refused to give his soul for you.
I would not weep these floods if my desire
Did not consume me in love's raging fire,
And if love did not burn my heart, my friend
Would not be these sad tears that never end;

The sun itself that lights the whole world's skies
Could be burnt up by all my fiery sighs.
O hidden candle of my soul, beware,
Don't immolate your moth that flutters there;
The magic of your eyes has robbed me of
My sleep, since all my vitals burn with love.
Grief for you soothes my heart; you are both pain
And balm, the wound that heals my heart again.
Your lips are sugar—if you can, bestow
On me a taste of them before I go;
Given the state I'm in, that cordial would,
I know, do me a world of honeyed good.
The evil eye has struck, because, O moon,
Your eyes no longer look upon Majnun.
I reached up for ripe fruit, and to my cost
It tumbled from my fingers and was lost.'"

MAJNUN GOES TO LAYLI'S HOME AND
SINGS THERE

One evening—when the twilight air was soft
As silken clothes, the haloed moon aloft
Was like a shining earring, and stars shone
Like drops of mercury beside the sun
That set in crimson fire—Majnun, whose heart
Like mercury would spill and split apart,
With his few friends set out impatiently,
Reciting prayers and singing poetry,
To where his love lived; since his heart was lost,
Like one who's drunk, he did not count the cost.
Where Layli sat within her tent that day
The flap was tied back in the Arab way,
She saw him and looked lovingly and long,
He saw her and began his loving song.
Layli a cradled star half hid from sight,
Majnun her chamberlain on watch at night—
Layli removed the scarf that held her hair,
Majnun began the song of his despair;
In Layli's heart a harp played plangently,
In Majnun's head a lute twanged desperately.
Layli the dawn's light when the dark's diminished,
Majnun a candle self-consumed and finished;

Layli a garden in a fruitful land,
Majnun the scar of self-reproach's brand;
Layli the full moon with her radiant light,
Majnun a reed before her, weak and slight;
Layli a rosebush, bright and beautiful,
Majnun a suppliant, bowed and pitiful.
Layli I'd say was like a fairy-child,
Majnun I tell you was a fire run wild;
Layli a field that was still freshly growing,
Majnun a field when autumn's winds are blowing;
Layli who with the dawn was glad to rise,
Majnun a lamp whose flame at sunrise dies;
Layli whose teasing curls fell like a wave,
Majnun whose earring marked him as a slave;[18]
Layli who drank her draught of wine at dawn,
Majnun who sang sad songs, whose clothes were torn.
Layli sewed silk within, Majnun burned rue[19]
Against the harm the evil eye might do;
Layli was like a rose, while Majnun's eyes
Shed rosewater, the tears a rose supplies;
Layli let down and spread her lovely hair,
Majnun wept pearls in his abject despair;
Layli drank musky wine; wine's musky scent
Rendered Majnun both tipsy and content;
Her fragrance charmed him, she was gratified
He'd searched for her and hurried to her side.
Afraid they'd be found out, of meeting's dangers,
They kept apart and acted like two strangers—
Their only messengers were covert glances;
They acted prudently, and took no chances,
Pretending that the bridge across the river
Dividing them was broken now forever.

MAJNUN'S FATHER GOES TO ASK FOR
LAYLI'S HAND IN MARRIAGE

Distressed they were divided in this fashion,
Majnun sang songs describing his sad passion,
Singing them as he went to Najd each night
With one or two friends in the same sad plight,
Fate's victims, heartsick, wild companions who
Together made a brazen, shameless crew.
His father pitied his unhappy son,
His relatives complained of all he'd done
And gave him good advice that he ignored
And told him moral tales that left him bored;
Advice can be extraordinary and splendid
But when love comes, its usefulness has ended.
Majnun's poor father seemed bereft of joy,
His heart in anguish for his suffering boy;
Bewildered and unsure, he tried to find
Some way to ease his son's tormented mind.
He asked his family what was going on
And heard the selfsame tale from everyone:
"His head and heart are in a crazy whirl
And all because of such-and-such a girl."
And when he'd heard their words, he saw he must
In some way cleanse his rose of grime and dust—[20]

He thought: "This pearl of such widespread renown
Would be a shining jewel in Qais's crown,
He'd call the loveliest of her tribe his wife,
The cherished charm and darling of his life."
None of the elders of the tribe opposed
The plan that Qais's father now proposed—
They swore this unpierced pearl was suitable
To be the partner of their peerless jewel
And as a group then they prepared to make
This journey for the grieving father's sake,
Saying that, if they could, they'd have Majnun
Wedded at last to his adored full moon;
When Seyed Amiri[21] heard this, he smiled
And stopped his weeping for his lovesick child.
The group set off and solemnly proceeded
With all the dignity the mission needed.
Nobles and commoners came out to meet them,
Hospitably to welcome them and greet them,
They hailed them kindly, and then set before them
A friendly spread of victuals to restore them.
They said, "What is it that you need from us,
What subject are you eager to discuss?
Tell us your aim, and if you've some request
We'll be delighted to oblige a guest."
And Seyed Amiri replied, "We seek
To get to know you better, so to speak,
And this is to promote the interests of
Two splendid children, whom our tribes both love."
And then he singled out specifically,
Of all the group, the father of Layli,
And said, "My hope is our two children may
Be joined together on their wedding day—

My son's a thirsty desert boy, he knows
And watches where your limpid freshet flows,
A stream that flows with kindness will revive
A thirsty soul and keep its hopes alive.
So this is what I seek, I'm not ashamed
To make the proposition that I've named;
You know my fame and worth, you understand
That I'm the first of chieftains in this land,
I've both the followers and fortune for
The ways of kindly peace or vengeful war.
I've come to buy, you've something fine to sell,
Be wise, and sell, and all will then be well—
Name me a price that's reasonable, I'll pay it
And more than that, you only have to say it."
When Layli's father'd heard him, he replied,
"It's not for us, but heaven, to decide
These things; and though your tempting words might
      charm me
I can't walk into flames that could well harm me.
Though friendship is involved in your request
There's much to say against what you suggest:
Your son's good-looking but unsuitable,
His willfulness is indisputable;
He's mad, and shows it; it's ridiculous
To think a madman's suitable for us.
Pray that God cures him; once his problem's over
Will be the time to praise this faithful lover—
Until your boy is competent and sane
Don't bring this subject up to me again;
Who'd buy a jewel that's flawed? And who would make
A necklace with a thread that's sure to break?

Arabs love gossip, as you know full well;
If I did this, who knows what tales they'd tell!
Forget we've had this talk, it's sealed and done,
So let's consign it to oblivion."
And Amiri and his companions then
Saw they would have to go back home again,
That unfulfilled and disappointed they
Must now set off upon their homeward way,
As sad as travelers bandits have attacked,
Whose caravan has been despoiled and sacked.

And as they went they tried their best to heal
The dreadful grief they knew Majnun must feel,
Though all they said was thorns thrown on a fire
That only made the flickering flames blaze higher.
They said, "Our tribe has lovelier girls than this,
Idols who'll saturate your soul with bliss,
They've scented limbs, and linen clothes, they're girls
Whose lips are rubies and whose ears are pearls,
Lovely as pictures, and in everything
They're more enchanting than the flower-filled spring;
We have a hundred like this—why should you
Pick out a perfect stranger to pursue?
Let it be one of us whom you decide
To choose as your auspicious, noble bride,
The helpmate who'll rejoice your heart, the friend
Whose sugared kindnesses will never end.
How Layli's hurt your soul! You shouldn't let her,
It would be best for you now to forget her."

MAJNUN'S LOVE FOR LAYLI DRIVES
HIM INTO THE WILDERNESS

Their words were bitter to Majnun, who acted
Like someone who's distraught, deranged, distracted;
He was a dead man tearing off his shroud,
Ripping his clothes, and clapping, crying aloud—
Since what were clothes to one who in his mind
Had left both this world and the next behind?[22]
And like Vameq whose search for Ozra[23] led
Him over plains and mountains, Majnun fled
His house abruptly, tortured by distress
And eager to seek out the wilderness.
He tore his clothes and made a patchwork cloak,
And all the ties that kept him home now broke
And as a stranger, with his garments torn,
Wandering unsheltered, ragged, and forlorn,
Ready to kill himself[24] in his despair,
Calling on God, frantically, everywhere,
He ran at random, crying his lament
Of "Layli, Layli," everywhere he went.
Bareheaded, with torn clothes, he soon became
An object of contempt, a source of shame,
Welcoming good and bad, as though he could
See no distinction between bad and good,

And singing songs as lovely as the light
Cast by the evening star in Yemen's night.[25]
And every line he sang was learned by heart
By someone ravished by its artless art—
Men followed in his footsteps, wondering
At his despair, and wept to hear him sing,
Though he took no account of them, or of
Their interest in his songs and in his love;
The world was nothing to him now, he led
A life not still alive but not yet dead.
He fell down on a muddy rock, and pressed
Another heavy rock against his chest—
His crushed flesh felt like dirty dregs that stay
Within a wine glass to be thrown away,
Or he was like a bird kept from its mate,
Or candles melted to their final state.
Dust on his face, his branded heart in pain,
He spread a prayer mat on the dusty plain
And sat there weeping, moaning, "What can heal
The sorrow and the passion that I feel?
I've wandered far from home, and I don't know
My way back now, or where I ought to go.
Far from my home, my family who'd defend me,
Far from my old companions who'd befriend me,
My name and honor are a glass that's dashed
Against a stone and is forever smashed.
For me, Good Fortune's drum has split apart,
The drum that beats now tells me to depart—
Men say I'm drunk, or sometimes they prefer
To say love's made me an idolater,
And that as men carve idols to adore,
Layli's the idol I bow down before.

Or I'm a Turkish hunter's chosen prey
That's caught and lame and cannot get away.
But I'm obedient to my love and in my heart
I kill myself for her and take her part;
And if she says I'm drunk, I'm drunk, so be it
And if she says I'm wild, I'm wild, I see it—
Not even Fate could tame me or restrain me,
Or overcome my wild despair and chain me.[26]
Would that this wind of grief that's laid me low
Would end me here and never cease to blow,
Or that a thunderbolt would strike this minute
And burn the house that's me, and all that's in it;
There's no one to set fire to me, to turn me
Into a soul-consuming fire and burn me,
Or feed me to a monster of the sea
And rid the world of my disgrace and me.
Unworthiest of my time, whom people call
A maddened demon who's despicable,
I'm like a thorn that wounds my tribe, and shame
Is all my friends feel when they hear my name,
And now my blood can legally be spilled—
No one is punished when an outcast's killed.
Farewell, dear friends, companions of my heart,
Our singing days are over, we must part—
The wine glass that we shared, our friendship's token,
Has dropped upon the ground now and is broken,
My leaving shatters it, and we can say
My floods of tears have swept the glass away
So that no shards or fragments still remain
To cut my friends' feet with unlooked for pain.
And as for those of you who do not know
Or understand my sorrow, let me go,

I'm lost, don't look for me, don't try to speak
With one who's lost; for how long will you seek
To tire your anxious hearts out to confront me,
To hurt me and to drive me off and hunt me,
When I myself want nothing but to leave
This place where I can only sigh and grieve?

"O my love, I have fallen, come to me,
And take my hand in loving sympathy;
This wounded soul is yours; better that I
Should live to be your lover than to die.
Be kind, and send a message to revive
My fainting soul so that I stay alive.
I'm crazy, mad, disordered in my brains—
Why is your neck encircled with such chains?[27]
Don't snare your neck like this, if there's to be
A noose around a neck it's meant for me.
My heart weaves hopes, your curls tear them apart—
Who taught your curls this cruel, destructive art?
But help me now I've fallen, rescue me,
Raise me from overwhelming misery—
Here, take my hand, drag me from grief's abyss,
Come, take my hand, or give me yours to kiss.
It's sinful to do nothing when you can
Give aid and succor to a desperate man.
Why don't you pity me? Don't scriptures say
We should be merciful in every way?
But one who doesn't suffer cannot know
The pains that those who suffer undergo,
Someone who's full thinks that a scrap of bread
Will fill a man whom hunger's left half dead—

A man will know what burning is when he
Grabs something burning inadvertently.
We're human, both of us, but you're a green
Fresh leaf, a dry twig's all I've ever been;
Or think of gold and gilt, an ounce of one
Is worth the other weighed out by the ton.
O comfort of my soul, why have you taken
My soul from me and left me here forsaken?
What is my crime, what is my sin, apart
From loving you with my remorseful heart?
Grant me one night from thousands, for one night
Say that what's sinful is allowed and right,
Don't draw your head back from accepting me,
On my head be the guilt! Your chastity
Remains unblemished and the sin's my own,
One of the many that are mine alone.
But if you feel unbridled anger, when
Shall I find mercy at your hands again?
Should anger flare in you like fire, then drench it
With all my tears, and they will quickly quench it.
O my new moon, whose star I am, your glances
Are like a spell that dazzles and entrances—
I shall not ask the shadows for some sign
Of you; I fear the shadows, I fear mine,
I saw you in the shadows and you stole
My shadow from me, and my heart and soul;
What kind of love is this, what kind of shame?
This is cruel force, not love's beguiling game.
What kind of reputation have you brought me?
To have no reputation's all you've taught me.
If I can't be with you, I won't complain
Since it will mean that I can hope again.

A thirsty child dreams of a golden cup
That's filled with water, and he drinks it up,
But when he wakes, the dream no longer lingers
And thirstily he sucks and licks his fingers.
Pain racks my limbs, they and my body's frame
Seem bent into the letters of your name;
Love for you overflows my heart, so be it,
But others must not know of it or see it;
It entered with my mother's milk, believe me,
And when my soul departs it too will leave me."
He fainted, and fell headlong to the ground,
And sadly those who'd watched him gathered round.

Kindly they lifted him, and gently bore him
Back to his home, hoping this would restore him.
Love that is not eternal love, in truth
Is no more than the lustful games of youth;
True love is love that does not fade, or care
To step outside itself or look elsewhere,
It's not the love that dreams are built upon
That's always weakening till at last it's gone.
Majnun's love's emblem, and its noblest name,
Love's insight, wisdom, and eternal fame;
He bore love's weight as though he were a rose
Accepting gratefully each wind that blows;
And now like rosewater that still retains
The scent of roses, so his scent remains,
And I'll distill the scent of this sweet rose
Within the fragrant verses I compose.

MAJNUN'S FATHER TAKES HIM TO MECCA

Just as the skies are governed by the moon
So love for moon-like Layli ruled Majnun,
And every day his reputation spread,
As still more lovelorn fancies filled his head.
The man whose nature's like this breaks each chain
That keeps us stable, self-controlled, and sane—
Fortune deserted him; his father had
Despaired of him, convinced that he was mad,
And sought for help from God throughout each night,
Anxiously praying till the morning light,
Traveling to every shrine and holy place,
Returning unfulfilled in every case.
His friends and relatives all crowded round
Hoping that some solution could be found,
Each setting out a strategy or plan
To see if they could help this helpless man,
Until they said, "Mecca will open wide
The door of where his difficulties hide;
Mecca resolves all men's predicaments,
Both earth's entreaties and the firmament's."
And he replied, "That's where I'll take Majnun;
The time for pilgrimage is coming soon."

*

The time came, and he strapped a litter on
A camel's back, and there he placed his son
So comfortably he seemed the moon inside
A cradle, loved and rocked throughout the ride.
Emotion surged within his breast as he
Drew near to Mecca and its sanctuary—
Humbly this dweller in a desert land
Wept tears as numerous as grains of sand,
As bright as strewn jewels, scattered without measure,
Making this treasured place a place of treasure.
Gently he took his son's hand then, and stayed
A moment with him in the ka'bah's shade,[28]
And said, "My boy, this is no joke; it's where
Men can be cured of every curse and care;
Circle the ka'bah once, and you will find
You can escape grief's circling in your mind;
Just say, 'O God, release me from this pain,
Grant me Your grace, and make me well again;
Save me from this obsession, comfort me,
Show me the way to health and sanity;
Know love is my addiction and my master,
Free me from love's injurious disaster.'"
Majnun heard all this talk of love, and after
He'd wept at first, he was convulsed with laughter.
He darted forward like a snake, and touched
The ka'bah's stone, and as he grasped and clutched,
He said, "I'm like a knocker on a door,
A ring that waits but can do nothing more,
My soul is sold for love, and from my ear
May love's bright earring[29] never disappear!
'Detach yourself from love,' these people say,
But knowledgeable folk don't talk this way!

My strength is all from love, so wouldn't I
Fall prey to death as well, if love should die?
It's love that's made me, formed me, fashioned me;
If there's no love, what could my future be?
And may the heart that has no love to hide
Be borne away upon grief's flowing tide!
O Lord, by Your celestial attributes,
And by Your perfect power that none disputes,
Convey me to love's limits and though I
May die in time, such love will never die.
From light's source give me everlasting light;
Don't keep such kohl back from my dazzled sight,
And though I'm drunk with love now, I'll soon prove
To be possessed of even greater love.
They say, 'Escape from love, and wholly free
Your heart from wanting Layli constantly.'
O God, increase my need to glimpse the face
Of Layli always and in every place,
Take back the years that I have left, and give
Them all to her as added years to live.[30]
I've withered to a hair in my despair
But I'd not have her lose a single hair,
And may the earring that I wear as proof
I'm hers be my continual reproof;
May my glass never lack her wine, my fame
Never be separated from her name,
May her pure beauty be the cause that I
Now sacrifice my soul for her and die,
And as I burn here like a candle, may
That flame not be extinguished for a day;
May all the love within me not grow old
But multiply and grow a hundredfold."

And as he spoke, his saddened father heard
His son's account, and didn't say a word;
He saw his heart was captive, and was sure
This sickness was impossible to cure.
He went back home and told his family there
All that he'd heard that proved his son's despair;
He said, "He touched the ka'bah, and the chain
Was snapped that keeps men sensible and sane.
The murmured sound of what Majnun was saying
Sounded like Zoroastrians when they're praying;[31]
I hoped the page he'd read there[32] would have taught him,
How to escape the grief that Layli's brought him,
But all his hopes and prayers were that he'd be
Cursed with this passion for eternity."

MEN FROM LAYLI'S TRIBE TURN
AGAINST MAJNUN

Because this news reached everyone, it fell
Into the hands of lawless oafs as well—
Men heard that love for his belovèd had
Driven a sweet young man completely mad;
The news intrigued them, they debated it,
Examined and exaggerated it;
While Layli sat enduring what they said,
Saddened by all the gossip that men spread.

And some of Layli's kinsfolk did not fail
To tell their tribal chieftain of this tale—
They said, "A crazy youth, a lovelorn stranger,
Is out there putting our good name in danger;
He comes each day, it isn't hard to find him,
A crowd of louts like dogs is right behind him;
Mournfully, crazily, he prowls around,
Sometimes he'll dance, sometimes he'll kiss the ground,
Or sing his love songs with a voice as sweet
As are the sentiments his songs repeat,
And every intricate sad song reveals
The secrets of the passion that he feels,
And from his songs men learn of shameful things
That wreck our reputation as he sings—

His sighs are hurting Layli, and his breath
Will give not life to Layli's flame but death.
He's like a goat, so drive him off like one—
Then we can start to mend the harm he's done!"
And when he'd heard them out, their warlike chief—
A violent, quarrelsome, hard-bitten thief—
Drew his bright sword and with a gruesome cry
Yelled, "If he's shamed us, this is our reply!"

Someone from Qais's family heard their plan
And quickly hurried to inform his clan
What he had heard, saying to Amiri,
"Prevent what could become a tragedy,
Their chief is fierce as fire, tumultuous
As flooding water, brutal, rancorous;
I fear that if Majnun's not heard the news
He's after him that it's his head he'll lose;
A dangerous chasm yawns before Majnun—
We have to bring him home again, and soon!"
You can imagine how the father of
Majnun responded with paternal love,
And set out riding like the wind to find him
Telling his friends to follow close behind him,
Hoping they'd find the suffering lad, and then
Gently and safely bring him home again.
This way and that they searched, but found no trace
Of Amiri's sad son in any place.
They said, "Perhaps death's overtaken him,
Or some wild beast has torn him limb from limb."
His fellow tribesmen mourned for him, and sighed,
Unsure if he had wandered off or died;

His family wept that nothing could be found
To show Majnun was dead or safe and sound.

*

For her part Layli waited patiently
Like a loved treasure hidden secretly,
Withdrawn from all the business going on,
Secluded, and ignoring everyone,
Watching the road, hoping to see dust rise
Above their hunting grounds and cloud the skies.[33]

Better to be a fox whose belly's full
Than be a mighty wolf that's vulnerable;[34]
A hawk that's eaten well will have no need
To envy other creatures when they feed,
And mounting hunger makes sour food taste sweet—
What was disgusting now seems good to eat,
But when we're sick, sweet halva's like a curse,
A poisoned food that only makes things worse.

Majnun was hungry, and he searched the ground
For anything to eat that could be found,
Forced by necessity to forage for
Food he'd have thought inedible before.
But in his suffering he remained content,
Hardship was not a burden to resent
Since it was like a promise that he'd be
Freed from his self[35] and its captivity;
He sought and suffered, though no suffering brought
Within his grasp the treasure that he sought.

*

But like an omen from a favoring sky
A member of the Bani Ma'd passed by
And saw him sprawled out on the desert sand,
A ravaged body in a ravaged land.
The man who's far from home, companionless,
Who has no friend to share in his distress,
No intimate with whom to pass the time,
Is like a line of verse without a rhyme,
His only friends his echoed cries that chide him,
His confidant his shadow's length beside him,
While like an archer his misfortune notches
An arrow to the string, and waits and watches.
The traveler recognized him as a man
Of some importance, from a noble clan,
And questioned him, but in response he heard
Not one consistent or coherent word,
And gradually gave up attempts to sound him
And traveled on, and left him where he'd found him.
He visited the young man's tribe, and said
He'd seen a man among the rocks, half dead,
And writhing like a snake, crazed in his mind,
Like a wild demon hiding from mankind,
At death's door, sprawled among the desert stones,
The marrow poking through his brittle bones.

His father heard the news and left in haste
His tribe and homeland for the desert waste;
Scouring each cave and cleft, he stumbled on
In his demonic search to find his son—
And then he saw him in a fissure, prone
And slumped down, with his head upon a stone,

And singing to himself and sometimes groaning,
Sighing from time to time and softly moaning,
And in his bloodshot eyes he saw tears well
And fall as quickly as his fortunes fell,[36]
So drunk within his dream, and so far gone,
He seemed oblivious of everyone.
But when he saw his searching father, he
Greeted him cordially and gratefully,
Then seeing how severe he looked, he bowed
Before him like his shadow, shocked and cowed,
And said, "O crown and scepter of my soul,
Forgive my feeble loss of self-control;
Don't question me, you see my wretched state,
Ascribe my desolation to my fate.
How can I bear to face you in this way,
And see you see me here on such a day?
I am ashamed you're here, how can your son
Plead for forgiveness for the things he's done?
You're well aware of how the matter stands,
My future is no longer in my hands."

MAJNUN'S FATHER ADVISES HIS SON

And when the father saw his son, he sighed
And snatched his turban off, and loudly cried
(As roosters do to greet the morning light),
Since their disgrace had changed his day to night.
He said, "Dear son, so wretched and forlorn,
Like a young rose whose petals are all torn,
Poor lovesick child, how you lament and grieve,
How burnt by love you are, and how naïve!
The evil eye has marred your charm, some curse
Has battered you and made your sickness worse,
Soaking your flesh with blood like this, and tearing
With prickly spines and thorns the clothes you're wearing.
You've given up on life, for what, and why,
What thorn is this that's festering in your eye?
Men suffer harm, but not as you have done,
And hardships come, but not like yours, my son;
You never rest from grieving, or from hearing
Your enemies' derisive taunts and sneering—
Hasn't their ridicule yet shaken you,
Doesn't their noisy scorn awaken you?
Forget this passion, it's dishonored me
And robbed you of your name and dignity—
The way you sweat and fret and make a fuss
About such trifles is ridiculous.

35

A friend should offer wise admonishment
Even for faults that are self-evident,
An honest friend can point things out, he makes
You want to rid yourself of your mistakes,
He's like a mirror showing you a room
So that you see the spots that need a broom.
Sit down, and free your heart from sorrow's hold;
It's no good beating iron when it's cold!
I see you haven't got the patience to
Be patient when no friends are close to you,
So visit us, don't stay away so long,
Come home more often, stay where you belong—
The heart's desires entice men who knows where
And then abandon them to their despair;
Be drunk, but not from wine, seek something higher,
And love desire while feeling no desire.[37]
You've let winds blow this scandal far and wide
And I'm the man our enemies deride;
Our hopes are coins, and yours is counterfeit,
It's useless to you, so get rid of it.
You sing your songs, I slap my thighs,[38] I tear
My soul apart, you rip the clothes you wear.
If love has lit a fire that's burnt your heart
Your burning love has torn my guts apart.
But don't despair of finding some way out—
Just sow the seed and soon you'll see it sprout.
Things that you think won't work may well produce
A hopeful outcome that can be of use,
There's hope still in what seems the darkest night
Since every night concludes with morning's light.
Spend time with those whose lives are fortunate,
Shun what has left you in this wretched state,

But keep ahold of wealth; when wealth is present
Your heart knows happiness, and life is pleasant.
Good Fortune unties knots, solves everything,
And is the turquoise in God's signet ring,
While anyone it favors finds that he
Is overwhelmed with wealth perpetually.
Be patient, seek for patience, nourish it,
And watch Good Fortune find you, bit by bit;
The sea that is so wide consists of drops
Uniting in a flow that never stops,
And that high mountain in the clouds is just
A vast accretion of small stones and dust;
Be patient, and you'll find that jewels are found
Slowly but surely, hidden in the ground.
Resourceful's better than robust and firm,
A man without resources is a worm—
A fox can manage things a wolf won't try,
The wolf is stronger, but the fox is sly.
Why would you give your heart to someone who
For years and years would never think of you,
She like a rose, you stuck in mud, her heart
The heavy stone that tears your life apart?
If people mention Layli's name to you
It means that they're imputing shame to you—
And when they stop, they're thinking well of you,
There's nothing shameful left to tell of you.
This constant moping is a poisonous thing,
It's drinking celery for a scorpion's sting.[39]
Come on, my boy, busy yourself, and find
Something to occupy your lovesick mind;
An elephant needs prodding to forget
His Indian home on which his mind is set.

Dear boy, of all that's dear to me most dear,
Stay with your family now, stop living here—
Apart from bringing you disgrace, my son,
What has your wandering in these mountains done?
Pitfalls and rocks make up the treacherous way here,
Why should you ever want to come or stay here!
Don't argue, there's a watchman watching you,
Chains and an iron door you can't get through.
You're like a child in this—look where you tread,
Watch Deceit's sword, and see you keep your head!
With friends enjoy yourself, do as you please,
Be happy, and annoy your enemies!"

MAJNUN'S REPLY TO HIS FATHER

Majnun's sweet lips sought words then to suffice
As answers to his father's sweet advice.
He said to him, "O glorious heaven I love
More than the glories of the heavens above,
Lord of the campsites of our wandering race,
Sweet mole of beauty on the Arab face,
It is to you I pray, my being lives
Within the blessings that your being gives,
I pray you live forever, and that I
Should not remain alive when you must die.
Your wise words are a treasury, a balm
To make my desperate fevers cool and calm;
What can I do, though, fallen in this place
Unmindful of myself, in deep disgrace
(As you well know), distracted and unable
To rule myself, unsettled and unstable?
I'm chained with iron chains, and what can aid me
When I can only be what Fate has made me?
Love's bonds won't open of themselves, love's weight
Can't be sloughed off once it's ordained by Fate—
I weep that I must suffer so, but all
My efforts not to are contemptible.
This searing thunderbolt could easily
Destroy a thousand others just like me;

Not only I have suffered, who is there
Who's not seen hundreds gripped by this despair?
No pit decides it should be dark, likewise
The moon does not decide when it must rise,
From ants to elephants there is no creature
Who's not compelled in some way by its nature.
If life went always as we wish, who would
Seek anything but what's desired and good?
My heartfelt grief would make hard granite melt,
Who'd willingly endure the grief I've felt?
Misfortune's marked me for her own; what man
Can drive off his misfortune? No one can!
If this way's travelers could be helped, I'd be
The sun or moon in heaven for all to see!
Whatever deeds are done, for good or ill,
They're not within the compass of our will—
Who'd choose to live a life like mine, hard-pressed
By love's disaster, weary and depressed,
Self-wounded in this way, confused, perplexed,
Incessantly preoccupied and vexed?
I let no laugh escape my lips, if I
So much as smile I fear I'd burn and die;
'Why don't you laugh?' men say. 'Tears indicate
A soul that's in a melancholy state.'
But I'm afraid my laugh would be a flame
That burned my mouth, and brought me only shame.
A partridge caught an ant once in its beak,
The wretch's prospects couldn't be more bleak;
The ant began to laugh immoderately
And cried, 'Hey, partridge, can you laugh like me?'
The partridge thought, 'What question could be dafter,
When I'm a bird that's famous for my laughter?'[40]

And so he laughed, his great beak opened wide . . .
Out hopped the ant, and scuttled off to hide.
A man who laughs out loud finds as a rule
He's not considered clever but a fool,
And misplaced laughter's more contemptible
Than endless tears wept by the bucketful.
Torture and pain are mine, frivolity
Is never going to help or comfort me.
A donkey that's grown old will carry on
Bearing its burdens till its life is done,
The only time its sufferings ever cease
Is when death comes at last, and it's at peace;
Don't say my love's a new-grown irksome thorn,
This thorn has grown in me since I was born;
Better a swordsman fight and lose his head
Than be a coward who has flinched and fled.
Love is no state for fearing thorns; regret
For lovers comes when thorns are *not* a threat!
A lover does not fear his fear, or fear
To fight with any foes who might appear,
And if my soul should fall in fire, I'd be
Cheered by the prospect of such agony.
My soul is so far gone, so broken, so unfit
For anything, what can you want from it?"

Majnun had told his tale, his father'd heard
His son's account, and wept at every word;
Here on one side the father sat down sighing,
There on the other side his son lay crying.

His father took him home again, and gave him
Into his friends' hands, hoping they could save him;

Majnun—lovelorn, grief-stricken—for his part
Tried to be patient, but it broke his heart.
For two days he endured such misery
That all who saw him wept with sympathy,
But then he burst from his confinement, sighed,
And in his frenzy pushed his way outside,
Running toward the foothills and the plain,
Eager to live at liberty again,
Though all his life was weakness, pain, and crying,
Not life so much as an extended dying.
Feverish with burning love, fervent and hot,
He made for Najd,[41] to him a sacred spot,
And reached there like a raging, warlike lion,
Striding and strutting as if shod with iron.

And as he went he sang in plangent strains
Love songs that told of all his lovelorn pains,
So that men gathered round the mountainside
To hear his songs that rang out far and wide,
Eager to hear such wonders and collect them,
And write them down so that they'd recollect them—
And so, in time, these echoes of his voice
Made other lovers marvel and rejoice.

LAYLI'S BEAUTY

Loveliest of miracles, and beauty's empress,
Throughout the seven climes[42] the prettiest temptress,
More gorgeous in her natural loveliness
Than seven caliphs' ceremonial dress;
The moon in heaven was envious of her face,
Tall cypresses resented her slim grace,
The instigator and destroyer of
Men's fearful hopes and hopeful fears of love,
Heir to the sun and moon's majestic light,
The house's lamp, the orchard's torch at night,
The idol idol-worshippers adore
And which they piously bow down before,
Bed-mate of love, and spouse of sweetest pleasure,
At once love's treasurer and shining treasure.
A merchant dressed in silks, glittering with gold,
Sugar and sweetness were the wares she sold,
Decked in a thousand pearls, a thousand were
Chained like Majnun by love's despair to her;
She was a miracle praised far and wide,
The cynosure of all the countryside.

A wine glass in her hand, her rose-like face
A bud that opened with a new-found grace . . .

43

With her no slender cypress could compete,
As for her lips, ripe dates were not so sweet,
A garden of delight, whose countenance
Lit fires of longing with each teasing glance—
With half a glance her eyesight's sorcery
Ruined a hundred kingdoms instantly,
With Persian, or with Arab, or with Turk
Her teasing glances never failed to work.
No one escaped her darts, her wondering stare
Enticed her prey into her ringlets' snare,
The arrows of her eyes brought down her prey
Like musk deer that successful hunters slay,
Just as her curls were like a chain that bound
The neck of any lion this huntress found.
Her cheeks and lips together were perfection,
Roses and honey mixed in one confection,[43]
A thousand gave their hearts away, and chose
To live in hopes they'd taste this honeyed rose.
Her curls swept clean the entrance way for guests,
Her lashes said, "Be off with you, you pests!"
Her curls entreated guests to come, but then
Her lashes' daggers drove them off again.
She was the queen in chess, whose moves defeated
The rooks and pawns against whom she competed;
Her stature was a cypress tree's, her face
A pheasant perched there in its topmost place.[44]
Her sugared smiles were sweets that put to shame
All other sweetmeats worthy of the name,
Her little ruby lips suggested bliss
That slighted sugar with their promised kiss,
Her dimpled chin was like a lovely well
In which a hundred hearts too rashly fell

But then her hair let down was like a rope
To lift them up again and give them hope.
And yet despite her coy coquettishness
She suffered to see others in distress . . .
And stayed withdrawn and unapproachable,
Behind her veil and irreproachable.
She went up on the roof where, out of sight,
She scanned the countryside from dawn to night,
Hoping to see Majnun,[45] and wondering whether
They might, for just a moment, sit together,
Uncertain which way she should look, unsure
How she could tell him all she must endure;
And fearing tattle-tales and dreading spies,
Even at night she stifled her sad sighs—
A trembling candle flame, half smiles, half weeping,
Sweet smiles and bitter tears instead of sleeping,
And all her outward suffering failed to show
The inward agony she'd come to know.
Grief's mirror was before her, and displayed
The image of her love her mind had made—
Her shadow was her only courtier,
Her veil her only friend to comfort her,
And secrets whispered for her shadow's sake
Kept her and her dark shadow wide awake,
While fire and water[46] made up all her nature
As though she were a flickering fairy creature.

As arrows are accoutrements of kings,
A woman's music's when her spindle sings—
But Layli in her sorrow now refused
The double-headed spindle she had used

And threw aside this homely spindle for
An arrow emblematic of love's war,
Whose single head seeks out the mark it's found
Unlike a spindle spinning round and round.[47]
Beneath her veil a sea of weeping drowned her,
Grief had ingested her and swirled around her.
Gold earrings in her ears, she laid her ear
Against the doors for any news she'd hear,
But kept her counsel still, not passing on
The thoughts that haunted her to anyone.
She sought the moonlight secretly at night,
Watching the road with her unwavering sight,
Wishing that she could send Majnun some kind
And peaceful greeting from her gentle mind,
Or waft from Najd a breeze's soft caress
Whose scent suggested loving faithfulness,
Or send the clouds from Najd to mass above
Majnun, and open there, and rain down love.

In every corner of her home she found
Love poems lying randomly around,
Each child come from the town's bazaar would share
Verses of love he'd heard repeated there,
Each passer-by beneath her roof passed on
A little verse of greeting, and was gone.
Now charming Layli had a talent for
Poetic meter, rhyme, and metaphor,
This unpierced pearl strung pearls of verse as pure
And virgin as herself, and as demure,[48]
And as his poems had invoked her name,
In answer to him she would do the same,

Though where she'd heard his fire and seen it glowing
She answered him with water gently flowing.
In secret she took paper then and wrote
In blood[49] her verses as a little note,
As if sweet jasmine sent, but stealthily,
A poem-message to her cypress tree.
Then from the roof where she kept watch she dropped
This message in the road; soon someone stopped
To pick it up and read it, and then dance
As if with joy at this strange happenstance.
He promptly took it to Majnun, whose strange
Behavior had inspired this strange exchange,
And who on reading Layli's words at once
Extemporized a poem in response—
And this is how love-messages between
This lovelorn pair passed safely and unseen.
The songs of nightingales could not compete
With their melodious songs, they were so sweet,
And many lovely songs were based upon
The lovers' story, and the songs they'd sung,
And harps, and lutes, and flutes, whatever tune
They played, it spoke of Layli and Majnun—
Their families' children heard these compositions
So often that they all became musicians!

They suffered from these slights, and wept to hear
The way such gossip made them both appear;
A year passed by, in which they had to be
Content with dreams, and hope, and memory.

A Description of Layli;
Layli Visits a Palm Grove

The sun's rose drew its veil back, and its light
Made all the roses of the lowlands bright,
Like glittering coins a lucky man has won
The blossoms on the fruit trees smiled and shone,
And like a red and yellow flag unfurled
Tulips and marigolds filled all the world.
The orchards' shade, the flower-filled gardens rang
With endless trills their avian songsters sang;
With dew the tender plants shone green and wet
Like emeralds round which glistening pearls are set;
Red tulips cast their petals, and you'd think
Their centers were calligrapher's black ink,
The lowly violet's scattered petals lay
Like glossy curls[50] let down in boisterous play.
New buds grew strong, as if preparing for
Their use as arrows in a threatened war,
The rose's armor was of silk, the breeze
Lay soft and low to ambush enemies,
And sunrise made the waterlily yield—
Without a fight it cast away its shield.
The box tree's leaves[51] were combed out by the breeze
That loosened flowers from pomegranate trees,

Curls of the perfumed hyacinth opened wide,
The rose inquisitively sought her side—
Narcissi blazed with fire, like one who seems
To start up suddenly from feverish dreams,
What looked like wine was drops of red rain blowing
From Judas trees as if their blood were flowing,
Jasmine seemed like a silver stream that spills
As if to wash the golden daffodils,
A timid rosebud opened up its eye
Then looked away as if it felt too shy,
A lily-of-the-valley seemed to sit
Among its sword-like leaves defending it.
In gardens songbirds sang, crows cawed and cried,
Filling with noise and song the countryside,
Hawks shrieked as if in love, a turtledove
Salted their pain with murmured tales of love,
Each ringdove high up in a plane tree cooed
Stories of lovers longed for and pursued;
And like Majnun himself, a nightingale
Raised up its head to sigh its lovesick tale,
While opening roses rose to shine and glitter
Like Layli's crowned head rising from a litter.
Layli allowed herself to stray at ease
Among the springtime's lovely flowers and trees,
Her plaited coils of hair seemed to bestow
Upon each flower she passed their lustrous glow,
And all the garden seemed to feast upon
Her moist, sweet lips that like red rubies shone;
She seemed a Turk[52] in Arab lands, her face
A Turk's, her body with an Arab's grace.

*

Surrounded by companions who'd protect her
(And may the evil eye's gaze not detect her),
This houri[53] went to see the garden's green
And shaded by a red rose sit unseen,
To lift the jonquil's goblet, to drink up
The new red wine within a tulip's cup,
To make the violets jealous of her hair
And roses weep in envious despair,
To teach the cypress what is meant by height,
And wash the lily's whiteness with her white,
To have the rosebuds pay their taxes to her,
The garden's wealth pay all the tribute due her;
To have her shadow stretched across the grass
Rival a palm tree's in its slender mass,
To smile to think her loveliness could be
Compared to roses or a cypress tree . . .

But no, no, this was not her aim at all,
To argue who was prettier or more tall—
Rather, she sought a safe place where she could
Sigh as those burnt in love's infernos should,
To tell the nightingales her secret pain,
To go through all she'd suffered once again
Hoping the breeze might bring some token of
The stranger-friend to whom she'd pledged her love,
Though doing this might mean that what had lain
Secret within her heart would be made plain.

There was a grove of date palms near that place
That had a Chinese painting's winsome grace,
Whose shady canopy and humming bees
Evoked Eram's enchanting paths and trees,[54]

A place for pleasure, rest, and privacy,
A special spot such as men rarely see.
Gracefully, slowly, with a distracted air,
Layli, with all her unwed friends, went there;
She sat down on the grass, and seemed a rose
That made the other bashful roses close,
A budding lily opened where she sighed
And other flowers grew graceful at her side,
And where her hand caressed the grass, a new
Tall box tree[55] and a cypress sapling grew.
Her cypress-slender, tulip-cheeked young friends
Had come for all the pleasures springtime sends—
They joked and frolicked there, but when their play
Had tired them out, they laughed and went away,
While Layli sat beneath a cypress tree;
The grass on which she sat appeared to be
A parrot's bright green feathers; on this throne
She seemed a gorgeous pheasant, all alone.

She wept, and in her secret weeping said,
Gently and kindly, through the tears she shed,
"O my loved friend, so faithful and so true,
So worthy of me, as I am of you,
O cypress among men, so young and bold,
Whose heart is warm, whose anguished sighs are cold,
Come to this garden now, take from my heart
This brand that burns me since we've had to part,
Sit with me here, my cypress, and I'll be
Beside you as your flowering cherry tree.
But now each moment spectral fears arise,
This garden is no garden in my eyes;

How long is it to be before you'll choose
To send a message to me with your news?"
Her words had hardly flown up in the air
When she heard someone softly singing there,
As if a passer-by sang both the tune
And words of verses first sung by Majnun:
"O my veiled idol, whom I hope will be
Unveiled at last by no one else but me;
Flailing in blood, Majnun sinks to perdition—
And how does Layli fare? What's her condition?
Majnun is wracked with pain in every limb—
Layli draws all his strength and will from him;
Majnun's pierced by love's dart, the wound is deep—
Layli lies sweetly, softly, sound asleep;
Majnun laments, his cries are never done—
Layli counts all her pleasures, one by one;
Majnun is branded and he writhes in pain—
Layli's all flowers and springtime's sweet refrain;
Majnun is stricken by necessity—
Layli is free, and laughs spontaneously;
Majnun's heart grieves that they must be apart—
Layli is calm, all's well within her heart."
When Layli heard this, she began to moan
And weep, as if her tears would wear through stone.
But then she saw, half hidden in the trees,
One of her mischievous accomplices
She'd thought of as a friend, but who'd betrayed her,
Whose notion of what friendship was dismayed her.
Once they were home, the pearl sought out her shell,[56]
But she who'd learned her secret sped to tell
The news to Layli's mother, who resolved
To find a way to have this problem solved.

She fretted like a bird caught in a snare—
What could be done? Her child was in despair,
And to herself she said, "Majnun's gone mad,
If I do nothing she'll be just as bad;
But if I tell her to be patient, she
Won't listen and she'll pay no heed to me—
She's been all patience since they've been apart
And still she longs for him with all her heart."
Layli still suffered, shut up in her room,
As faint as shadows in a litter's gloom.
Her sighs were choked, as if a fog possessed her,
And sorrow like a hidden thorn distressed her;
So Layli lived, heartsick, in love—and who
In love escapes the grief that she went through?

Ebn Salam Asks for Layli's Hand
in Marriage

This garden's gardener, poet-author of
These words, brands with his speech this tale of love:

Layli, that moon who was so beautiful
It seemed she was a moon that's always full,
Went one day to her garden, where her face
Was like a rose that topped a sapling's grace,
And where her scent and beauty were so prized
Both roses and their attar were despised,
And as she walked her tumbling curls descended
As though they were chained links that never ended.
It happened that a dignified young man,
A member of the Bani Asad clan,
As he was passing by caught sight of her
And thought no blossom could be lovelier.
He was a wealthy, well-liked man, whose name
Was Ebn Salam; he had a certain fame
Among his fellow Arabs for good sense,
Someone to watch, a man of consequence.
And seeing that bright torch, he felt desire
Like wind rush up in him to grasp this fire,
Not thinking that when any fire is lit
A wind is likely to extinguish it.

When he reached home, he longed to be united
With this bright moon, and have his love requited,
Forgetting that no man could ever clasp
The shining moon within his eager grasp.
He set to work, and chose a messenger
To ask if he might be betrothed to her,
To have that fairy creature be his bride
And brought within her litter to his side;
He promised love, said he'd be dust before her,
Pile gold like dust heaps (that's how he'd adore her),
Offered a thousand treasures, said that he'd
Provide more livestock than they'd ever need.[57]
The go-between arrived in hopes that he
Could make a pact with Layli's family
On Ebn Salam's behalf, as had been planned;
He ceremonially kissed her father's hand,
Then set out the proposal that he'd brought
Announcing Ebn Salam politely sought
That he and their child Layli should be wed.
And in reply young Layli's parents said,
"Your proposition is appropriate,
But as things are at present we should wait,
Layli's unwell and weak; after a while
She'll be quite well again, and make us smile—
That's when the marriage plans can go ahead
And sugar will be sprinkled as you're wed;[58]
This marriage will be good for all of us,
Let's hope it will be soon, and prosperous—
But not quite yet, we need a small delay
And after that we'll have the happy day;
The garden will be cleared of thorns; our rose
Will flower, her budding petals will unclose;

We'll put a gold chain round her neck, and then
She and the chain will both be yours. Amen!"
So Ebn Salam was what he'd wished to be,
A chosen suitor waiting patiently,
Who rode home, now the dust of doubt was laid,
Pleased with the promise Layli's father'd made.[59]

NOFAL SYMPATHIZES WITH MAJNUN

Veiled Layli's secret was now out, her name
A bandied byword for disgrace and shame,
And harps and lutes joined in, so that among
Men everywhere the lovers' tale was sung
By sweet-voiced singers, whose beguiling art
Enchanted each delighted listener's heart;
Confused now as her curls, poor Layli lay
Alone, awake, as day succeeded day.

Majnun meandered through the wilderness,
Sunk like his fate in tangled hopelessness,
Chasing wild horses with a thousand pains
While love songs in their thousands filled the plains.
King-like, enthralled, he came to Najd, although
In Najd he'd nothing kingly left to show;
His feet were bruised by love, his heartfelt sighs
Dispersed the pathway's dust into the skies,
Lovers who heard him struggling in love's throes
Would fall into despair and rend their clothes,
And hearts that had seemed proof against attacks
Now found their tempered steel had turned to wax.

Nofal was someone who by bravery
Had boldly broadened his authority

Until he'd rendered all the nearby land
His own, subservient to his command:
His sword could make an army flee in fear,
In wrath a lion, in gentleness a deer,
With many followers, magnificent,
Wealthy, and in his wealth beneficent.
Mounted upon a fearsome horse, one day
This hunter sallied out in search of prey,
Searching among the hillside caves he found
A man whose moaning made the hills resound,
With blistered feet, one beaten down by Fate,
Far from his friends and in a wretched state,
A wild man who it seemed was glad to shun
Mankind and live apart from everyone,
Singing such songs of anguish and complaint
Whoever heard them would collapse and faint.
Nofal inquired about this fugitive—
What kind of man was he? How did he live?
His fellow hunters said, "This started when
He fell in love; he first grew sad, and then
His sadness turned to madness—as you see,
His mind's surrendered to insanity,
He sings his love songs night and day, and tries
To catch his lover's scent from windy skies,
And if a breeze should bring her scent, he'll make
A hundred songs and verses for her sake,
And clouds that come from where she lives he'll greet
With grateful poems that are sugar-sweet;
And now he spends all day and every day
In this sad way, and in no other way.
Men come from far away to bring him wine
And food—a thousand times he will decline

Their generous gift, then finally he'll take
A single glass for his belovèd's sake."

When he had heard them out, Nofal replied,
"It would be chivalrous if someone tried
To help and comfort this unhappy man,
And I'm determined to do all I can.
It's prey that I've been looking for today
And now I've found some quite unlooked for prey!"
Then lightly from his courser he alighted
And had a little meal spread, and invited
The poor emaciated wretch he'd found
To eat, and sit beside him on the ground.
He told sweet tales, his words were soft and warm
Like pliant wax that takes on any form
Though to his listener every tale he'd tell
Appeared to be an empty useless shell—
If it was not the tale of Layli he
Was deaf to it, whatever it might be.

Nofal saw this young man would not partake
Of any food for absent Layli's sake,
And gradually he changed the subject of
His stories to sweet Layli and her love,
So that the wild, sad wanderer became
Peaceful and calm, distracted by her name,
Delighted that he'd found a willing friend
Whose talk of Layli seemed to have no end.
His spirits rose and he began a song
Of love that was both passionate and strong—
With every line he laughed, completing it
With sparks of unpremeditated wit;

And then he didn't hesitate to dine
But gladly ate the food and drank the wine.

Nofal's sweet eloquence, his charming chatter
Made every problem seem a simple matter:
"Don't be a candle guttering as it dies
Because she's like a lamp in distant skies,"
He said. "With gold or strength I shall not fail
To make you both like two pans on a scale,
Equal and side by side; if she's a bird
Desire will bring her down, you have my word,
Instinct will grasp her by the neck, and then
She will be brought back to the earth again;
If she's like sparks in flint, I will contrive,
Like iron, to make those sparks leap out alive.
My lariat won't rest till at your side
I see that lovely moon's become your bride."
Majnun became so hopeful that he bowed
His head in prayer, then spoke his thoughts aloud:
"Your words are wonderful—that is, if you
Are saying something that is really true.
But then, her mother shouldn't offer her
To one like me of doubtful character;
One shouldn't leave a rose in windy weather
Or pair a demon and the moon together,
And it's ridiculous to think that she
Could ever wed a crazy fool like me.
They've washed my filthy shirt, time after time,
But they can't wash away the dirt and grime,
They've tried to silver-coat me and renew me
But underlying blackness shows the true me;

Your hand is generous, but what's wrong with me
Cannot be cured by generosity.
I think that in the way of friendship you
Will leave me when there's still so much to do,
Your hunt for her will be in vain, you'll see
She can't be caught, and you'll abandon me!
We bluster like the wind, we puff and blow,
But empty vessels . . . well, the rest you know.
If you should keep your promise, may the Lord
Make your life prosperous as your reward,
But if your vow is just a mirage, you
Should leave me, it's the best thing you could do,
And I'll return to what I was before—
Just as I was, and trouble you no more."

Hearing how desperately he groaned and sighed,
Nofal was quick to hurry to his side—
Nofal, a young man with a noble mind,
A stranger to Majnun, whose heart was kind
(They were the same age, and this gallant stranger
Pitied his grief and his condition's danger).
He swore by God, by all that He had wrought,
And by the message that the Prophet brought:
"My wealth and sword I shall devote to you
Not as a wolf but as lion would do,
From now on I shan't eat or sleep or rest
Till I've completed this praiseworthy quest—
I'll stay with you until I've seen you're free
From your bewilderment and misery.
Sit now, be patient for a while, and start
To calm the fire that rages in your heart,

And meanwhile I'll unbolt the iron door
That leads to confrontation and to war."
To Majnun, then, this cordial seemed to be
The drink to save his soul and sanity.
His mind grew calmer, he was less afraid,
He trusted in the vow his friend had made,
And he was patient, pouring water on
His inward fire till it was almost gone—
His friend was his asylum, it was best
For him to convalesce with him, and rest.

He bathed, and put clean clothing on, and chose
An Arab turban to complete his clothes,
Then sat together with his friend to dine
And hear musicians play, and savor wine,
And write sweet verses on the beauty of
The sweet girl who commanded all his love.
Well clothed, well fed, respectable again,
He seemed to be the healthiest of men—
His sallow face was pink and flushed, he stood
Erect—not bowed now—as a young man should;
His pitch-black perfumed beard encircled all
His face again, grown thick and beautiful,
It seemed the breeze both borrowed and then lent
His breaths as they exhaled their rosy scent;
He seemed a shining laughing dawn, and when
He smiled the rising sun appeared again—
The plants rejoiced, and as a wondrous sign
Red roses glowed like goblets of red wine.
Majnun grew sensible, intelligence
Returned to him, and with it his good sense,

And all the time his noble host expressed
A hundred kinds of kindness to his guest—
Away from him he knew no happiness
And only drank to him and his success;
So for two months they drank their wine, and spent
Their time at ease, in negligent content.
As day succeeded cheerful day these two
Rejoiced, and happiness was all they knew.
Sometimes Majnun would write a few lines of
Protesting poems that condemned his love:
" 'O you, beyond my bitter sighs and cries,
Blowing my dust about with windy lies,
You made a hundred vows you would be true—
Not half of one of them was kept by you,
Happy to have my promises, and yet
Happy as well to have yourself forget,
Leading me on with your deceitful heart,
Leaving me restless once we had to part—
Your tongue so glib then with each loving vow,
Your tongue so chained up and so silent now;
A hundred ways your tongue has wounded me,
Your heart withholds its soothing remedy—
My patience flees, my intellect is going,
Save me, or where I'll be there is no knowing.
Should lovers show no love? Should they retract
The promises they make each time they act?
Though you've forgotten magnanimity
True lovers act with generosity—
To call someone who doesn't keep her word
A human being is to me absurd.'

*

"Without my friend I'm weak, in constant pain,
Like one who craves life's water, but in vain—
Life's water given to a man who craves it
Is treasure for a ruined town that saves it:
Bring Layli to me soon and I'll revive,
Without her though I know I won't survive."

NOFAL FIGHTS LAYLI'S TRIBE
ON BEHALF OF MAJNUN

Reproved so charmingly, Nofal became
As soft as wax before a roaring flame;
At once he leaped up, put his armor on,
And drew his sword, determined to be gone.
He chose a hundred warriors, horsemen who
Galloped as speedily as wild birds flew,
And with them he set off without delay
Like a black lion when it stalks its prey.
As he neared Layli's tribe a man was sent
Ahead to spell out what his coming meant,
To say, "I and my men have reached your lands
To fight if need be for our just demands;
Give Layli to us now; if not, our swords
Are ready—we're not here to bandy words—
Gently I'll give her to one worthy of
Her hand as he is worthy of her love,
His thirst will then be slaked, his health restored,
Which is a deed to gratify the Lord."
But when Nofal's prompt messenger had spoken
The glass of mutual respect was broken.
They answered, "What you ask's impossible,
Our Layli is the moon when she is full—

She's not a cake for you to feast upon!
Who steals the moon? Not you, nor anyone!
We'll kill your slashing swordsmen, we'll drive back
With stones your spearmen if they dare attack!"
The messenger repeated every word,
Telling Nofal each syllable he'd heard—
Furious, Nofal insisted he retrace
His steps back to the former meeting place
And say, "You senseless fools, you'd better be
Prepared to fight a breaking wave or flee."
Once more the messenger returned, once more
He brought back insults as he'd done before.
Nofal flared like a fire then to engage
The enemy, so violent was his rage—
He drew his sword and with his cavalry
Fell like a lion on the enemy.

Like mountains then the two sides clashed, and cries
Of violent rage rose up into the skies
As Nofal's enemies received the lion
With drawn swords like a barricade of iron.
The battlefield became a sea that rose
And fell with surging battle-cries and blows,
As blood shed by sharp swords dripped down and sank
Into the earth made drunk by what it drank.
Warriors' massed lances held off the attack
Until by lions they were beaten back,
And feathered arrows swooped like birds that kill
With thirsty beaks and drink the blood they spill.
Swords lopped off horses' heads, and on the ground
Chieftains' and horses' heads lay scattered round—

The yells of horsemen rose into the skies
Till sun and skies were deafened by their cries,
And when death's thunderbolt crashed down, the shock
Struck even iron ore concealed in rock,
Catastrophe's sharp lance, its honed point like
A crowbar's hair-thin head, prepared to strike,
And earth became a sea of surging blood,
Its stones like stars that rose above the flood.
Black horses reared like lions on each side,
Or like black snakes whose mouths gaped open wide,
Like black lions in their fury, and like white
Foul demons in the swiftness of their flight.

Majnun thought all who fought there on this grim
And fatal battlefield supported him—
Each horseman whom he saw he prayed that he
Would soon be granted peace and victory,
And felt he'd die for everyone who died
Whether from his or his opponents' side;
He wandered like a lover here and there
Never at peace in his confused despair,
And were it not for shame he would have waged
War on his own side as he stormed and raged—
If scorn had let him, he'd have fiercely fought
Against his allies and the men they brought
And slashed his friends' heads off, did he not see
The sneering laughter of his enemy.
If Fate had willed it, he'd have drawn his bow
Against his friend as often as his foe
And had his heart not stopped him, he'd have slain
His faithful allies on that dreadful plain.

On one side warriors valiantly tried
To triumph over their opponents' side,
On this side horses were urged onward while
On that prayers rose up from the rank and file;
When one from his side was struck down, he'd kiss
The warrior's hand that had accomplished this,
When one from Layli's tribe was struck and died
How inconsolably he raged and cried!
When his side's lances were victorious, he
Wished his opponents' lances victory,
And when his forces had the upper hand
Arrows were rained on them from Majnun's hand—
If Layli's side seemed stronger, he was sure
To show his pleasure with a lion's roar,
And when one asked him, "Why are you
So contrary in everything you do?
Why is it you support your enemy
When it's for you we fight so desperately?"
He said, "But when my enemy's my friend,
Who is it that my falchion should defend?
With mortal enemies we have to fight
But war against our friends cannot be right.
Warfare means wounds, but here I catch the scent
Of peaceful friendliness and sweet content—
When it's her soul's scent the belovèd sends,
The lover sends her his, and they are friends,
She sends me honeyed drinks, shall I send her
A drink concocted from sour vinegar?
Hers is the hand of friendship—who'd refuse it?
And foolishly pass by it, and so lose it?
She is my heart's desire, and she is where
My soul is—she's my soul, and I am there;

I give the soul she takes, to have her cherish
My soul's a joy for which I'd gladly perish—
Giving my soul like this, how am I fit
To pity your poor soul or care for it?"
And hearing him, the man he spoke to shed
Tears of concern, and humbly bowed his head,
While Majnun danced away half hidden by
The battle's dust that darkened earth and sky.

Meanwhile Nofal fought wildly, sword in hand,
A maddened elephant that scoured the land—
Each side he struck a man lay dead, each thrust
Reduced a world of enemies to dust,
Each way he turned heads fell, and men's blood flowed
In running rivers everywhere he rode.
All day these swordsmen fought, until the light
Began to fade with the approach of night,
And when the scented curls of darkness lay
Upon the pallid forehead of the day
That like a Georgian girl shone palely white
Till daylight was a curl cut off by night,
The armies parted, they no longer fought;
Now it was sleep their weary bodies sought.

Like a black serpent then Zahhak[60] awoke
And smiled, and plucked the stars till morning broke;
Now in his hand each waking warrior takes
His spear as fatal as Zahhak's black snakes,
But hidden by the night, from far and wide,
Allies had flocked to Layli's kinsmen's side
And from their camp new forces loosed a rain
Of arrows that obscured the sky and plain,

And seeing how things stood, Nofal grew sure
That it was peace he needed now, not war.

He sent a messenger to sue for peace,
To say, "Hostilities should hereby cease
Since swords are not the method to decide
The matter of a suitor and his bride;
To gain your angel, who is worthy of
My noble friend's devotion and his love,
I'll gladly sacrifice my personal treasure
And give you wealth beyond all count or measure.
Sweeter than anything I say would be
To end our anger and our enmity;
If sugar's not for sale, let us prefer
At least that we don't deal in vinegar,
Since even if you won't do what is right
There's no necessity that we should fight."
The envoy spoke, and hardly had he started
When both the armies disengaged and parted;
They heard each other's words, and turned aside,
Tugging their reins now for the homeward ride.
Peace came between them, and they thought no more
Of enmity, or stratagems, or war.

MAJNUN'S ANGER AGAINST NOFAL

But as Majnun became aware of this retreat
His fury flickered with intenser heat.
He leaped up at Nofal: "Is this," he cried,
"How you bring lovers to each other's side?
Well done indeed! Bravo! What better end
Could I have hoped for from my faithful friend?
Is this the sum of all your chivalry
And how your sword defeats an enemy?
Is this the most your mighty strength can do?
Is this how devilish foes are trapped by you?
This is your horsemanship? This is the way
You fling your lariat and seize your prey?
You've gone against my wishes . . . what a fine
Success you've made of this affair of mine!
You've made my dearest friend my enemy
And closed a thousand doors in front of me;
Your friendship made me lose my friend, you stole
From me my occupation and my soul—
This is how friendship's threads are snapped, and how
A splendid horseman is unseated now!
A shepherd sees a wolf—he aims at it
And shoots, and sees that it's his dog he's hit.
You're famous for your generosity
And what a splendid gift it's given me!

I never was so wounded through and through
As when I rode to battle next to you;
You sowed, and when no harvest came you tore
The ground you'd sown with this divisive war.
You! Who began so well, whose kindly ways
Befriended me and brightened all my days,
Who made my dark heart bright again, whose balm
Tended my wounds, and made my spirit calm."
With soft, smooth words Nofal tried to evade
The accusations that Majnun had made:
"We were outnumbered and I saw we'd lose,
The peace that I suggested was a ruse—
Now we've escaped their swords, from far and wide
I'll summon hardy tribesmen to our side;
I'll smash this stone, I shan't sleep till I make
Their high-flown obstinacy yield and break."
As far as Baghdad and Medina then
He sent out messengers to gather men,
In secret seeking hardened soldiers he
Could lead against his stubborn enemy,
Then brought his gathered forces primed for war
To where the battle had been fought before;
Meanwhile his enemies were unaware
Of all the forces that he'd summoned there.

NOFAL'S SECOND BATTLE

The poet opens speech's treasure chest
To lay before us what is in his breast:

Someone who watched Nofal that day would find
Wonders enough to daze his marveling mind.
The massed troops felt the earth begin to shake,
The slopes of Bu Qubays[61] to crack and quake,
Nofal's war-cry rang out, and at the sound
His enemies prepared to stand their ground.
Their chief then climbed to where he could assess
Both armies and their battle readiness,
And saw to the horizon, everywhere,
Soldiers whose spears and lances thronged the air—
The din of drums, the bugles' blasts, would jolt
Hearts of dead men to rise up and revolt.
This chief had no desire for battle, nor
Would shame permit him to evade this war—
He made a stand; the flood came, and he bore it
Although it swept away his wealth before it.
The two wings of his army turned and fled,
Each flashing sword that struck, struck off a head,
The blood flowed on the sand, and where it flowed
The tumbling sand grains like carnelians glowed.

73

Hearts trembled at the slaughter, swords held back,
Ashamed to cut off heads in their attack—
Nofal though pressed on with his sword, and made
A mountain piled from corpses with its blade,
He fought there like a dragon dealing death
With every stabbing wound, with every breath,
And every man his mace struck, one and all,
Had they been mountains, still they'd reel and fall,
His lance pierced every shield, and now bereft
Its bearer's book had no more pages left.
Majnun fought just as hard, as if he'd give
His life away and had no wish to live,
So long and hard they fought, it was as though
They slaughtered mounted men at every blow—
When partners ride together they can split
A stone, and make fresh water gush from it
(Discord will bring defeat and misery,
Alliances bring partners victory).
That day Nofal's men triumphed as they fought
And so achieved the conquest they had sought,
Killing the stragglers on the battlefield,
Forcing all those they didn't kill to yield;
Those who'd survived lay wounded, half alive,
And no one who was wounded would survive.

Their tribal elders mourned, and bowed before
Nofal, acknowledging they'd lost the war—
Weeping and moaning then, they wailed and pleaded,
And begged him that their just requests be heeded:
"Your enemies are dead, we who remain
Are captives here whose kinsman have been slain;

What will it profit you to slaughter us?
To shed our blood would not be chivalrous;
You don't need spears and arrows to subdue
This wounded remnant that submits to you;
Judge us with charity, choose mercy's way,
Be mindful of God's final Judgment Day.
Employ your sword against armed enemies,
Against belligerent adversaries,
But who will fight when unarmed men admit
They've lost the war and willingly submit?
We've humbly thrown away our shields before you
And it's for mercy that we now implore you,
We are defenseless here, and you've repaid us—
You don't need spears and arrows to persuade us.
And when a battle's fought, the one who wins
Is satisfied, and can forgive past sins."

Nofal responded, "I must have the bride,
At once, if I'm to leave here satisfied."
Layli's sad father spoke; he bowed his head
Down to the dust before Nofal, and said,
"Most worthy of all Arabs in renown,
Worthy of leadership and of the crown,
I am an old, sad man, my heart is broken,
I'm one of whom contemptuous things are spoken
By Arabs who revile me as a stranger;
This blood that has been shed, this mortal danger,
I take upon myself, since it's for me
Our tribe has suffered this catastrophe.
For all this sinfulness I am to blame
And wish to purify myself of shame.

If you entrust my daughter to my care
You'll have my endless gratitude, I swear,
But I shall not protest now or demur
Whatever you decide to do with her,
Not if you light a fire in which she would
As an example burn like sandalwood,
And if you were to kill her with your sword
Or throw her in a well, you have my word
Your slave will not object, or turn away
His face from anything you do or say.
But God forbid I'd give my lovely child
To this Majnun, who's so deranged and wild;
Madmen should be chained up, not handed over
To a young girl to be her husband-lover—
For me to grant his devilish desire
Would be like throwing brushwood on a fire.
The man's a fool, he reels from whim to whim,
A scatterbrain, no good can come of him!
He wanders in the mountains and the plains,
A spectacle no decency constrains,
Consorts with vagabonds, and makes his name—
And mine—a byword for disgrace and shame.
In Arab countries, everywhere he's gone,
My daughter's name's now known to everyone;
No one had heard of her, but he has made
Her every spiteful gossip's stock-in-trade,
And if I let him lead her off, I'll be
Scorned as a fool for all eternity;
Better a crocodile devour someone
Than that he be derided and live on!
Don't shame me in this way, I beg of you,
Think of the consequences if you do;

And at the least, if you don't pity me,
Depart from me in peace and let me be,
And if you don't, I swear I'll make your name
As much as mine a source of grief and shame.
I'll cut her head off, throw it in the street,
And let it lie there for stray dogs to eat,
And in this way at least I will be free
From all this horror that's tormenting me;
For dogs to eat her would be better than
For her to marry that disgusting man.
When dogs bite someone, ointments can restore
The patient to the health he'd known before,
A thousand ointments cannot cure the bite
Of humans spewing mockery and spite."

Hearing his words, Nofal became tongue-tied,
And slowly, sympathetically replied.
"Stand up," he said. "Though I have won
This battle, still, when all is said and done,
You have to give us Layli willingly;
If you are still convinced you cannot see
Her leave you and feel happy in your heart,
What man would force the two of you apart?
A woman who is taken off by force
Is bread that's indigestible and coarse.
I came here to do good, I can't allow
Myself to be involved in evil now."
His closest friends agreed with him and said,
"The old man's right, it would be wrong to wed
His daughter to a man who's so impulsive,
So lustful and so foolish and repulsive—

Her life would be a donkey's! Woe betide
The wretched woman who becomes his bride—
It would be nothing short of a disaster
For her to have him as her lord and master;
It's clear you can't give her to him, he's so
Unstable who could say how things might go?
And yesterday we fought for him while he
Quite blatantly cheered on the enemy,
We faced their arrows, while in front of us
He prayed that they would be victorious—
He cries and laughs at random, and this plainly
Points to the fact he isn't thinking sanely.
Hard on the heels of when their troth is plighted
Sorrow will come if these two are united—
This cannot turn out well, you will be blamed,
Her father will be wounded and ashamed.
It's best to extricate ourselves while we
Retain some semblance of integrity."
And when Nofal weighed their advice, he saw
That he and all his forces should withdraw.

Majnun was heartbroken, bereft, forlorn,
Wounded within by this unlooked-for thorn;
He said, "Today Good Fortune left my side,
The luck that lay asleep in me has died;
I cherished it in all simplicity—
Would that Good Fortune had kept faith with me."

Weeping, Majnun turned to Nofal, and felt
His rage like molten lava seethe and melt:
"With friendship you began, but in the end
You went back on your promise to your friend;

How bright the dawn was, but that morning light
Turned to the hopeless darkness of the night!
What happened to your hand that almost caught—
And then declined to catch—the prey I sought?
You led me thirsty to Euphrates' brink
And then before I had the chance to drink
You shoved me into hell, as if you made
Then snatched away from me cool lemonade;
You set sweet cakes before me, but when I
Reached out for them . . . swatted me like a fly.
The thread is knotted and its goal's forgotten;
As weightless as a bit of airy cotton."
And having said all this, he tugged his reins
As if to gallop off across the plains.
Nofal perceived his anger then, and tried
To comfort and console him; he replied,
"I'll search this land and find a woman who
Will make a flawless, worthy bride for you,
Who's modest, rich, whose breasts are silvery white,
Whose lovely buttocks gleam quick-silver bright;
With her you'll find good luck, and wealth will bless
Your home again with prosperous happiness."
They tried to give him hope, but could not make
The chain about his heart unlock or break;
Majnun rode off as his confusion grew,
Till like a cloud he disappeared from view.

Once back at home, Nofal would sit each day
With friends and talk, to while the hours away,
Chatting about Majnun, and endlessly
Recounting this poor outcast's history,

Whose whereabouts were all unknown, whose name
Seemed struck abruptly from the roll of fame;
And as they questioned him, Nofal's friends heard
Majnun's sad tale, recounted word by word.

MAJNUN FREES DEER FROM A HUNTER'S TRAP

Here are the things the teller of this tale
Revealed next as he drew aside its veil:

Majnun was like a bird that soars on wings
Of thwarted love, and as he soars he sings;
When he had left Nofal's men, he made haste
To fly like wind across the desert waste,
Singing of Sheikh Nofal's cruel treachery,
Of his betrayal, his inconstancy,
Singing in every hamlet, everywhere
Complaining of his fate and his despair.

And as he wept he glimpsed far off one day
A trap that had been laid for wandering prey,
And saw a few deer had been captured there
With hooves caught tightly in the huntsman's snare.
He saw the hunter's knife was raised to shed
Their blood, and wildly urged his horse ahead
To stop him if he could, and loudly cried,
"I am your guest, it's me who should decide
If they should die, and I say, 'Let them be!'
Open the trap and set these creatures free—
We all have souls, and what makes you so fit
To say who keeps his soul, who loses it?

Such lovely hindquarters and eyes, you'd swear
They're marked, 'Preserve, and treat with utmost care!'
How can you contemplate this brutal deed,
To stab these strangers, and to watch them bleed?
You'd be a savage wolf if you could bring
Yourself to do this loathsome, wicked thing.
Isn't their scent like spring, don't you surmise
You see your lover when you see their eyes?
For love's sake let them go, cherish them, make
Life's joyous freedom theirs for springtime's sake;
Those throats should not be cut, those necks should feel
A golden necklace there, not tempered steel,
Those eyes as dark as kohl should never be
Mixed with the trampled earth's impurity,
Those flanks that silver envies aren't mere meat
To quarter cruelly and then grill and eat,
Those gorgeous hindquarters were never made
For wounds inflicted by a dagger's blade,
Those navels where musk's fragrance forms and grows
Should never be the places where blood flows,
Those delicate, small hooves should never be
Subject to anguish and to agony,
Nor those strong, never-burdened backs be found
Laid low and broken on the dusty ground."

The huntsman wondered what on earth he meant
And bit his finger in astonishment;[62]
He said, "I hear you, and I might agree,
If I weren't thwarted by my poverty;
Two months of hunting's brought me what I need
And I've my children and a wife to feed.

How can a man in my position give
The prey I've hunted for, the right to live?
If you're so anxiously affected by them
They're yours, provided you've the means to buy them."

At once Majnun leaped from his horse, and handed
Its bridle to the man he'd reprimanded.
"Take this," he said. The huntsman grasped the reins,
And rode off happily across the plains.
Majnun then, as he kissed each deer's black eyes,
Murmured, "These aren't the eyes I idolize,
But even so they bring me memories of
The lovely eyes with which I am in love."
He bowed before the deer repeatedly
As if he worshiped them, then set them free.
They dashed off quickly, and Majnun made haste
To chase them as they crossed the desert waste,
Calling them as he went; his armor weighed
Him down and slowed the progress that he made,
As if it were a rosebush briar that grows
So densely it obliterates its rose.
He reached a sandy place that was as hot
As boiling water seething in a pot;
His clothes in tatters, it began to seem
His heart would soon volatilize to steam,
But then the air grew dark; the world was shaded
By night's black banner as the sunlight faded.
A path of moonlight lay across the land
Like a thin thread, a glittering strand—
The night was dark as Layli's curls, the light
As slender as her body, and as bright.

Now in a cave Majnun moaned like a snake
A lizard's bitten, wretched, wide awake,
Curled like a snake, or tossing there and turning,
Like thorns thrown on a fire that's fiercely burning;
He sighed and sang his songs, and groaned and wept
Throughout the night till dawn, and never slept.

MAJNUN FREES ANOTHER DEER
FROM A HUNTSMAN

Morning shone brightly; Ethiopian night
Frowned and then fled before the dawning light
That rose from China to pervade the skies.
Majnun awoke, and was as quick to rise
As scent diffused by fire, and like such scent
His sweetness seemed to fill the firmament.
Now like a lover singing sad refrains
He started off across the barren plains;
How ardently he sang, and may God bless
His songs that echoed in that wilderness!

And then before his eyes, what should appear
But one more trap, and in it one more deer,
And there another lion-like hunter bent
On slaughtering this rosy innocent
Whose neck was stretched before the lifted knife
About to shed its blood and take its life.
His shout was sharp,[63] as when a doctor needs
To lance a lesion and ensure it bleeds:
"Hey you, you domineering dog, release
That helpless creature, let it go in peace;
Set your poor prisoner free to roam and graze
And know contentment for a few more days,

Let him rejoice now, while it's not too late
To be together with his chosen mate.
Tonight, how will his doe address you when
She sees he's gone and won't return again?
She'll say, 'Now that you've taken him from me
I wish for you a condign misery;
May you not see one happy day, may you
Be tortured by the torments I've been through.'
If you're afraid of how the anguished sighs
Of wretched sufferers ascend the skies,[64]
Don't do this deed; what will you think when you're
The fated prey the hunter's hunting for?"
The huntsman stepped back from the deer and said,
"And if I spare this animal instead
Of killing it, what can you offer me?
You can't expect me to do this for free.
Hunting's my livelihood; show me what you
Might pay me, and I'll see what I can do."
Majnun set down his weapons, then unbound
His armored gear and laid it on the ground;
The huntsman made off with the lot, and thought
His haul far better than the prey he'd caught.

Then as a father comes close to his child
Majnun approached the stag and gently smiled;
He calmed it, stroked it, as a friend caressed it,
And where he saw a wound he soothed and dressed it;
He rubbed the deer down, brushed dust from its hide,
Then brushed away the copious tears he cried.[65]
He said, "You're like me, love has been denied you,
You've lost the one who ought to be beside you;

Dear mountain dweller, matchless liege-lord of
The upland plains, how you recall my love—
Your scent evokes her fragrance,[66] and your eyes
Resemble hers in darkness and in size,
Now may your hooves be freed from where they're caught,
Now may you lie beside the love you've sought,
Now may no devious hunter's traps confront you
Or monarchs with their lariats try to hunt you.
Nestled within your mouth, adorning it,
Your teeth are lovelier than a golden bit,
No splendid clothes could be more dignified
Than is the glory of your leathern hide,
Your tears are poison's antidote, although
It's better that these tears now cease to flow.
Dear noble beast, open your heart to one
Whose burning heart's despair is never done—
I know that in these parts there's gossip of
The presence of that full moon whom I love;
If, as you graze, you see her, oh explain
To her the nature of my grief and pain;
Tell her, 'O prisoner of my enemy,
I'm such as you would never hope to see—
We're far from one another, and I'm sure
That you endure the grief that I endure;
An old man with no news of you is like
An arrow that shoots wide and fails to strike,
And I don't pay the least attention to
Breezes that bring to me no scent of you,
As thoughts that aren't of you cannot remain
Embedded anywhere within my brain.'"
A hundred times and more, he told such tales
Of all his anguished sorrows and travails,

Then kissed the deer's dark eyes, and dexterously
Untied his hobbled hooves, and set him free.

When he had gone, Majnun set off again
Wandering at random through the empty plain.
The moon shone in the heavens as night fell
Like Joseph's face within his darksome well—[67]
The stars were like the Nile, foaming and flowing,
The heavens like Egypt glittered with their glowing,
And like the Nile Majnun moved on and on;
Unsure of where he was and where he'd gone,
Haphazard as a slithering snake's tongue darts,
Or like a hen that pecks by fits and starts,
A twisting injured snake that cannot rest,
A wing-clipped hen uneasy on her nest.
As oil burns in a lamp he felt desire
Flare up in him, his brain blazed like a fire—
He was a candle burning through the night,
Unresting, self-consumed by fire and light.

Majnun Talks to a Raven

Gold streaked the purple heavens as dawn's light
Spread through the dark and drove away the night;
That smiling yellow rose, the bright sun, spread
Its petaled beams and stained the sky rose red.
Majnun was like an autumn rose that's dying,
Wet with the tears that he was always crying;
Dawn's breeze dried all his fiery tears, but soon
He felt the burning of the blaze of noon.
His clothes were no protection, so he found
A tree, and sat beneath it on the ground,
And there a pool (whose limpid waters' gleam
Was like the purity of Kosar's stream)[68]
Was bordered by clean, verdant grass that made
The shady place a paradisal glade.
Hot now and thirsty, gratefully he sank
Down on the lush, fresh grass and deeply drank,
And for a while he rested from his seeking,
From hearing nothing and from always speaking.[69]

The grass he lay on seemed like green brocade
Beneath the lovely tree's enchanting shade;
He saw a raven perched there, on a tree,
Its eyes like lamps in their intensity;

Its blackness was as dark as Layli's hair
And seemed a sign of heartfelt, deep despair;
It sat there silent, sharp-eyed, watching him,
A jet-black stone within a turquoise rim.[70]
Majnun thought, "This black traveler seems to be
A stricken being who is much like me."
He cried, "Hey, Blacky! Tell me why you're dressed
In black like this? What's made you so depressed?
Why are your clothes so dark? The day is bright,
What's made you choose to be as dark as night?
Grief's fire has charred my heart, but why are you
Dressed in this melancholy, mourning hue?
And if you're heart's not burnt, what's made you choose
The pitch-black color men with charred hearts use?
And if you're one of us, why would you flee
Elsewhere, abandoning the likes of me?
Where have you sprung from, Blacky? Who are you?
The offspring of some pillaging Hindu?
Am I a king, and you're up there to shade me?
If not, what's all this spectacle you've made me?
The day you find my friend, say that I say,
'Without you I'm a floundering castaway,
Save me, and if you can't . . . then there will be
No hope for me, and there'll be no more me.'
Tell her, 'Don't be afraid, don't hesitate,
I fear I'll die in this heartbroken state.'
Say to her, 'Hurry, when the eyes are gone
Applying kohl's no good to anyone,
And when the wolf has seized the lamb, how can
A shepherd's shouting help the wretched man?
When once a flood has swept away a wall
No iron or plaster's any use at all,

A rock-strewn, barren field cannot bear crops
Whether rain never comes or never stops.'"
He shot his speech's dart so forcefully
The startled raven flew from tree to tree;
Majnun spread wings of all he had to say—
The raven spread its wings and flew away;
His vehement ranting made the bird desert him,
The raven left, and this surprised and hurt him.

Night like a raven's sable wing descended,
Bats woke up from their sleep, and day was ended;
You'd say the stars were lamps that lit the skies,
Or that they shone like ravens' glittering eyes.
Majnun was like a lamp that gives no light
As raven-darkness blotted out his sight;
He fell, and till the dawn broke never slept,
A candle self-consumed that burned and wept.

MAJNUN DELIBERATELY BECOMES
AN OLD WOMAN'S PRISONER

When morning's veil was lifted and dawn's light
Made all the waking world and heavens bright,
Gardens came into flower on every side,
And heaven's lamp spread glory far and wide.
Majnun flew like a raven here and there
Or like a moth that flutters through the air,
Drawn by a lamp, and as a pining lover
He made for lands that Layli's tribe ruled over,
Until at last he caught the longed-for scent
Of human presence, or a settlement.
He sat, and pressed his hand against his side
And like a weakened man who's almost died
But then revives again, he caught his breath
And sang like one who has evaded death.
He saw an ancient woman then, who had
A wanderer with her who appeared quite mad,
And whom the hurrying woman held in check
By a long rope she'd tied around his neck,
And chains festooned him head to foot, though he
Seemed happy in what looked like misery;
The woman scurried forward, pulling on
The rope as if to make her prisoner run,
And seeing this, Majnun was horrified—
"For God's sake, woman, don't do that!" he cried.

"Who is this man? Whatever did he do
That he should be chained up like this by you?"
"If it's the facts you want," the woman said,
"He's not a crazy madman to be led
Around in chains like this, and truth to tell
Neither does he deserve a prison cell.[71]
I am a widow, and my friend here's poor,
It's need that's made us wander door to door—
Chained up like this, folk think he's mad, and give
Us scraps of this and that on which to live.
Whatever we receive I always see
Donations are divided equally—
There's half for him and half for me, not one
Last crumb remains uneaten when we're done."
Majnun fell at her feet, as though he were
A bird with broken wings entreating her,
And cried, "Take off your friend's chains, set him free,
Take *me* now as your prisoner, chain up me;
Your friend does not deserve those chains—I do,
It's me who should be led around by you;
I'm *really* mad, I'm crazy, I don't care
Where you might drag me—here, there, anywhere!
And any alms that we might get I swear
They're wholly yours, I won't demand my share."
And when she'd grasped what he'd proposed to her
The woman couldn't have been happier.
She undid all the chains—her friend was freed—
And tied Majnun up just as they'd agreed,
Binding him well, and lastly making sure
The knot about his neck was quite secure.
Then she set off, and forced Majnun to run
From place to place, hurrying him on and on,

And men came out to see him everywhere;
Some laughed at him, some wept to see him there;
The ignorant and careless laughed, the wise
Wiped brimming tears from sympathetic eyes
While he himself seemed unaffected by
The chains and wounds that made them laugh or cry.
As they drew near to campsites, he would start
To sing of Layli and his broken heart,
Then wildly dance before each tent they found
Until he stumbled on the stony ground,
And once near Layli's neighborhood he caught
A subtle fragrance that the breezes brought,
And sat there in the dust, convinced this scent
Was wafted on the wind from Layli's tent,
And like rain-laden clouds when spring appears
He wept into the soil his endless tears
And beat his head against the ground and cried,
"We're separate, but in grief we're side by side,
And I'd be guiltier if I should be
Freed from these shackles that imprison me.
I'm chained like this because my actions ended
In guilt for something that was unintended,
Which was that you were hurt, and I submit
To any punishment that you see fit—
Despite my weapons, and the war I fought,
I stand here as a prisoner whom you've caught.
It was your tribe's terrain that I attacked
But it's myself I wounded by this act,
And if my wayward feet sinned then, look how
My neck is yoked with chains and shackles now;
The hand that loosed those arrows aches with pain,
Broken and useless, twisted by a chain,

And for the sin that I committed I've
Suffered so much I'm scarcely still alive.
Don't leave me in this state you see before you,
If you're to kill me, do it, I implore you!
I grow from you, uproot me, don't deny me,
Hammer four nails in me, and crucify me.
Your loyalty has shamed my treachery,
Your innocence my infidelity,
It's I who've sinned against you, and the sin
That I convict myself of lies within.
You must be faithful now, don't hesitate,
The sin is yours now if you vacillate,
Don't wish me a long life, don't praise or bless me,
Don't think to wish me well now or caress me,
My hope is that you'll kill me, that you'll find
Some cause to do this somewhere in your mind.
If you should draw your sword against me, I
Shall gladly sacrifice myself and die,
I'll be like Esma'il, rather than be
A brute convicted of apostasy.[72]
My heart's resplendent candle will still shine
If you remove this foolish head of mine—
A candle's head must hurt, it's always burning,
So snuff it out, and pacify its yearning;
Better I die before you than survive
Bereft of you, in pain, but still alive.
Since there's no way that I can reach you, I
Shall choose some corner, and sit there and sigh,
Grieving alone so that I won't remind you
Of all my pain, and I shan't try to find you.
May you rejoice unhurt, and may there be
Grief from now on for me and only me."

Then when he'd spoken, he exerted all
His strength and felt his fetters snap, and fall—
At once he leaped free from his broken chains
And like an arrow sped across the plains;
Wild in his madness now, he wept and cried
Until he reached a barren mountainside,
And made his way to Najd, traveling alone
While never ceasing to lament and moan.

Not knowing that he'd no wish to be seen
His family sought him everywhere he'd been;
But when they met him, both his parents knew
That there was nothing useful they could do.
He answered randomly; they left him there
And traveled home defeated by despair.
Majnun thought only now of Layli's name,
And towns or ruins were to him the same;
And when another name than hers was said
He beat himself, or fell asleep, or fled.

LAYLI'S FATHER GIVES HER TO EBN SALAM

The diver for bright pearls of meaning spread
His pearls before his audience, and said:

When Nofal won his battle, Layli heard
In detail everything that had occurred
And whispered to herself, "How glorious,
The man I love has been victorious!"
But then her father without more ado
Came in to her, his turban all askew,
And told her of the trick that he had played
With all the smooth talk of his long tirade:
"Ah, what a fine show I put on today,
I've saved us from that madman, come what may;
I listened to their claims, disputed them,
And at a single stroke refuted them.
Nofal is finished, he's been shown the door
And won't be coming back here any more;
As for Majnun, he's gone off who knows where,
And won't come courting now, he wouldn't dare.
Thank God that such a suitor's gone for good
And everything has turned out as it should!"
But Layli, hearing what her father said,
Felt only boundless misery and dread;

She hid her grief from him, and silently
Heaved desperate heartfelt sighs, but inwardly.

Her father left, and her narcissus eyes[73]
Grew rose-red with their weeping; piteous cries
Accompanied her tears that flowed pell-mell
As though they'd lay the dust on which they fell,
And seeing they were both lost equally[74]
She bit her hands and arms unceasingly,
While blood-red tears stained both her face and clothes
Like Judas blossoms or a crimson rose.
There was no friend in whom she could confide,
And she was helpless, as though caught inside
A wicker cage, twisting and turning there
Like a trapped snake that's injured in a snare,
While breezes blew her scent from place to place
Like whispering harbingers of her sweet face.
Gossip about her spread throughout the land
And eager suitors came to seek her hand;
Chieftains and princes, wealthy merchants vied
To claim this wondrous beauty as their bride,
A thousand marriage brokers said no pearl
Could be as precious as this lovely girl—
One suitor thought of wedding rites, one of
The honeyed sweetness that is found in love,
And all the while her father thought it best
To hide her like a pearl placed in a chest,
To keep her silver body safe, alone,
To shield her honor's glass from every stone.[75]

She drank wine outwardly, but inwardly
All that she drank was grief and misery,

She seemed to be a smiling candle while
She burned like melting wax beneath her smile;
She seemed a budding rose, in truth her life
Was like a lamp beneath which lurked a knife—
Her manner was all smiles and welcoming
While inwardly she feared what Fate would bring.
She was the glorious moon surrounded by
A hundred planets scattered in the sky.

When Ebn Salam heard of these rivalries
He thought at once of former promises,
And went with dignity and stately pride
To claim and welcome Layli as his bride.
He brought such gifts it seemed they'd never cease,[76]
Ass-loads of rubies, sugar, ambergris,
The finest musk that musk deer ever made,
And camel-loads of carpets and brocade;
On every kind of mount men could conceive
He brought more gifts than men could well believe.
He gave gold fine enough to start a war
And poured it out like sand grains on a shore,
Scattering the grains with such a generous hand
The mound collapsed like houses built on sand.

For two whole days he rested, then he sent
His messenger, a man so eloquent
He could have shamed a stone with his quick wit,
Making it malleable and softening it—
His talk, like Jesus's reviving breath,
Could bring a soul back from the point of death.[77]
The messenger brought gifts from far away,
From distant Rome and from remote Cathay,

And placed within the tribal treasury
The treasures that he gave so generously,
Then opened with the key of speech the lid
Beneath which more persuasive treasures hid.
He said, "Behold my lion prince, the sure
Defender of our warriors in war,
The noblest Arab sheikh, whose worldly treasure
Exceeds all computation and all measure;
If you want blood, like water he will pour it,
If you want gold, like sand he'll sift and store it,
With him come all the comforts you'll require,
From him come all the judgments you'll desire."
And with his talk the messenger succeeded
In softening Layli's father, who conceded
The promise of betrothal he had made,
And swore his promise wouldn't be betrayed,
That he was ready now, by nuptial laws,
To place the moon within the dragon's jaws.[78]

Dawn broke, when heaven's bride[79] began to shine
And lifted Jamshid's goblet[80] brimmed with wine,
And night's Arabian dark was nullified
In favor of day's pallid Russian bride.
Once Layli's father finished with adorning
The streets and markets for the wedding morning,
He called the bridegroom and his guests inside
Into the presence of the waiting bride
Where celebrations for the wedding day
Were happily and briskly under way.
Following the Arab custom, in the room
The bride was seated now beside her groom;

And then, as ritual required, once more
They swore the marriage oath agreed before.
The bridal price was settled then and there
And storms of coins rained down upon the pair—
Sugar was ground and sprinkled,[81] sandalwood
And sugar burned together as they should,
While from sweet Layli's lips a sigh as burning
Betrayed as fragrantly her hidden yearning;
Her harsh rosewater tears brought no relief
As she exhaled the scented breath of grief,
Her ruby mouth breathed fragrant fiery sighs
While rosewater descended from her eyes.
All that could be prepared for her was done
While all that she'd prepared for once was gone;
How close to her parched lips the cup had seemed—
It broke, and with it all that she had dreamed.

Step on a thorn and it will disconcert you,
And fire put in your mouth will surely hurt you,
A limb that is rebellious won't submit
To any orders that you issue it;
Someone who goes against her tribe will be
An outcast soul in perpetuity—
Severing a finger bitten by a snake
Becomes the best precaution you can take;
One must accept reverses, since defying
What comes one's way is tantamount to dying.
The world knew Layli as a wondrous creature,
But death would come from her defiant nature;
She'd gained a princely lamp; but in her sight
The lamp she longed for was the morning light.

*

When dawning sunlight struck night's purple tent
Pink stained the Tigris and the firmament,
And then the happy groom brought for his bride
A curtained litter all bejeweled inside,
And when she'd entered it, his camel train
Set off auspiciously across the plain.
His realm was hers, he said; his choices were
Whatever she decided to prefer.
For two or three more days he gently tried
To soften into wax his virtuous bride,
Then he grew bold in seeking out the prize
Of sweetly ripened fruit before his eyes—
He sought sweet dates, but they were well defended
By thorns that scratched the hand that he extended;
The shock of this so disconcerted him
That for a few days sleep deserted him—
Indeed, the blow that Layli struck had rendered
His will as weak as someone's who's surrendered.
She said to him, "If you try that again
I'll wipe your name out from the ranks of men;
I've sworn by God, and His supremacy,
By Him who made the man I love and me,
I won't submit to you, you have my word,
Not if you shed my blood now with your sword!"
And Ebn Salam saw that her oath implied
All hope of happiness for him had died;
He was her husband, but another light
Than his illumined Layli's day and night.
Though when it came to leaving her, he knew
That this was something he could never do,
His heart was hers, he had to be assured
That he could see the full moon he adored.

He thought, "Now that I've learned of how things are
It's better that I see her from afar,
To lose all sight of her would sorely grieve me,
Better a stolen glance than that she leave me."
He wept, and begged forgiveness, and admitted
It was a dreadful sin that he'd committed;
He said, "I'll only look at you; if I
Do more than this, then I deserve to die."
There would be no persuading or pursuing her—
From that time on, to look was all his wooing her.

That lovely garden, and that lamp that glowed[82]
And lit the budding roses, watched the road,
Hoping for wind-blown scattered dust to wend
Its way to her from her cave-dwelling friend;
She'd sing sad songs, and go continually
To scan the road, but always fruitlessly—
She'd stumble like a drunk, and cast such glances,
Sadder than are a thousand sad romances,
She'd seek to find out where Majnun was hidden
And hurt her soul with things that were forbidden,
And how impatiently she would complain
About her lover's absence, but in vain.
What had been covered was now on display,
Her secret love was now as clear as day,
And her impatient pain was mixed with fear
Of what her husband or her father'd hear—
But who's afraid, once love is in the soul,
Of husbandly or fatherly control?

MAJNUN LEARNS OF LAYLI'S MARRIAGE

That learnèd singer of Baghdad, behold,
Here is the stirring story that he told:

The man who'd broken all his chains, and who
Was crazy for the moon he couldn't view,
Majnun, whose liver smoldered and became
Like grilled kebabs in passion's ardent flame,[83]
Majnun, proprietor of a little town
Whose ruined buildings had all tumbled down,[84]
Frequented all the caravanserais
With no companions but his anxious sighs.
The scent of Layli's litter seemed to bring
To him a fragrance sweeter then the spring,
But as he breathed it in his limbs all showed
A sallow color[85] that like amber glowed;
Black melancholy had affected him
And showed its influence in every limb;
Weak and confused he fell beneath a tree
That had a thorny trunk and canopy,
And he was so perplexed he couldn't tell
Whether it was on thorns or flowers he fell.
And then he saw a female camel pass
Swift as a snake that's twisting through the grass;
Its pitch-black rider pulled back on his rein
And like a demon yelled out in disdain,

"You're so in love, you fool, you're so far gone,
You've no idea of what's been going on;
Tug at the reins and turn your horse's head,
You'll find no faith in love, you've been misled;
The business you're involved in's dark as night,
Your lover has moved on, gone out of sight—
It's pointless, useless, everything you're doing,
You'll finish up with nothing from your wooing!
You never thought the one you love would be
Unfaithful to you, and your enemy?
Well, she's your enemy and faithless too,
And doesn't want to see or hear of you!
She's thrown you to the winds and she forgets you,
Gone back on what she promised and rejects you.
They've given her away, and she's a bride,
Her husband's young, and now she's satisfied;
She serves him as she should, and in his arms
She doesn't struggle or withhold her charms,
Each day she's with him, always, face to face,
Clasping her husband in her close embrace;
Her days are spent in kisses, hugs, caresses,
So why should you care how her love progresses?
She's far away from you and you're alone
So smash this love of yours against a stone!
For years to come she'll have forgotten you,
And now it's up to you, forget her too!
A thousand women are to blame, not one,
The promises they make are soon undone—
Men thought up vows and wrote them out, but when
It came to women's vows they broke the pen;
Women can be your friend, but in the end,
You'll find out that they've found another friend,

And when she's cuddled by another love
It won't be you that she'll be thinking of!
Women have more desire than men, for sure;[86]
Domestic duties are what keeps them pure . . .
And women won't play fair, they like to cheat,
All that they're really good at is deceit.
Many've committed crimes, they're criminal,
Not one of them is faithful, none at all!
And when a man is with a woman, she's
The one to watch for infidelities;
What is a woman but a showcase for
Deceit? Outwardly peace, inwardly war,
The worst of enemies, the killer of
Your soul when she declares undying love.
You say, 'Do this,' she's other things to do—
'And don't do that,' she's still ignoring you;
When you're depressed she hasn't got a care,
When you're delighted she's in deep despair;
This is the way that women are, my friend,
And tales of women's evil never end."

The demon's wild offensive talk provoked
An inward blazing fire that almost choked
With smoky anger poor outraged Majnun,
Who fell as if an epileptic swoon
Had toppled him, and as he fell his head
Struck hard against a stone that turned blood-red;
He fell among sharp rocks, his soul was shattered
And all his worn-out clothes were torn and tattered.

Even the demon whose foul words had maimed
Majnun's sad soul felt sorry and ashamed;

He watched, and as he watched he saw that soon
Awareness was returning to Majnun—
A thousand times he asked for pardon then,
Saying he was the most ashamed of men,
Saying, "All that I told you was a lie,
Forgive me, let such silliness go by,
Do as you wish with me for my offense,
I offer you my soul in recompense.
Your chaste, veiled love still loves you, and her heart
Is still as broken that you're far apart;
If she has wed another it's still you
She thinks and dreams of, and is faithful to,
She speaks of no one else but you, throughout
The world it's you she cannot live without
And every moment, always, she will find
That you and only you are in her mind.
As for her husband, that poor man she's wed,
He hasn't spent one night in Layli's bed;
She's been a wife to him now for a year,
But you have all her love still, never fear,
And if she lives a thousand years without you
Nothing will make her yield to him, or doubt you."

His talk seemed like a mirror from which two
Dissimilar faces peered, but which was true?
Though even so, Majnun's despair grew less
And he was comforted in his distress.
Now like a bird that has a broken wing,
Despite his head wound, he began to sing
A song like threaded rubies—one that dealt
With broken vows and all the grief he felt;
But still his mind was hazy, clouded, dim,
And still his love had heard no news of him.

MAJNUN COMPLAINS OF LAYLI TO THE WIND

The bride's maidservant led the dazzling bride
Down from her litter to the world outside.[87]
This bride no artist's brush could represent
Descended from her litter's traveling tent,
Constrained to join the husband she must meet
As if she'd journeyed there with shackled feet,
And grieving inwardly, still brokenhearted,
Longing for him from whom she had been parted.

When Majnun heard about her married state
His grief redoubled and he cursed his fate;
His knowledge that his love was now a bride
Strengthened the madness that his name implied;
He stumbled like a bird whose wings have failed,
As weak as was the breath that he exhaled.
He set off for her home, weeping and moaning,
Grown thin now as a hair with all his groaning
And still obsessively addressing her:
"You're happy with the man whom you prefer,
But what's become of us sat side by side
And of the thousand love-knots that we tied?
Where are the hopeful plans that we prepared,
Where are the humble promises we shared,
Now that you break your vows so carelessly
And hide your sinless face away from me?

I think your heart is done with loyalty now,
And where's the friendship in a broken vow?
I gave my soul to you, and I received
From you glib words that flattered and deceived,
The soul I gave deserved your love, but you
Bestowed love owed to me on someone new.
You're happy with your new love—I can see it;
And you neglect your old love—well, so be it.
But still I ask, when you're in his embrace,
See that you don't forget my name and face;
In your sweet garden all my youth was spent,
And oh, the agonies I underwent—
I was the dove that labored . . . even so
The ripened fruit was stolen by a crow;
Your dates are sweet, but still they ought to be
Like spines and thorns to everyone but me;
What scorching ardent sighs I heaved for you—
No one deserves your garden as I do.
I was the first love whom you chose, but then,
You chose to treat me as the worst of men;
I gave my heart to you, and on that day
I never thought that you would act this way.
You tricked me with your vows, but I have stayed
Loyal to you, true to the vows I made—
Look at your vows, the loving words you said,
Then look at what you've done, and who you've wed;
Your heart was heated by another's flame,
Before my eyes you showed you felt no shame.
If we cannot distinguish good from ill
Others will follow us who can and will,
And they will be the arbiters who should
Decide what's bad in us and what is good;

They'll see how I have suffered, and they'll see
What I have done to you and you to me.
I think that I've been blind, they'll think so too,
And that the one who broke her vows is you.
A chastely budding rose will have no thorn—
It opens, breaks its oath, and thorns are born;
Wine's not a matter of acclaim or shame
Till drunken ruffians give it a bad name;
It's when the waning moon has gone that night
Becomes a fearsome dark bereft of light.
All of my life was tied to what you swore,
For you it was an oath you could ignore,
And you don't act to please me now, but I
Will not forget you, not until I die.
For all the suffering that you've put me through
I'd suffer more if I resented you—
You've filled my heart with grief, and there's no space
Remaining to be shamed by my disgrace.
You've changed, and I don't know you; I can't say
It's *your* heart that's disloyal to me today;
I'm helpless, wondering whether it's the same you,
And now I've no idea how I should name you.
Your cruelty takes away my wish to live,
Your beauty tells me that I must forgive;
It's surely licit—if such beauty dares to—
To take the life of anyone it cares to;
You're dawn's light, I'm a sputtering lamp; it's clear
That lamps aren't needed when the dawn is here.
You are the moon if moons are sweetest things,
If kings are two-faced, you're the best of kings;
Fire's mouth will water at the distant sight
Of your magnificently shining light,

A garden's full of flowers, and should it meet you,
Your lovely charms would make it want to eat you,
A silken ruby-colored cloak's disgrace
Is that it looks like straw beside your face,
Your eyebrow's curve is like the new moon's when
It shows a feast-day has come round again,
Aloes and sandalwood are valueless
Beside your face's shining loveliness,
Your pallid face that's shadowed by your hair
Shows China's wealth and Africa's are there.[88]
How hard to separate oneself, to leave
The loveliness of such a face and grieve,
But I know nothing else that I can do
Except to sacrifice my soul to you;
I offer up my patience, and I wait
To see which way my reins are tugged by Fate."

MAJNUN'S FATHER GOES TO SEE HIS SON

In fluent verse a Persian nobleman
Renews the Arab story he began:

The father of Majnun groaned, brokenhearted,
As Jacob did when Joseph had departed;
Knowing Majnun was mad with love, no rest
Or hope could now reside within his breast—
Sighs punctuated his persistent pain,
Life passed in expectation but in vain;
Always he thought up schemes and plans, but then
Washed Africans can't change to Turkomen.[89]
He spent vast sums, seeking him wildly, blindly,
But Fate did not reward his efforts kindly
And he lost hope of finding his mad son,
And when he'd realized that all hope was gone
He sat withdrawn, within a little room,
Alone, expecting nothing but his tomb.
But then he feared that death would come before
He'd set out searching for his son once more,
And in his old age, feeble now and weak,
His voice so strangled he could hardly speak,
He took his staff, and set off once again
(This time accompanied by two young men),
In search of his lost son, hoping that God
Would look with favor on the path he trod.

He went back to the rocks and fertile land,
The green earth and the deserts of black sand,
But though he went in hope, he saw no trace
Of his lost sought-for son in any place.
But then he met a man who told him where
A wretched outcast lived, not far from there,
And that he'd find him in a grim defile,
A dreadful place, repulsive, bleak, and vile,
Like a foul grave, a lowering cloud, a pit
Of fire, of oily flames and blackened grit.
Traveling along the indicated way
The old man hurried onward for a day,
Then saw his son, frail and emaciated—
His anguished heart was deeply agitated
To see him in this state, bereft, alone,
His scrawny body now mere skin and bone,
Lost in an unreal world, and given over
To being an idolatrous mad lover,
A splinter stuck within a dream of dread,
A hair a hair's breadth's space from being dead,
More fretful than a scurrying searching hound,
More hidden than dark demons underground.
The cauldron of his body had boiled dry,
His mind was too far gone to function by,
Bareheaded, writhing like a snake, he wore
A skin around his waist and nothing more.
His father ventured close and sat beside him
And gently stroked his head, and pacified him;
Majnun, aware of someone near him weeping,
Opened his eyes as though he had been sleeping
And saw a man he didn't recognize
And started back from him in mute surprise.

(How could he know another man when he
No longer knew his own identity?)
He questioned him: "What brings you here today?
Leave me alone! Who are you? Go away!"
The man said, "I'm your father, you're my son,
I've wept and longed for you since you've been gone."
And when Majnun saw who he was, he crept
To him, and bowed down at his feet, and wept;
Both wept together then, each kissed the other
And whispered how he'd sorely missed the other.
The father dried his eyes at last and then
Examined this most miserable of men,
And saw he was as naked as the way
That all mankind will be on Judgment Day;
He pulled fine garments from his bag, and put
Them on his son, and clothed him head to foot,
And from his turban to his shoes his son's
Attire was now as fine as anyone's;
Then as a father he began to give
His son advice on how he ought to live.

"Now by your father's soul this is no place
For you to sleep; time in its endless race
Is rushing on—what's here to lie upon
But rocks and thorns? The sooner that you're gone
From here the better! Look how heaven's dart
Has cruelly spilled your blood and pierced your heart,
A few more days with boulders as your bed
Will surely finish you and you'll be dead,
You'll be a body, decomposing meat
For animals like wolves and lions to eat;

Better to be a dog in streets you know
Than suffer all that exiles undergo;
Where have you reached by running on and on?
Somewhere it's better that you'd never gone!
It isn't reasonable to grieve; grief makes
A man so weak that his resolve soon breaks;
Look how a flood that's unforeseen will burst
A river's banks and leave a plain submersed,
Or how a flood roars down a mountainside
Causing its slopes to crumble and subside;
Your grief's like this—if you were iron you
Could not resist the harm such grief will do,
Stubborn rebelliousness fills all your days,
Now for a few days try more yielding ways;
Your head tugs at the reins, your heart's on fire,
But still you can't accomplish your desire—
Stop urging this steed on, it's foolishness,
So stop all this ridiculous excess,
Stop acting like the demons' honored guest
Or like a pit that demons have possessed!
Be patient, strong, let all this turmoil leave you,
And don't let silly specious lies deceive you.
Be happy, life's mere wind, intelligence
Says pleasure is the soul-mate of good sense.
If pleasure is a lie or if it's real
Its presence will enhance the way you feel—
Better to be content and happy than
To chase vague fancies like a foolish man;
Unhealthy longings have no solid bases,
You can't rely on them, they're empty spaces;
Men store up grain they have, since all men know
Many won't eat the harvest that they sow.

Now life is yours, it's in your hands, today,
So see that you enjoy it while you may—
Tomorrow death will surely come for you
And no excuse will work when death is due.
The drink death brings you isn't new, it's made
From all you brought to life's long cavalcade—
As women wear the garments that they've sewn,
So men will reap the harvest that they've grown;
If you act well today, the day of death
Will be made fragrant by your actions' breath—
Know death before it comes, and pass away
Untouched by pain or suffering on that day,
A soul escapes death's talons when it dies
Before the body's subsequent demise,[90]
How a man fares in death depends upon
The many deeds he has already done—
He'll smile on this last journey if good deeds
Provide him the provisions that he needs.

"It's up to you what happens next, but sit,
Be calm, forget this madness, banish it!
Each moment every sorrow will diminish,
And every grief eventually must finish.
Even dogs have a home, and you have none—
Aren't you a man still, when all's said and done?
If you're a man then be one! And if you're
A devil, vanish! What're you waiting for?
Ghouls who live on the earth possess the guile
To show themselves as humans for a while,
But you're a man, the noblest, wisest being,
So what's this ghoul's behavior that I'm seeing?[91]

For these few days that I have left, let's ride
As sociable companions, side by side;
We are one flesh, so be my friend, and be
A comfort in my weak old age to me.
If you leave me tonight, tomorrow when
You look for me, you won't find me again—
If what I'm saying seems too burdensome,
Remember, heaven decrees when death must come;
My end is close, accept this and be strong,
Consent to what must come before too long.
My page is written now; live cheerfully,
Drink wine, rejoice when there's no trace of me—
Sadness has killed me and my life departs;
Be safe, be happy in your heart of hearts.
My sun's traversed the skies, and, now it's near
That point when yellow sunset must appear;[92]
You are the dawn, my day fades into night;
My son, my soul is ready to take flight.
Oh come to me, my soul, my boy, before
Your father's spirit will be here no more;
When I have gone from here, see that you make
Your house both warm and friendly, for my sake,
So that before I die, I'll know someone
Is there to take my place when I am gone,
And when my body's taken you will be
My true successor, here in place of me.
No friend or enemy, when I am dead,
Will stand for it if you're not there instead,
A stranger will appear, and soon despoil
Riches that represent a lifetime's toil—
If you won't take my place, who will be there
To guard the wealth I gathered with such care?

This is my swansong, spoken from my heart,
My time has come, I'm ready to depart.
Alas, that when I'm gone you'll come and keep
Your vigil at my grave and grieve and weep
And bow your head down to my dust and mourn
My passing deeply, wretched and forlorn.
But should your soul go too, what will survive
Of all my clan when you are not alive?"

MAJNUN ANSWERS HIS FATHER

Majnun heard all his father's words and tried
To show him that his heart was satisfied,
And, for a few days, struggled not to grieve him
While wondering all the while how to deceive him.
He tried renouncing love, but love betrayed
Soon boxed his ears and made him more afraid
(Love's like an elephant, and when it starts
It tramples heroes with the stoutest hearts,
The arrows that are shot in love's disputes
Wound both the target and the one who shoots).
Majnun's head turned in turmoil, listening to
His father's thoughts on what he ought to do;
He said, "The words you utter vivify me,
Your thoughts resolve the problems that defy me,
And as my teacher the advice you gave
Instructed me and made me like your slave,
Your words are like my soul's lamp . . . but I fear
They're words of wisdom I no longer hear.
I know what you advise is right, but I
Can't act like this, no matter how I try!
Why mint me wisdom's coins? You ridicule
The coins I deal in, thinking I'm a fool;
It's love that rules me now and in my brain
The world itself's not worth a barley grain!

My fate is such that all the words I hear
Disperse upon the wind and disappear.
All that I knew is gone, and in my mind
Only forgetfulness is left behind,
Every last little scrap of what I heard
Just yesterday is gone now, every word,
And ask me what I'm doing now, this minute—
My mind's a total blank, there's nothing in it!
I know you're my respected father, though
Your name is gone, that's something I don't know,
It isn't just my father—I'm not sure
Inside myself who I am any more;
My own name's gone now, and I can't discover
Which one I am—the loved one or the lover?
The lightning in my heart has lit a fire
That's burns my inmost being with desire.
I live off plants and herbs, my hunger's died,
Raw vegetation leaves me satisfied—
I think this means I don't need food to fill
The maw of my digestion's little mill.
I'm lost in wildness now, and men like me
Can't live in civilized society,
Who'd want to be the friend of someone wild
Or learn the habits of a savage child?
The melon's fly-blown now, better to slit
My stomach than have someone munch on it.
I fear, when all men know my situation,
The harm done to our friends' good reputation—
When someone's skin's all blisters children should
Be kept away from him, for their own good.
My longing is to be in ruined places
Whose past inhabitants have left few traces—

Take no account of me, my life is done,
Imagine that you never had a son.
Think of a man in love as one who's dead,
Who's left this world now, and gone on ahead;
You say the night of your last journey's near
While I am lost within my journey here.
Your journey means my autumn's come, alone
We travel to what's certain but unknown.
Those who are living will soon weep for you,
What can a dead man, such as I am, do?"

Majnun's Father Bids Him Farewell

His father saw the pain his anguish brought him
And how the world of love had wholly caught him,
He gave up hope that he could heal his son—
Such feverish knots could never be undone.
He said, "O loved and wearisome sweet boy,
You're both my shackles and my crowning joy,
I've heard your hopelessness, your misery,
And said farewell now to both you and me;
Your father weeps for you, tears blear his sight,
And you should weep too, as is only right,
Stand up, embrace me now before we part,
And pour your tears into my grieving heart—
They'll cleanse me as I die, and they'll bestow
Consoling dreams upon me as I go.
It's readiness, not kohl, a traveler's eyes
Require on this last journey as he dies,
So now, before I leave you, hold me fast—
How long the warmth of your embrace must last!
I'm entering the other world, I know,
My tent is folded, I'm prepared to go,
But I shan't travel far from you, I'm leaving
But still in death I'll join in all your grieving.
Farewell, I'm going to that place whence men
Who've traveled there cannot come back again;

Farewell, my self dissolves, I cannot stay,
My caravan's already on its way."

He turned aside then, and along the track
By which he'd come began his journey back
And reached home wearily and sick at heart
Knowing his soul was ready to depart.
Weakly, for two more days now, and in pain,
His soul traversed the last of life's terrain
And when death stepped forth from its ambush, he
Quitted his mortal substance willingly.
The heavenly bird flew upward from its snare
And in truth's realm shed every earthly care—
His soul grasped heaven's rope; his earthly frame
Descended to the earth from which it came.

The soul at rest is one that had no rest
But like the moon relentlessly progressed
Through earthly life, and like the lightning's light
Came and departed quickly in the night.
Don't pause here, since this fleeting world begets
Sorrow and pain and infinite regrets,
The man who thinks this world his home will find
That peace is banned forever from his mind,
While one who looks to heaven knows that he
Will never die but lives eternally.
The world's a devil with an angel's face
And you must perish in its cruel embrace,
Or it's a bowl of bleeding entrails cut
From our and every human being's gut.
If in this world you cherish anyone
The world ensures that he will soon be gone,

It is the devils' home, a place of grieving
That floods of pilgrim-souls are always leaving.
The world's mouth seems as sweet as dates; take care!
Her kiss will show you thorns are hidden there.
Your cypress grows in water that's unfit,
And brackish, spiky spines encompass it.
How long will you endure this, to attack
And ignominiously be driven back?
Take life for what it is, the world is pain,
You're part of it, it's pointless to complain.
A clever thief will steal a precious jewel
From everything around it, he's no fool;
A snake though doesn't know what jewels are worth,
He lets it go, and dines on slime and earth—
You are the flower that lights the world, don't be
The earthbound snake that acts so foolishly.

Great kings and holy men once ruled the earth
Whose rulers now are of inferior worth,
Look who has taken those past sovereigns' place—
The leavings of a rabble-rousing race.
You won't attain those former heroes' fame
Unless you leave behind a righteous name;
Renounce all evil, act then as you should,
Good fortune follows those whose deeds are good;
When you've been harmed, this wasn't done by those
Whom you believe to be your mortal foes,
All of the harmful things they seemed to do
Derived in truth from no one else but you.
Act well then, and reflect upon this fact,
An actor's the recipient of his act—

It's like a voice that travels out, and then
The echo of that voice comes back again;
Whisper your secrets to a mountainside,
And as they come back they are multiplied.

Consider heaven's ways with careful eyes,
And you will understand, if you are wise,
Nothing outdoes the heavens, no man's look
Deciphers what's inscribed in heaven's book;
No mangonel, no mighty catapult,
Can break the battlements of heaven's vault
That are so far from earth they have no fear
Of any taunts or threats that rise from here.
Don't peer with purblind eyes around this pit,
Many like you have fallen into it,
And do you think that some long winding rope
Will come to haul you out? Is this your hope?
The feast that's spread out here will prove to be
No feast at all, since it's illusory.
Where you see noble buildings, all around
Ruins of noble buildings can be found,
These ruins were once buildings, firm and strong,
These buildings will be ruins before long,
And every village shows how buildings fall
And wise precautions are no use at all.

MAJNUN LEARNS OF HIS FATHER'S DEATH

One day by chance, in the late afternoon,
A hunter happened to pass by Majnun;
It was a lion that the hunter sought
But when he saw Majnun, sunk deep in thought,
He stopped, and angrily spoke up, as though
A sword and not his tongue would deal the blow:
"What are you doing brooding here, so far
From where your friends and all your family are?
Caring for Layli only, unaware
Of how your home is, or what's happened there,
Forgetful of your parents and their name—
You shameless oaf, shame on your lack of shame!
A son who's dead and buried's better than
A son unworthy to be called a man!
Your father was alive when some rash whim
Made you decide that you'd abandon him
And now he's dead I wish long life to you,
But honoring him's the least that you can do—
Come to his grave, show sorrow and respect,
Seek pardon from his soul for your neglect."
Hearing such words, Majnun's frail body bowed,
Bent like a harp, crying his grief aloud,
He threw himself headlong, and with loud moans
Battered and bruised his forehead against stones,

126

And desperately began to weep and rave,
Running until he reached his father's grave,
And when he found the place it was as though
He'd found a diamond shattered with a blow;
He fell upon the dust and wildly grasped it
And like a lover to his body clasped it,
He wept such tears of filial regret
The dust upon his father's grave grew wet;
How he embraced the dust he clung to there,
Then poured and smeared it on his head and hair
Until, worn out and feverish, he lay
Upon the ground as night imprisoned day.
How much he'd suffered—one who from his first
Short steps had been a prisoner and accursed
(Whoever he may be, a man resembles
An orphan when fear traps him, and he trembles);
Suffering an orphan's and a prisoner's fate,
He was reduced now to this desperate state.
He writhed and twisted, wishing he could find
A friend there with a sympathetic mind,
But no one came in whom he could confide,
There was no friend to make him turn aside
From all this grief, and so he wept so much
The tear-soaked earth grew sodden to the touch.
He cried, "O father, where have you now gone?
You've shown no sign to your tormented son—
Where can I seek you, find the love you taught me?
Who can I speak to of the grief you've brought me?
You found it best to have no son, descended
Into the ground, and so your life was ended—
For me though there is only bitterness
Now I've become this new thing—fatherless!

I cry for help, but who can I cry to
Since help has always come to me from you?
You were my friend, my ally, and the source
Of all my heart's vitality and force;
You taught me what is right, you sympathized
With all I sought and suffered and devised;
I'll be a phantom without you, no one,
Alas that I am here and you have gone.
Don't use your absence as my punishment,
I am ashamed enough and I repent,
Ah, how I blame myself, and weep and rave
When I recall the good advice you gave—
You were the happy trainer, I the colt
Who'd bridle at the bridle and then bolt,
You were an earring fastened to my ear
With gentle guidance I refused to hear;
I was unmoved by all your kind advice,
You were so warm, and I as cold as ice.
I never spoke the words you wished I'd spoken
Or lay beside you till the dawn had broken,
But in a hundred different ways I hurt you
While I went wandering, happy to desert you;
You were my pillow, but I spurned all sleep
To gad about, and stay awake, and weep;
You had prepared a feast for me, I fled
And fell, and broken boulders were my bed;
Your prayed for me, to no effect; I planted
A fruit tree whose sweet fruit I wasn't granted.
Now I remember your kindheartedness
And every moment deepens my distress;
I'll wear dark blue, I'll weep a Nile for you,[93]
And bruised and blind,[94] I'll be both black and blue.

O my dear father, oh, what have I done?
A thousand pains are heaped upon your son.
I hurt you, O my father, and if I
Am not forgiven by you, I must die—
May all my sins and my iniquity
Be overlooked and not redound on me.
You are my star, shine on me, don't forget me,
And solve for me the problems that beset me—
Pardon your slave, I fear that if you sever
Forgiveness from me I'll be lost forever!
You said I am your vitals, your bones' marrow,
Are you to shoot me with your anger's arrow?
And is your wrath to roast me now like meat?
If I'm your vitals, it's yourself you'll eat,
If my blood's shed in this, then yours is too,
If I'm to roast in fire, then so will you,
And if I've sinned against you, I am caught
And punished by the ugly sins I've wrought.
I was the foolish child who never hears
His father's words, and so you boxed my ears,
As I deserved." He wept, and was all tears and sighs,
Turning the day dark with his piteous cries,
Beating the drum of sorrow, until night
Descended and dispelled the day's last light.

The moon moved into Pisces and the night
Was like a black shell brimming with its light,
Its radiance flooded from the shell, a flow
Of bright pearls scattered on the world below,
And Majnun's eyes, as dark as that black shell,
Scattered their pearls upon the world as well.

Seated beside his father's grave till morning,
Majnun sang threnodies of grief and mourning,
From end to end it was as though this dust
Were now the only home that he could trust;
As if he drank deep draughts there through the night,
He bowed his head until the morning light.
A new day dawned, and from the mountainside
Dawn's banner streamed out as the darkness died,
And like a wondrous alchemist—behold,
The morning light transformed earth's dust to gold.
Majnun, that thing of earth, weeping in pain
Set off across the earth to Najd again—
He wept, but this time all the tears he shed
Were not for someone loved but someone dead.
Each labored, bitter breath he drew distressed him,
A hundred thousand agonies possessed him,
And as he traveled on his tortuous way
His day seemed night, and night was turned to day.

MAJNUN AMONG THE ANIMALS

This is the way the lord of eloquence
Resumed his telling of this sweet romance:

Majnun, that basil in a barren land,[95]
His pillow stones, his tablecloth dry sand,
Still grieving for his father, always questing,
Crossed over plains and mountains, never resting.
One day he passed through country not far from
The place where Layli's people made their home
And saw a piece of paper lying there
On which two words were written as a pair—
Layli–Majnun. He picked it up and ripped
The scrap in half, dividing up the script
And then destroying half; he kept the bit
That had his name, *Majnun*, inscribed on it.
Some bystanders reproached him: "Why did you
Tear them like that? Why separate these two?"
Majnun replied, "The writing showed a pair—
Lovers are one, just one name should be there;
Look at a lover truly—you'll discover
That both are there, the loved one and the lover."
"But you kept your name, not her name," they said.
"Isn't it better to keep hers instead?"
He said, "I shouldn't be the one within,
Invisible, while she's the outer skin;

131

I ought to be her veil and hide her well,
She is the hidden pith, I'm just the shell."[96]

He left the bystanders, like Rabe'eh,[97]
Impatient to be on his wandering way,
Singing his love songs since he knew they brought
The medicine that his desperate sorrows sought.
He was a wild man now, the bonds that tied
Him to society were cast aside,
He sought out isolated desert places
And roots and leaves for food, in green oases,
And animals, but not to trap or eat them,
Rather to live with them, and gently greet them,
And humbly, like a servant, he drew near
The animals he found there, lions or deer,
Whatever beasts he saw, he was the same,
Their lowly servitor in all but name,
Till lions and deer and wolves and foxes soon
Seemed like an army summoned by Majnun,
And they became *his* servants, flocking round him,
And as their own King Solomon they crowned him.[98]
Majnun was not much more than skin and bone
But hungry vultures left their lord alone
And over him, with eagles, spread their wings
As parasols are opened over kings;
Wolves did not trouble sheep, and lions kept
Their talons from wild asses as they slept,
Wild dogs and rabbits were at peace, among
A pride of lions deer could nurse their young;
Majnun was safe, as if his life were charmed,
And mingling with them he was never harmed.

At night, a vixen swished her tail and swept
His sleeping area clean before he slept,
A deer came, and with dexterous holds and moves
Massaged his legs with her four tiny hooves,
His head and body were supported by
An ass's neck and a gazelle's plump thigh,
A lion knelt beside him like a sentry
Whose drawn sword would permit no others entry,
A lurking wolf kept watch too, prowling round
On guard to keep his master safe and sound,
The leopard skin on which he lay seemed like
A living leopard that's prepared to strike.
He seemed, surrounded by his followers,
A king encircled by his warriors,
And no one feared that some bloodthirsty beast
Would eye his body as a helpless feast.
Any who seemed like enemies were soon
Disposed of by these guardians of Majnun,
And no one dared to hurt or give offense
To those to whom he granted audience,
And friend or stranger no one could come near
Unless his order rang out, loud and clear.
He healed the wounded in his retinue
Tending them as kindhearted shepherds do,
But he was savage to all savage men,
Having no wish to mix with them again.
Among the fawns around him there was one
Whose nature was all play and prancing fun,
Skittish and agile, prompt to dodge and jump,
She had a graceful neck, a fleshy rump—
Majnun loved all the fawns, both big and small,
But this one was his favorite of them all;

He'd call her to him when she shied and fled,
And he was always stroking her smooth head,
Each day he'd kiss her eyes with heartfelt sighs
Since they reminded him of Layli's eyes.
Men were amazed to see how meek and mild
These beasts were that were normally so wild,
And travelers came each day to stop and make
A gift of foodstuffs for devotion's sake;[99]
Majnun sat on a lion's back to greet them,
Alarming them as he rode out to meet them,
And ate a little of the food they brought,
Then gave the rest to his attentive court.
In every passing season he made sure
His animals were well provided for
And they in turn bowed down to him, agreeing
That he'd become the source of their well-being,
And since self-interest made them all respect him
They trailed him always, anxious to protect him.
Kindness to all creation will preserve you,
And free men will be slaves who long to serve you.

A TALE

I heard that once, according to a story,
There was a king of Marv who reigned in glory;
He kept a pack of dogs chained up, fierce, savage,
Demonic animals, disposed to ravage
Whatever they encountered—in a fight
They'd tear a camel's head off with one bite;
And when the king was angry he'd condemn
The miscreant to be consigned to them—
They were the gory means of the removal
Of anyone who lost the king's approval.
Among the king's companions there was one
Who was accomplished, elegant, and young
But also frightened that one day he might
Become abhorrent in his sovereign's sight.
He thought he'd go and see the dogs, and show them
Just who he was, and slowly get to know them;
He feared the dogs, but made friends with the men
Who fed them and had access to their pen,
And afterward, each day, he threw sheep's meat
Before the slavering dogs, for them to eat,
And gradually these savage beasts became,
For him at least, calm, tractable, and tame;
His openhandedness meant that they'd greet
Him happily and lie down at his feet.

*

135

One day the king in fury turned against
The young man; now beside himself, incensed,
He ordered that the wretched youth be thrown
Straight to the dogs; his sycophants had grown
More dog-like than the dogs, and cruelly seized
Their victim to ensure their king was pleased.
They trussed him up, and pushed him through the gate
Into the pen, and left him to his fate.
At first the dogs crouched, ready to attack,
And snarled and growled at him . . . but then drew back,
They'd recognized their friend, and came around him
Wagging their tales, delighted to have found him,
As if they were his nurse and he their child;
They nuzzled at his hands, no longer wild,
And sat beside him, keeping watch all night
Until the first signs of the morning light.

The next day dawned; night's dusky silken veil
Turned to a dazzling gold, and then grew pale.
The king regretted last night's deed, and blamed
Himself for what he'd done, and felt ashamed.
He said to his companions, "I was foolish,
What was I dreaming of to be so mulish
As to destroy a youth whose company
Always diverted and delighted me?
See what my murderous dogs have done to him—
They must have torn the poor lad limb from limb."
The dog's chief keeper came before the king
And said, "You majesty, a wondrous thing
Has happened to that man who's not a man,
Who must be more a heavenly angel than

A human being; come yourself and see
The power of God's redeeming clemency—
He sits surrounded by your dogs, their paws
Caress him, and affection's locked their jaws;
Your wolfish dogs have not disturbed, I swear,
Upon that young man's head a single hair."

Courtiers were promptly ordered then to bring
The lost young prisoner quickly to the king;
They scurried off and solemnly they brought
The young man from the dog pen to the court.
The king stared at him, wondering and relieved
To see unhurt the man for whom he'd grieved.
He stood and wept and asked time after time
For absolution for his wicked crime,
Then said, "How is it that you still draw breath
And stand here when you were condemned to death?"
The young man said, "For some time I've been giving
Your dogs fresh meat, and that's why I'm still living,
For those few scraps I gave them they behaved
So lovingly to me that I was saved.
Ten years I was your slave, and now we've learned
Exactly what my years of service earned—
You threw me to your dogs for one offense,
But dogs don't eat their friends, they have more sense!
Your dogs became my allies, you accused me,
And they were kind to me, while you abused me.
A bone contents a dog, but men reach higher
And it's your soul itself that they require."
And when the king had heard him out he knew
What was the right and human thing to do;

The drunkard was now sober and commanded
The business of his dogs to be disbanded.

My point in telling you this tale's to make you
See kindness guards you well, and won't forsake you;
By feeding his wild friends, Majnun erected
A wall by which his life would be protected;
Those whose good deeds protect them find a fence
Surrounds them as a firmly fixed defense,
And whether active or at rest or sleeping,
They're always in their followers' safe-keeping,
And if you act as this youth acted, you
Will be secure from worldly suffering too;
A caliph, once he's dined with you, will waive
His status and become your grateful slave.

A Description of Night;
Majnun's Invocation to the Heavens

The night was bright as day, the skies as glowing
As gardens are when spring's new growth is showing,
And hung with stars the shining heavens revolved
Resplendent in their sheen of glittering gold.
The planets linked their hands and danced upon
Fair carpets where the far horizons shone,
While meteors pierced the demons of the night,
Calling on God to aid them in their flight.
The heavenly air seemed scented with fine musk,
The moon's jewel made earth glimmer in the dusk,
Beneath the sky's six vaults[100] their scent and light
Made the horizons odorous and bright.
Heaven above higher heaven rose, and made
About earth's pole a lofty barricade.
A hundred different stars contributed
To one vast dazzling pageant overhead:
The Pleiades' bright banner's silken glow
Was made of starry gold and indigo,
Across the skies its bright expanse unrolled
Affixed there by a nail of heavenly gold;
Like silk the full moon shone with golden light
Its halo was spun linen, pure and white;
The stars seemed changed, as though they were revealed
As glittering gems upon a heavenly shield.

*

You'd say the shadows on the moon were like
Marks where our glorious monarch's missiles strike,[101]
Or that the planet Mercury was one
Such glistening missile passing by the sun;
Venus is like his glittering saddle now,
Sweet-smelling as the sweat upon his brow,
The sun's his royal sword that's sheathed at night
And in the day subdues the world with light,
Red warlike Mars is hastening through the skies,
Eager to pierce his hostile rivals' eyes.
Jupiter bears the royal seal, the clasp
That brings the whole wide world within his grasp,
And Saturn is the whetstone that will render
His sword unrivaled in its dazzling splendor.
May no clime be deprived of such a king
Or of the glories that his reign will bring,
O Nezami, what could be greater than
To serve as we do such a glorious man!
The zodiac itself, the bright moon's phases,
Shake in amazement and proclaim his praises,
The archer Aries shares their perturbation
And laughs and urges on their celebration.

The shining pearls of Taurus' necklaces
Are stars he's borrowed from the Pleiades,
Gemini's there, the twins, never alone,
Two beings seated on a single throne,
Like houris dressed in linen they appear
Together, side by side and ear to ear,
Cancer is there, the crab, sidling to snatch
And tear whatever its sharp claws might catch,

And Leo's there, his blazing heart a fire
Of sandalwood whose flames flare ever higher.
There Virgo clasps her wheat stalks to ensure
No grain is lost, her harvest stays secure,
Orion with his hunting dogs prepares
To seek out lions in their hidden lairs;
Libra is there, her scales are true and just,
Like words of wise men who deserve our trust.
The stars of Scorpio are surmounted by
A crown of stars that curves across the sky,
Aquarius is mute, his mouth is filled
With precious water that must not be spilled—
Beneath him golden verses introduce
His silent meaning and his mantic use
(And in the heavenly highways there are those
Strange stars whose hidden meaning no one knows).
Capella is so bright because she takes
The light each other star beside her makes,
The brightest star in Canis Major glows
Like shameless dancers who have shed their clothes,
And like a traveler now one star shines high
And solitary in the southern sky
While Aquila extends its pinions there,
A hovering eagle in the darkened air;
Close to the Bear a star now fades, as though
Its death knell were proclaiming it must go.

The fainter stars were now invisible;
As pale as Joseph hidden in his well[102]
The dawn began to break, and as the night
Drew back, the heavens were suffused with light.

Majnun gazed up at the deceitful sky,
Reproaching Venus with his heartfelt cry:
"O Venus, O bright star of providence,
Benign bestower of magnificence,
The shining torch of those who seek delight,
Bright emblem of all those who sing and write,
You hold the key to every joy, you shine
In every goblet as the purest wine,
Your seal confirms great monarchs, and you are
Of every human bliss the guiding star;
Sweetest of noblewomen, those you bless
Live in the fragrance of your happiness—
Out of your kindness now, I beg you, be
Kind to Majnun, open hope's door for me;
Waft me my dear friend's scent, it's time, I swear,
For her sweet scent to cure me of despair."

And then, above the far horizon's rim,
Jupiter rose, and Majnun called to him:
"O most auspicious star, O guarantor
Of vows, whose promises are true and sure,
O quickener of the soul, whose sanction brings
Triumphant conquests to world-conquering kings,
O scribe whose writ proclaims supremacy,
Success in war and final victory,
O arbiter whose absolute command
Determines lawfulness in every land,
Of all my destiny the one decider,
Of all my heart's resolve the sole provider,
Look down on me now with benevolence,
If you can help me, come to my defense:

Drive sorrow from me, free me from distress,
Treat me with chivalry, with manliness,
Show me your heavenly friendship, and oh leave me
One rose from all life's roses, don't deceive me!"

For all he said, the heavens moved as though
They had no notion of the world below,
And Majnun saw they were oblivious of
His ardent supplications and his love.
He cried out then to Him whose might had made
The world itself to hasten to his aid.
He said, "O my secure asylum, who
Can I fly for assistance to but You?
Venus and Jupiter serve You alone,
The name preceding all names is Your own.
You know far more than mankind can conceive,
You give far more than mankind can believe;
Resolver of all knots that hinder us,
Lord of existence, wise and generous,
The true performer of each hero's deed,
The comfort of all those in desperate need—
We are your slaves, and there is no one who
Bows down in prayer to any God but You.
The seven heavens are the gift you gave
And all but You must be your abject slave,
By You the six directions were first made
And always it is You they have obeyed,
If any eye should glimpse Your radiant light,
It would be blinded and bereft of sight;
The dog You favor is made wholly pure,
And cursèd be the man whom You abjure.

My flesh dissolves before You, look on me,
Witness my weakness and infirmity—
Do not withhold Your grace from me, a stranger,
Leaving me here defenseless and in danger,
But by Your Godly favor turn my night
Of wretchedness to dawn's resplendent light
So that Good Fortune's mine, and I can be
Saved from this life of constant misery."

He spoke his words more weakly now, and wept,
And gradually sank down, and softly slept;
He dreamed a tree rose from the earth beside him—
A bird flew down from it as if to chide him
But from its beak it dropped a jewel instead
That landed softly on his sleeping head.
When he awoke, a new dawn had begun
And earth's rim glittered with the rising sun,
And he too felt refreshed and born anew
As if he flew just as the dream-bird flew:
In fancies or in dreams, comfort can bless
The lovelorn in their lonely wretchedness.

A Message from Layli Reaches Majnun

The new day dawned, but what a day! All eyes
Rejoiced and shone that saw the sun arise,
The dawn partook of paradise, the breeze
Was like the breath of Jesus in the trees[103]
And Fortune's right hand seemed to cast a spell
Ensuring that all deeds would turn out well;
So many grievances had come from Fate
It sent Good Luck (though laggardly, and late).

How much Majnun had suffered! His poor heart
And vitals were worn out and torn apart.
He sat among the mountain slopes, around him
Were all the animals who'd sought and found him,
When from the plain he saw dust clouds arise
As dark as kohl around a woman's eyes;
Her veil was lifted and the dust clouds cleared
And from their midst a rider soon appeared—
A man, but what a man! He seemed all light
As he dismounted, an enchanting sight;
Majnun saw that he was a worthy man,
A jewel of virtue from a noble clan,
And clapped his hands, and his wild retinue
Dropped to the ground and docilely withdrew.

Majnun stepped forward and began to speak,
His tone was kindly, welcoming, and meek:
"But who are you, O shining, splendid star?
Why have you come here? Tell me who you are.
Your face is kindly, and your manner's mild,
But all men know that I am mad and wild;
A dragon's jaws[104] once robbed me of all hope—
I saw that serpent, and I fear a rope,[105]
What happened once has made my doubting mind
Imagine snakes and thorns are all I'll find—
That bite, that thorn within my heart, is like
A festering wound made by an iron spike;
If you have only similar ware to show
You'd better not say anything, just go."
The traveler fell before him and lay prone
As if he were the shadow that he'd thrown
And said, "My lord, you shelter in your shade
Such savage beasts, and yet you're not afraid,
The deer adore you, and the lions lie
Calmly and peaceably with you nearby.
I am a friend to friends, a go-between
Whose back and forth stays secret and unseen;
I have a message for you, one I'm sure
No passer-by has brought to you before;
With your permission I shall pass it on,
If you don't want it, then farewell, I've gone!"
Hope filled the lover's heart; he cried, "What is it?
Out with it! Tell me what's provoked this visit!"
The messenger replied, "I know the course
Fate's given you is like a stubborn horse,
Refractory and wild, but all the same
I hope the news I bring will make it tame.

I passed a group of dwellings yesterday
And saw there, to my wonder and dismay,
A lovely woman sitting by the road;
Despite her linen veil, it seemed she glowed
More brightly than the sun, a cypress tree
Lovelier than any cypress tree could be,
A garden, but a garden to suffice
To be the garden of God's paradise.
Her voice was sweet and liquid, like a stream
That lulls all other streams to sleep and dream;
Her eyes like doe's eyes, whose dark gaze would make
A lion lie down dazed, and half awake.
She seemed an alphabet of loveliness,
Curved letters were the curling of each tress,
Straight letters were her stature, and her lips
Were like a letter formed as an ellipse,
And all the letters made her like that bowl
That shows the world as an enchanted whole.[106]
Her eyes were like narcissus flowers that grow
Beside a stream whose waters gently flow,
Her eyebrows met,[107] and made an arched shape there,
So lovely that it was beyond compare;
Her breath was sweet as basil, and her nature
Made her a magical, enthralling creature;
In short she was so finely formed that she
Seemed air's and water's child exclusively,
And it would be impossible to start
To tell the kindness that was in her heart.
Her body's arrow has become a bow
Bent with the weight of never-ending woe,
She's grown as thin and meager as bamboo
Her cheeks have lost their pomegranate hue;

The golden child is sallow now with pain,
As sweet and slight as reedy sugar-cane;
The heavens have laid siege to her, they've made
This bride a burning castle that's betrayed,
Her father and her husband have conspired
To make her act as they, not she, desired—
She longs still for her friend, but as a wife
Sits with her husband, fearful for her life.
Her rose-like eyes wept attar's drops, as though
The sun were flooded with the moonlight's glow,[108]
She wept so much I pitied her, and said,
'What dreadful wound has caused these tears you shed?'
Poison was in her smile as she complained,
'You rub salt in the wound that I've sustained—
Oh I was Layli once, but now you'll see
How much more mad than my Majnun I'll be—
He is a black star, a besotted child,
But I'm a thousand times more crazed and wild,
And though pain seeks him out, I'm still the one
Who has to suffer more than he has done.
I am a woman, as a lover he
Can be as reckless as he wants to be,
Go where he wants . . . a man need never know
The wasting agonies I undergo.
But I'm alone and wretched, too afraid
To make the kind of protests that he's made,
I'm inexperienced, and fear that I
Will fail at any venture that I try;
I drink the awful poison that I'm given
And hide the hell I'm in and say it's heaven.
On this side I see unfamiliar strangers,
On that side I see too-familiar dangers,

I'm pulled this way and that between the two,
And know I've no idea what I should do.
I daren't defy my husband, and I lack
The nerve to answer my strict father back.
At times my heart says, "Like a partridge rise,
Flee from these kites and crows and seek the skies."
Then honor says, "Don't listen to his squawks,
Partridges finish up as prey for hawks!"
A woman might put up a fight, but she's
A woman, helpless against enemies,
She might be like a mighty lioness—
But she's still hemmed in by her helplessness
And since I can't escape this endless grief
I bow to it, and look for no relief.
But still I suffer sorely, without end,
Wondering about my lonely, absent friend,
Thinking of how his days pass, and how he
Must count them off, and always without me.
Where does that lord of wandering go, and where
Does he sit down to eat what travelers' fare?
Who does he sup with then? Who does he find
To sympathize with his poor, troubled mind?
If you know where he is or where he's gone,
Tell me what distant road he's traveling on.'

"And when I'd heard her out, I knew that I
Would be at fault if I did not reply,
Since as a seal impresses wax I knew
Within my heart the tales concerning you;
I knew you'd lost your wits for love, and were
Content to have no friends, remembering her,
That you owned nothing but the wind, and that
Shy deer were now the friends with whom you sat;

And that if love had broken you before,
Your father's death then broke you even more,
That all your life was thorns and misery,
An endless cycle of adversity,
And that at times you sang sad ballads of
The depths and sorrows of your desperate love,
And then you'd sing sad elegies, and make
The rocks resound for your dead father's sake.

"I sang a few lines from your songs that made her
Sigh from the sorrow that she felt pervade her;
She trembled then, and hung her lovely head
And swooned as if without you she were dead,
And when she'd caught her breath, again she sighed
And sobbed repeatedly and wildly cried,
Mourning her love and yours with every breath
And grieving for your noble father's death,
Grieving that he had gone, but grieving too
That you had no one left to comfort you.
Then, as her sobbing lessened, she addressed me;
Determinedly, and earnestly, she pressed me
To help her; this is what she said: 'My lord,
You seem like someone who will keep his word;
You see the state I'm in; look there, that tent . . .'
(And here she pointed to the one she meant)
'Is mine; give me a day, then come to me,
Pass by my tent as if fortuitously,
I'll write a letter—somehow, undetected
I'll pass it to you so we're not suspected;
God speed you, then, and see the letter ends
In no one else's hands but my dear friend's.'

She stood and left; she'd nothing more to say
And I continued on my previous way.

"So yesterday I wandered past her tent
As if at random and by accident;
Dressed in dark blue,[109] I saw her watching me . . .
She slipped the letter to me secretly,
The wax that sealed it seemed an emblem of
Her inward seal of sorrow and of love."
At that, he took the letter from his cloak
And humbly held and kissed it as he spoke:
Majnun stared wildly, grabbed it, whirled around
A hundred times and sprawled upon the ground;
Losing control as he held on to it,
Stumbling like someone in a drunken fit;
He held the letter as he fell, and then
Turned to it when his wits returned again.

MAJNUN READS LAYLI'S LETTER

Eager to read it once the seal was broken,
Impatiently he tore the letter open
And read, "In His name Whose divine decree
Preserves the soul as wisdom's sanctuary,
Whose knowledge is beyond man's furthest reach,
Who knows the speech of those who have no speech,
The King Whose will apportions day and night,
Who feeds the fishes and the birds in flight,
Who lights the stars and heavens, Who designed
The world and all its beauty for mankind,
Eternal in Himself and all He's made,
Whose life cannot diminish, change or fade,
Who made the earth and life, Whose mercies give
These treasures to mankind that they may live,
Who lights the soul with sense, Whose beams illumine
The universe itself and all that's human . . ."
When Layli'd scattered these bright jewels, she turned her
Attention to the matters that concerned her:
"This letter is like silk, and it is sent
From one who grieves to one our fates torment,
That is, from me, who locked up weeps and rages,
To you, who's broken free of paltry cages.
How are you, my lost love, who has to live
Beneath the light the seven planets give?

O treasurer of former love, whose light
Illumines love itself and makes it bright,
Whose drops of blood shed on the earth must shine
As glittering rubies deep within a mine,
O stream of Khezr,[110] deep in the dark of night,
O dazzled moth that seeks dawn's candlelight,
O you who's caused such uproar, and whose home
Is hidden where wild asses choose to roam,
O you who's caused me such disgrace, who'll be
On Judgment Day together there with me,
O heart that's faithful to my faithful heart
That's never wished or hoped that we might part,
How do you fare, and what now can you do
In this sad game love's played with me and you?
And how can I endure this destiny
Which keeps my partner now so far from me?
This so-called partner-husband they've supplied me
Has never lain with me or slept beside me,
He wears my life away, but he's been taught
Mine is a diamond that he hasn't bought,
My treasured jewel remains intact, as though
It were a rosebud that refused to grow;
Spouses are fine . . . but what's this spouse to me
Who's not the lover whom I long to see?
Garlic and lily plants look similar,
Their scent soon tells you which of them they are!
And unripe cucumbers might look as sweet
As citrons when they're ripe enough to eat,
But bite them and they're bitter, and their taste
Shows that your trust in looks has been misplaced.
My wish was always that I would be blessed
With someone just like you to share my nest,

And that if anyone should thwart you he
Should be dispatched from life immediately;
How's it a sin, if I can't live with you,
For me to live as I'm now forced to do?
The heart that doesn't please you has no place
On earth, and she should perish in disgrace,
And she who seeks to hurt you, may her hand
Dry up and may she vanish from this land.
To me a single hair from you is worth
All of the wondrous treasures of the earth,
And gardens filled with roses are less sweet
Than dust that has been walked on by your feet.
Oh, in your wanderings in the desert be
The sacred water that Khezr guards for me;[111]
I am the moon and you're the sun, you are
The shining light I look on from afar—
Forgive my staying here; you know, Majnun,
The sun can't be accosted by the moon.
I heard about your father's death and tore
In my unhappiness the clothes I wore,
I clawed my face in grief and wept and cried
As if it were my father who had died,
I wept so long and hard my eyes grew red,
I dressed in dark blue to lament the dead,
I mourned in sympathy with you, to share
Your heartfelt agony, and your despair,
And I did everything but come to you
Which was the one thing that I couldn't do—
My body's parted from you, even so
My soul is with you everywhere you go.
I know your heart's grief, but I also see
That patience is our only remedy.

We're guests here for a brief two days, and Fate
Is something that we have to tolerate,
This inn[112] that seems so lovely has waylaid us
And soon enough we find it has betrayed us;
Don't be deceived, see what life has in store,
And see how short it is, and say no more.
Try to mourn less, be patient, for who knows
The ways by which this crooked heaven goes?
Stay strong within your love for me, and see
How patience overcomes adversity—
I suffer as you do, but I endure
More patiently, my step is strong and sure.
It's wisest to stay out of sight, and tears
Provoke your enemies' derisive sneers—
A man who's sensible will never voice
Sadness that makes his enemy rejoice;
Be as you are, yourself, but also strive
To be content, while you are here, alive.
The world and heavens turn, and you must learn
Not to be outraged by them as they turn—
Don't watch the sower; when the wheat has grown
Watch as the reaper harvests what he's sown;
The palm tree that's all thorny spines creates
In time a bounteous harvest of sweet dates,
And that tight, tiny bud that hardly shows
It's living, opens as a lovely rose.
Don't grieve that you have no one; you have me,
And isn't that enough? It ought to be!
Crying that you're alone is wrong of you—
It's only God of Whom this claim is true!
Grieve for your father, but don't be the flash
Of angry lightning or the thunder's crash,

And don't be like the lowering cloud that rains
Its tears so copiously it drowns the plains.
Your father's gone, but you're alive; the ground,
The rock, is broken, but a jewel is found."

Majnun read through the letter and he fell
Like a pistachio loosened from its shell,
And cried out, "God . . . O God . . ." now unaware
Of who he was, or how he was, or where,
And when he came back to himself, all he
Could do was weep and wail unceasingly
And kiss the messenger's two hands, and then
He'd kiss his feet, and then his hands again,
And moan in his despair, "But, oh, I lack
Both pen and ink, so how can I write back?"
The messenger produced a bag (the sort
A lawyer always has when he's in court),
And from it gave Majnun all he required
To write whatever message he desired.
Majnun took up the fluent pen and wrote
A thousand greetings in his hasty note,
Setting out all the sorrows he'd been through
In language that was beautiful and true,
And gave the missive to the messenger,
Entreating him to carry it to her.
The messenger set off, and made good speed,
And gave the note to Layli as agreed,
Who, when she saw it, wept with old regret
And, as she took it, made the missive wet.

MAJNUN'S LETTER REACHES LAYLI

The letter opened with the glorious praise
Of One Who is unequaled in all ways,
The King of all that's known and is unknown,
Who hides the shining ruby in the stone,
Upholder of the Great and Little Bear,
And of the heavens, and all stars everywhere,
Foundation of our hearts, Bringer of light
That heralds day and banishes the night,
Who irrigates the laughing spring, Who's there
To answer every needy suppliant's prayer . . .
Majnun then spoke of all his woes, and of
The pains he'd suffered for the sake of love:

"I'm writing now, unhappy with my fate,
To you, who's left me in this wretched state;
You are the locked, forbidden treasury,
I've still to forge the iron that makes its key.
I am the dust beneath your feet, but you—
Who is it whom you give life's water to?
I bow before you, clutching at your dress—
Who is it whom your lovely hands caress?
How much I've suffered as I weep and wait—
Whose sufferings does your kindness mitigate?

I bear your burdens, toiling in despair—
Whose is the earring that you humbly wear?[113]
My ka'bah is your lovely face, I pray
In one direction—to your alleyway;
You are a pearl dropped in a glass of wine,[114]
You heal a thousand breasts, but never mine.
You are a crown, but you have never crowned me,
Instead you rob me, harry me, and hound me;
You are a treasure strangers freely take,
But when friends come, you're guarded by a snake;[115]
You're Eram's garden,[116] which is locked to me,
And you're a paradise I never see,
But then you are what frees me from my grief,
The medicine that must bring my love relief.
Don't take an axe to this poor tree that's grown
From your encouragement; for you alone,
I lie in endless pain, reduced to dust—
Heal me, caress me, as is only just.
If you are kind, I'll give the spring to you,
If you are cruel, dust's all I'll bring to you—
Kindness renews the earth, whose dirt discloses
From kindness's effects the sweetest roses.
I bow before you at your feet, don't send me
Away from you with arguments; befriend me;
I bring you water—see it doesn't spill,
And I shall be obedient to your will,
But even the most passive subjects are
Prone to rebel if they are pushed too far.
I am your slave, but don't think you can leave me—
I'd soon become your enemy, believe me!
Treat a dog badly and he'll turn into
A ravening wolf that wants revenge on you;

Don't be at every beggar's beck and call,
Handing your treasures out to one and all.
I'll be your slave, in all humility,
If you'll act generously and graciously.
But I can't fight you, I'm content to yield,
And look, I gladly throw away my shield,
But don't attack your friends—to fight your own
Is wearing weapons out against a stone,
And why assault yourself, when all you'll do
Is tear apart whatever's left of you?
Be friendly, and free men will then behave
As if each one desires to be your slave;
Those who aren't kind in this way can't be sure
That they'll stay safe, unchallenged and secure,
While those who act humanely quickly find
Servants will flock to them because they're kind.
Anger resides in everyone, within
Each mind a devil lurks who savors sin,
And if your devil rears its head, its evil
Will be confronted by another's devil.
How long will you destroy me and oppress me?
Can't you relent for one day and caress me?
So cold are all my sighs, in my despair
They freeze the very dust that fills the air.
You've crept off, and found somewhere else to hide,
And chosen someone else to lie beside,
And my neglected name's inscribed upon
A block of ice that melts until it's gone.
Your words to me are worthless, substanceless,
And all that's in them is an emptiness;
You've turned my days to night and given me
Nothing but wounds and sighs and misery,

And kept your heart while I gave mine to you,
And when you've killed me, you'll forget me too.
Your words to me are brands that wound and burn me,
But you don't care, and ceaselessly you spurn me;
My love for you was visible upon
My face and obvious to everyone,
Where can your love for me be seen? What sign
Shows me that you're still longing to be mine?
There's none, you broke your vow to me, and now
You've made another man that selfsame vow,
For him you've words of kindness and desire;
To me your words were false, you were a liar.
If you're in love, where is your honesty?
Where are the kindly sighs you owe to me?
Without them what you call love is oppression,
You want me as a conquest, a possession;
You're free of heartbreak and its lovelorn sighing,
For you love's selling, bargaining, and buying.
I've longed to see your face, I've bowed my head
Upon the dusty street where you might tread,
I've cast lots, trying to find out when and where
I ought to wait in hopes you'll pass me there.
The man who sees you is the happy one,
Not one who waits in vain as I have done,
You are a jewel, luck loves whoever can
Possess and hold you—I am not that man;
Though nightingales make gardens sweet, it's crows
That eat the juicy figs the gardener grows,
And from his pomegranate tree the fruit
Is given to some sick, bedridden brute.
The world was ever thus, and what we prize
Lies in the ground, it's hidden from our eyes:

Tell me I'll see my longed-for ruby shine
Freed from the darkness of her stony mine,
Tell me the pale moon will break free at last
From the fell dragon that has held her fast,[117]
Tell me that the officious bee has flown
And left the lovely honey all alone,
Tell me the garden's nasty owner's gone
And that the hideous crows there have moved on,
That nightingales replace them, that the rose
Is cleansed of dust and wears her loveliest clothes,
Tell me the blackguard's forfeited his head
And that the treasure's guardian snake[118] is dead,
Tell me the castle jailer's dreadful fall
Has left him dying by the castle wall,
And that, after her long captivity,
The castle's lady once again is free.

"I'm exiled from your flame, but I wish no
Harm to the moth that hovers in its glow,
Sorrow and scorn may kill me, but I bless
Your Ebn Salam, and wish him happiness.
My good and evil come from you, my grief
Derives from you and so does its relief;
An iron wall's between us, but I'm sure
The shell still holds its pearl, unpierced and pure;
Within your tumbling curls, and guarded by
Your dragon will, your untouched treasures lie.[119]
You know a lover's heart can harbor spite
And every kind of evil appetite,
A lover is the blindest man, his eyes
Will see a fly take on a vulture's size—

I'm restless as an ant to make this fly
Fly from the sugar that has caught his eye,
By which I mean this fine young man[120] has made
A nasty profit from a lawless trade,
He's seized upon an unpicked rose, his gold
Has bought a pearl that shouldn't have been sold.

"Oh, I know well enough that love's a name
For something difficult, it's not a game;
How can I *not* weep, when you're unaware
Of all my agonies and my despair?
I'm worse than you have seen me, in a word
I'm far more crazy even than you've heard,
And now that we're apart I travel on
A path that's purposeless, whose meaning's gone,
In love's religion, love without such pain
Has no more value than a barley grain.

"Your lips cannot touch mine, so let it be
That in your kisses you'll remember me;
When you use musky scent, when you prepare
The fragrance that pervades your lovely hair,
Let the breeze waft these sweet aromas near me
And they'll revitalize my heart, and cheer me,
And in my dreams I'll taste the sweetness of
The dates your face's garden gives your love,
And I shall taste once more your noble wine
Imagining that once again you're mine.
O God, how wonderful it is to think
That you might hand me that forbidden drink,
That you might sit with me, and that I'd be
Drunk with the wine that's you sat next to me,

And that I'd savor in alternate sips
Wine from your hands and kisses from your lips.
But oh, your little lips, how will they bear
The ardent kisses I shall give them there?
They're agate and they're honey, how will they
Endure such amorous and boisterous play?
At times I'll kiss your lovely lips and face,
At times enfold you in my strong embrace,
At times caress your apple chin,[121] and then
Steal sweetest sugar from your lips again.

"All that I've said's a dream you can ignore,
A way to write to you, and nothing more;
I long for nothing now but tales of you,
Of how and where you are and what you do,
My love for you's so strongly set in place
Why do I even need to see your face?
It's blasphemy to say we're two, to say
Love is between us now in any way—
When love displays its face, it's a disgrace
For me to see your actual living face.
Love's my companion, may its wounds caress
My inward being with untold distress,
My wounds cannot be cured, but I shall dwell
In happiness if you are whole and well,
And if I suffer from your absence, may
Such absent suffering never come your way.
If my poor donkey falls down dead, may your
Swift Arab horse's hooves be strong and sure,
If hidden grief besets me, may you be
Endowed forever with nobility,
May those who would oppose you know defeat
And be the trampled dust beneath your feet."

MAJNUN'S UNCLE, SALIM AMIRI, COMES TO SEE MAJNUN

The golden words this storyteller said
Were precious stones strung on a jeweler's thread:

There was an uncle of Majnun who cared
About his nephew's state, and how he fared;
An old man, who had great experience,
Someone endowed with kindness and good sense,
Skillful, astute in an emergency—
His noble name was Salim Amiri.
For years he'd soothed his nephew's agonies
And sympathized with all his miseries;
At times he'd take him food and clothes, and then
After a month he'd do the same again.
One day he set off on his horse to find
This youth who'd been so pitied and maligned,
And like a violent blustery whirlwind he
Searched the land eagerly and ceaselessly
Until he found him in a rocky cleft,
Careless of all the comradeship he'd left,
Surrounded by a few wild beasts, but sure
He wouldn't see wild humans any more.
Salim was fearful of these wild assistants
And hailed Majnun, but from a prudent distance.

Hearing a human voice, Majnun inquired
First what his name was, then what he desired.
"I am Salim," he said, "a wanderer who
Has known the buffetings of Fate like you,
I am your uncle, but I'd hardly know it,
If we're alike your strange face doesn't show it,
Your skin's so weathered you're a different man,
You look as black as any African!"
Majnun was quick to greet him and assure him
That he was welcome there, and knelt before him,
And asked for news of all that he was missing,
Happy to hear his uncle's reminiscing.
Salim saw he was naked, comfortless,
Without provisions in the wilderness,
And showed him clothes he'd brought (and meanwhile he
Apologized for their poor quality),[122]
Saying, "They're honest goods, why don't you use them?
Take them for my sake; come on, don't refuse them."
Majnun replied, "My body's fire will turn them
To smoke and ash, it will completely burn them;
Imagine I've accepted them and worn them,
Then ripped them up, and shredded them, and torn
    them!"
Salim insisted, though, till he relented
And wore the clothes his uncle had presented.
Quickly Salim produced a meal, roast meats
Of various kinds, and various kinds of sweets,
But then, no matter how much Salim pleaded,
Majnun said there was nothing there he needed—
He didn't taste the food, but handed it
To all the beasts around him, bit by bit.

Salim said, "But you're in a desperate plight—
What is it that you live on day and night?
It's food that gives men strength to stay alive,
So if you're human how do you survive?"
Majnun replied, "My heart's poor faculties
Come from the presence of the morning breeze,
I eat so little that I haven't fed
My body's appetite and now it's dead,
But if a breeze brings Layli's fragrance, then
Surely my soul revives, and lives again.
I sleep on stones each night, by day I find
Little to eat, and still less peace of mind;
I tear off bark from trees, and use my teeth
To gnaw the gums and resins underneath,
Or I eat plants, but not each week; a diet
Of plants once every month keeps hunger quiet.
I eat so little now that I've been freed
From flesh's every mortal want and need,
I can't eat bread, the tiniest little bit
Would make my gullet gag and choke on it.
And this not needing food means that I've grown
So thin now I'm no more than skin and bone,
But I accept your present as a treat
For all the others here who need to eat—
For me to see the deer and lions feed
Is all the sustenance I'll ever need."

And when Salim saw he was satisfied
To live on what the desert's plants supplied,
He sympathized with Majnun's situation
And answered him with friendly admiration,

Not least because Salim was well aware
Of how gross appetite can be a snare—
Of how a greedy bird can easily
Be trapped, then realize that it can't get free.
If plants are what a man's content to eat,
He'll be a king whom no one can defeat.

A TALE[123]

"One day a king decided he would ride
With regal pomp around the countryside,
And passed the hovel of a hermit who
Thought always of the world he'd travel to.
The king was shocked a man should choose to live
In somewhere so run-down and primitive
And asked his courtiers, 'What's he doing here,
Living in such a wretched atmosphere?
What does he eat? How can he sleep? How can
He bear to live here? Just who is this man?'
They said, 'He is a saint, a man who's quit
This world and everything to do with it;
He neither eats nor sleeps, but patiently
Subsists, and shuns all human company.'
Apprised of this, the king resolved to meet him
And sent his chamberlain ahead to greet him;
The chamberlain approached the man to bring
Him forward to the presence of the king
And said, 'You have renounced the world, and choose
To live somewhere that most men would refuse;
You've no friends here, so why should you remain here?
Stuck in this den, what can you hope to gain here?'
The hermit had some plants he'd picked to steep
And crush, gathered from where the wild deer sleep,

He showed them to the chamberlain and said,
'This is my fodder for the path ahead.'
The haughty chamberlain said, 'Why should you
Live in the shameful, wretched way you do?
If you should serve our king, you can be sure
You won't be eating plant stems any more.'
The hermit said, 'But what are you implying?
This is a syrup, sweet and fortifying;
"Plant stems," you say! Taste this, and I've no doubt
That you'll forget the king you boast about!'
The king had heard their talk, and with remorse
He hurriedly dismounted from his horse
And knelt before the hermit reverently,
And kissed the ground there deferentially.
Contentment is a quality that brings
A kingdom greater than an earthly king's."

Majnun was cheered to hear this tale, and sat
Beside his kindly guest, prepared to chat—
He asked about his friends, seeking to know
Details that he'd forgotten long ago,
And then how his poor mother was now keeping,
And suddenly he found that he was weeping;
"That broken-winged, poor bird I left behind,
How is her health, what occupies her mind?
My face is black[124] to think what I have done,
I ought to be her slave now, not her son—
And is she sick or well? I long for her,
To be her confidant and comforter."
Salim knew Majnun's mother well, and went
To fetch her in response to his lament,

He would not leave the jewel without the mine[125]
From which it came, where first it used to shine,
And brought her from her house to see her son,
And seeing him she saw what grief had done—
The red rose had turned yellow, rust had shrouded
The mirror's brightness now grown dim and clouded;[126]
And almost fell and fainted as she felt
The strength in all her limbs dissolve and melt.
From head to foot she lavished all her care—
Washing his face with tears, combing his hair,
Cleansing his scars and skin as she caressed
Each part of him, seeing his wounds were dressed,
Rinsing his hair of dust, making it neat,
And drawing thorns from his sore, blistered feet.
When she'd done all a mother's love could do
And eased his pain in every way she knew,
She said: "My son, what are you thinking of,
Playing this violent game of pointless love?
Death waits, and wields a sharp two-handed sword
That in your drunkenness you have ignored,
Your disillusioned father's dead, and I
Know that it won't be long before I die;
Listen to me, come home again, don't scorn
And foul the humble nest where you were born.
Though birds might fly, though animals might roam
As long as day lasts, far away from home,
When twilight deepens they all know it's best
That each of them should seek his natal nest.
Worn out and sleepless, how long will you flee
From every kind of human company?
Life lasts two days, no more; why don't you spend them
Resting at home? What better way to end them?

Why haunt these caves? Why tread on stony ground
Where only ants and slithering snakes are found,
Where snakes can bite you, and where ants are all
The company you can expect to call?
Rest from all this, your soul is sensitive,
It isn't stone to crush, it needs to live!
Your heart's not iron, your soul's not stone, don't act
As if they're enemies to be attacked!"

Hearing his mother's words, Majnun became
Like fire that flares up with a flickering flame;
He cried: "Humbly I bow my head to you,
You were the shell in which my being grew,
I am the seed you've sown, and may there be
No other heaven but your door for me.
It's true my wits have wandered; all the same
You know I'm innocent, I'm not to blame,
All that's occurred is not because of me,
All this was fated from eternity.
The time's long past when I could hope to find
Some remedy to heal my heart and mind—
You know such violent love's not ours to choose,
It's not a thing to want or to refuse.
My soul is like a trapped bird,[127] and I long to see
My soul escape this cage, alive and free;
My sorrow isn't something you'll assuage
By trapping me within a second cage.
Don't ask me to come home, to weep and sigh there,
I fear I'll be so desperate that I'll die there—
The wilderness is life to me; I dread
The thought of home, where I would soon be dead.

Better I sing to these wild beasts than stay
Among mankind and sulk my life away;
If I come home, all I will do is grieve
Distractedly, and look for ways to leave,
I'll be a checker in backgammon when
It's been hemmed in and cannot move again—
Mother, go back, you've traveled here in vain,
And leave me to my wilderness of pain."

He fell, and like a shadow in the street
Stretched out upon the ground, and kissed her feet;
With these sad kisses he apologized,
Knowing he could not do as she advised.
He said farewell, and left his mother there—
Weeping, she turned, and went home in despair,
Where longing for her son intensified,
Just as his father's had, till she too died.

Each day the world will snatch more souls away;
Acknowledge that it's faithless while you may,
But though the world is fickle, still men act
As if they were oblivious of this fact.
Inconstant Fate has like a peasant sown
A few seeds, which she harvests when they've grown,
And for the soul it lights a lamp each night
That wind extinguishes with morning's light—
The turning heavens signify our pain,
The lamps they light for us they light in vain.
Problems impede us everywhere we run
Like Gordian knots that cannot be undone
Until we're free of those four elements[128]
That constitute our earthly residence.

Be as a pure soul, free of quandaries,
Not like a sickness nothing can appease,
If sandalwood makes coils of smoke, then be
The source that solves all coils invisibly.

Majnun Is Told of His Mother's Death

Then like a mounted king whose rivals yield
Before him and forsake the battlefield,
The rising sun put all the stars to flight
And filled the firmament with morning's light—
Dawn broke the victor's goblet raised on high
And red wine poured from it across the sky.
Majnun still sang his songs that boasted of
His solitary existence and his love,
And he forgot his mother, unaware
That death had come for her in her despair.
Salim came bravely to his friend once more,
Bringing him food and clothing as before,
But also with a mourner's woeful cries—
"Oh, far from you, your mother's closed her eyes,
Longing, as did your father, for her son
She's quit this world forever now, she's gone."
Majnun, distraught at what Salim had said,
Repeatedly and wildly struck his head,
Groan upon groan he wailed, moan upon moan,
And fell down like a glass smashed by a stone—
Smearing his head with dust, wildly he cried
For both his parents' deaths and how they'd died.

He hurried to their graves, and bent his head
Down to the dust that lay upon the dead,

Sprawling on each of them, knowing no one,
No balm, brings back the dead when they are gone.
His relatives heard all his endless crying
And saw the graves on which Majnun was lying—
They sympathized with all his misery
And tried to find some helpful remedy.
They saw he'd fallen, at his feet they fell,
They saw him weeping and they wept as well,
And as they shared his desperate sorrow, soon
Like rosewater their tears revived Majnun[129]
And as he struggled back to consciousness
They greeted him with earnest friendliness,
Saying that now he'd come back home he should
Stay with them there, and settle down for good.
But heartfelt sorrow and his mind's distress
Urged him to seek the empty wilderness;
He sighed, and left them there, and set off for
The mountain fastness where he'd lived before;
Wild beasts fell in behind him, but no one,
No human friend, pursued him once he'd gone—
The world of humans seemed to him to be
A place of evil and iniquity.
He left as lightning flashes disappear,
Or as a cloud does when the sky grows clear.

Be it a thousand years, or but a day,
Our earthly life's foundations fall away;
Life bears the seal of death, no matter how
Its sweetness flatters and deceives us now;
Ah, you forget that one day you must die,
That you must bid your precious soul goodbye.

How long will you applaud yourself, and scoff
At death, and say it's still a long way off?
Your mind is feeble, and it cannot give
You any notion of how long you'll live.

Every detectable small speck of earth
Is satisfied with its extent and girth—
Compared to Mount Qaf,[130] though, a speck is just
A useless scrap, a tiny bit of dust.
Look at yourself—what leaf, what tiny tree
Are you in all the countryside we see?
Look at how small you are, beneath the high
And overarching vastness of the sky—
Examine who you are, do it with care,
Your own assessment says you're hardly there.
You thought you were a great thing on the earth,
Well satisfied with your extent and worth,
This "greatness" though, is relatively small,
So low you'll think you're scarcely there at all,
If you go further on, if you persist,
You'll find you even doubt that you exist.

Be humble, sit upon the earth, pour dust
And dirt upon your shame and self-disgust;
You grasp a few old coins within your hand
And boast the world is yours now to command,
But while you're in this world, your neediness
Will always bring you failure and distress.
Your wanting earthly friends still hasn't gone,
It's still this world that you depend upon—
In all your fawning, though, be careful that
You're not some begging dog or wheedling cat!

LAYLI SENDS A MESSAGE TO MAJNUN

Layli preserved her chastity, but she
Could not keep secret all her misery
Which made her like a lover's anguished sighs
Choking a thousand times with stifled cries—
Missing Majnun, imprisoned by her pain,
Grief's anxious captive, chained without a chain.
Her husband's watchful jealousy was spread
Like broken glass wherever she might tread,
So that she wouldn't slip away at night
Like drunks in search of dubious delight;
He humbly, kindly, humored her all day,
Indulging all her whims in every way,
But still, whatever strategy he tried,
She brushed him off, and coldly turned aside.
And then, one pitch-black night when not a fly
Was stirring and the watch was not nearby,
She stole into the street, not thinking of
Her husband's presence but her absent love.

She found a spot beside a thoroughfare
(No enemy'd suspect that she was there),
And sat to wait for someone passing who
Had seen her friend to tell her what he knew;

177

And there the old man came, the one who'd taken
Her letter for her when she'd felt forsaken.
He came on foot, deliberately but slowly,
And seemed like Khezr, a man both wise and holy;[131]
The lovely captive asked if he could give
Her news about the man who chose to live
Among wild beasts, deep in the wilderness,
Whether he lived in joy now or distress,
The one whose talk was always verse and rhyme,
Who made up songs and sang them all the time.
Kindly the old man said, "Dear beauteous moon,
He's Joseph in his well,[132] this poor Majnun,
Now he's without you, wandering and wailing,
Like a town-crier whose cries are unavailing.
Every two steps he takes he cries for Layli,
And everywhere he stops he sighs for Layli;
Careless of who he is, he has but one
Obsession, which is: where has Layli gone?"

And Layli wept, as if that cypress tree
Would shrink into a reed from misery;
Narcissus eyes shed agate tears that shone
Against the jasmine skin they fell upon.
She said, "I am his friend, and it's for me
That he endures such daily agony;
We two are one in this sad state, we share
Our endless misery and our despair,
The difference is, he sighs on mountain tops,
While in this pit my sighing never stops."
She took off her jeweled earrings then, and kissed them,
Relinquished them, and happily dismissed them,

And said, "Take these, they're yours, go back and spend
A little time with my unhappy friend,
Then bring him here by back-roads and conceal him
Somewhere secure, where nothing will reveal him,
And, once you have him hidden, let me know
Exactly where it is I have to go
To catch a glimpse of him—like him I'll stay
Invisible, and hide my self away.
There I shall find out how he is, and whether
His love for me is still as strong as ever;
It may be that he'll sing a line or two
About his love and sorrow, something new—
Oh, all the knots within my soul will be
Untied if he should sing like this for me!"

The old man took the pierced pearls from the girl
(Who was herself as yet an unpierced pearl)
And tucked them in his sash. Without delay
He set off, and procured along the way
Some new clothes, since the ones Majnun had worn
When last he'd seen him had been frayed and torn.
He went through towns and empty wildernesses,
And like the wind through mountain fastnesses
Without success at first, but then he found
Majnun stretched out upon the stony ground
In mountain foothills, while around him lay
Wild animals to drive mankind away.
Majnun saw him approach, and couldn't rest
But like a baby fretful for the breast,
Waited impatiently, then shouted to
His beasts to part, and let the old man through;

The beasts drew back respectfully, contritely,
And Majnun came to meet his guest politely.
Down to the earth the old man bowed his head,
Greeted his host, apologized, and said:
"Upholder of love's realm, may you survive
As long as love itself remains alive,
Drink from your source like Khezr, like Alexander
Traverse love's world and be its sole commander.[133]
The paragon of beauty has stayed true
To all her promises of love for you,
Layli sends greetings to you, and assures you
That as she always has done she adores you;
It is so long since she has seen a trace
Of you, or heard your voice, or glimpsed your face,
She longs to see you and to sit beside you
Just for a moment—and I've come to hide you
Where you can see her face and put an end
To your extended exile from your friend,
And you can comfort her by singing of
The past you shared together and your love.
There is a grove of palms where undergrowth
Is so entwined that it'll hide you both,
A pleasant patch of green surrounded by
Tall palm trees towering up into the sky.
Spring's sweetest flowers await your meeting there,
There is the key to all you long to share."

He showed Manjun the clothes he'd brought, and
    dressed him,
And made him kindly promises, and blessed him.
Majnun stepped free of all his old distress
And fastened on the belt of sure success

And followed the old man, feeling he'd found
Life-giving water welling from the ground;[134]
He moved like the Euphrates' eager flow
Or like the air when scented breezes blow,
Behind him came his animals, all following
Their liege-lord, their commander, and their king,
A splendid and obedient retinue
Traveling behind him to the rendezvous.

When they arrived at the appointed place
Majnun sat at a towering palm tree's base
(They had agreed his retinue should stay,
Apart from him, a bow-shot's length away),
While the old man went quickly off to tell
Layli Majnun had come, and all was well.
The lovely tent-dweller leaped up, as wild
And swift as is a headlong fairy-child—
She came within ten paces of her friend,
Then felt her fortitude and willpower end;
And said, "Old man, your kindness made me strong,
But now, believe me, I cannot go on,
I'm like a candle, one more step I know
I'll melt away within the candle's glow.
I have a husband, and it's true he's sleeping,
But God knows this, and he is in His keeping;
I never gave my heart to him, but I'm
Not base and cruel enough for such a crime.
I can't look further, doing so would be
Against all reason, and the death of me.
Better no words at all than words that mean
Things that are evil, noxious, and unclean,

Though it might heal my sorrow, all the same
I can't do something that will bring me shame.
Even Majnun who lives for love must know
That further on than this we cannot go,
But ask him if he'd make my heart rejoice
With one or two lines sung by his sweet voice—
If he brought wine, I'd drink it willingly
And if he sings, the sound will nourish me."

Spring's charm was in these lovers, and they both
Shone with the loveliness of spring's new growth;
The old man went from this sweet spring to that
And saw Majnun had fainted; he lay flat
Upon the stony ground, worn out and weak,
With tearful traces smeared across his cheek.

Majnun revived, and slowly sat up next
To the old man, and smiled as if perplexed,
And said, "What springtime flower is this that's lent
The air that comes to me such lovely scent?
But it's no flower I know, it's Layli's hair
That gives this fainting fragrance to the air,
So delicate, so sweet, I'd sacrifice
My aching heart for such a paradise."
Touched by such love, the old man said, "It's wrong
That you've been forced apart, and for so long;
But you must call her first, then she'll appear
In all her loveliness beside you here . . .
She's not here, and you don't know what to do!
How will you be when she's in front of you?"
Majnun replied, "You have a good heart, so
Don't tell me old things I already know.

It's true that I have caught the scent of wine,
That doesn't mean the wine itself is mine."
Then he began to sing a few lines of
The poems he'd composed in praise of love.

MAJNUN SINGS IN LAYLI'S PRESENCE

"Where am I? Where are you? How were you made
That I am yours no matter where I've strayed?
I am a tuneless song, and God help me
If you're my rival or my enemy.
I'm driven from my home, I reign and roam
As does the full moon when she's halfway home;
Hardship is mine—give me fine clothes, I'll tear them,
But give me sackcloth garments and I'll wear them,
Fate doesn't own me, grief delights in me
As I delight in grief's sweet company.
I feel I die of thirst, and yet around me
The water rises quickly and has drowned me,
I am a bat who loves the night, but one
Who is the dearest friend now of the sun.
I've lost my way, and claim that I'm a guide,
Homeless, I boast I own the countryside;
I am a fraud, and claim I'm Solomon,
Horseless, I claim it's Rakhsh I ride upon,[135]
I long for you with every step, my friend,
And have no longing that this longing end;
Inactive outwardly, within my heart
I'm all impatience, chafing to depart.

*

"Surpassing wonderful in all you do,
I'm a mere bandit who's in love with you
But when a bandit grabs an enemy
He pulls her with him and she can't get free;
The reckless man who isn't fearful whether
He lives or dies, kills good and bad together;
The wolf who fears his prey can only blame
Himself for his embarrassment and shame.
Before you've come, you'd leave me here alone . . . ?
How can you harvest what you've never sown?
And don't wish me, 'Good night'—how can it be
A 'good night' when you won't remain with me?
And are our souls in separate worlds that you
Can't step in my direction? Is this true?
Give me another soul to bear it, then,
Or treat me better when you come again.
If you won't treat me generously, I fear
My soul is leaving me and death is near,
While any soul your lips speak kindly to
Enjoys eternal life because of you.
So many men desire to be your slaves—
As I behave, though, none of them behaves,
As long as I remember you my mind
Is humble, happy, gladdened, and resigned—
And may the night that I forget you be
The night my heart becomes your enemy.

"From now on you and I, and I and you,
May one heart beat for us although we're two
And it is right that heart be yours, since my
Poor heart is broken and expects to die.

Like dawn, we'll have a single sun—one heart—
When it appears a hundred suns depart,
And we two shall be one, a single coin
On which on either side two figures join,
Or we shall be a single almond, but
Two kernels will be in that single nut,
So we'll be one, and all that made us two
Will be cast off like a discarded shoe—
With you my being turns to light, flown far
From every entity but what you are.
Whose body's this, what can it rightly claim?
It's like a coin reminted in your name—
At such a feast no sadness should be there,
Nor when your banner flutters in the air,
Our single soul is yours, and you are free,
More noble than a single cypress tree,
While I'm all yours, my dearest, like a rose
You've tucked inside the sash that binds your clothes.
The breeze that brings your scent revives my soul
And scours my heart of rust and makes it whole,
And heals me in the way that mummia heals[136]
The pains a feverish, sick body feels.
If you're a dog at heart, then I shall be
Dust in your street for dogs to tread on me,
And if you keep a pack of dogs, I'll take
My humble place among them for your sake,
And all the beasts within my retinue
Will dedicate their services to you.
I'm poor and you are rich, this is my duty,
I'm nothingness and you are all of beauty,
Your beauty spots are silver coins, discreet,
Your golden coins are bracelets on your feet,

And seeing all your beauty and your grace
I long to take those golden bracelets' place.
Clouds' rainy tears announce that spring is here,
Majnun for you sheds many a flowing tear,
Men set an Indian guard to watch and wait,
Majnun's the Indian guard who's at your gate,
The heavens take their beauty from the moon,
Just as your face tells fortunes to Majnun,
And far from you Majnun's the nightingale
Who sees his longing for the roses fail;
Men mine the earth for rubies, but to find
Where you are, it's his soul Majnun has mined!
Oh God, how wonderful if you could be
Filled with impetuous desire for me!

"Moonlight would make the night as bright as day,
I'd be alone, and see you make your way
Through flowers to me, and I'd sit next to you,
And we'd be side by side at last, we two,
And like a harp[137] I'd clasp you for my own
And hide you like a ruby locked in stone . . .
Now drunk with your narcissus eyes I stare
And dare to touch your hyacinthine hair,
My fingers play among your curls, then trace
The contours of your eyebrows and your face.
I grasp your apple chin,[138] my body rests
Upon the pomegranates of your breasts,
I fondle them like apples, and I bite
Your pomegranate chin with fictive spite;
Across your shoulders I push back your hair
To steal the pretty earrings hidden there,

I move your veil aside, and in small sips
I taste the dates of your delicious lips;
I frame your face in tumbling curls, as though
Violets enclosed a rose's modest glow,
And then I sweep the curls back, and your face
Is there again in all its radiant grace;
And now I have you lean against my chest
To read how lost I've been and how distressed
In poems that I give into your hand
To have you sympathize and understand . . .

"O God, that this enchanting fantasy
Could really come to pass for you and me!
Unless my little harp should chance to break,
This is the song I'll sing for your sweet sake;
Ah, don't torment me so, don't sentence me
To such prolonged and dreadful misery.
Don't summon me to you, would that you knew
How happy life with me could be for you,
There'd be no shame for you, there'd be no strangers
To threaten us with trouble or with dangers,
Lie still with me or wander, for it's clear
No one you know is going to appear—
And my kind animals can't say a word
About whatever they have seen or heard.
Wherever else you go, whatever pit
You hide in, others can discover it,
Friends might surround you, but wherever you
Find friends, your enemies will be there too;
How could I keep you safe in distant places
Where you're hemmed in by unfamiliar faces?

With me, though, you'd be safe, you could be sure
Of being always happy and secure.
Life is our friend now, we must grasp it when
We can, this chance will never come again!
Don't be a dazzling sun that's counterfeit,
Or cheat me with a mirage's deceit.
Thirst for your beauty has disfigured me—
And you've shown not one jot of sympathy.
Without you I can suffer; just as true
Is that I could rejoice and drink with you,
It seems that you've forgotten this, as though
It were a waking dream dreamed long ago—
Wine drunk with you would surely be forgiven
Since wine is not forbidden us in heaven!
I'd drink an ocean from your hands, I'd drain
The draught, not half a droplet would remain,
And poison given me by you would be
A draught that I would swallow willingly,
And I'd be drunk, and you'd respond, and then
You too would fill your empty glass again."

He spoke, and turned, impatient to depart,
As melancholy filled his aching heart,
And that sweet cypress started to retrace
Her journey home, with sadness in her face.

SALAM BAGHDADI COMES TO SEE MAJNUN

The skillful teller of this story says
That in Baghdad in those now distant days
A lover lived, a youth so young his beard
And lip's first growth had hardly yet appeared;
Love's troubles had already reached him though
And he knew well the setbacks lovers know,
Love's smoky fire had choked him, and he'd borne
Love's miseries, its vigils, and its scorn.
Salam was this youth's name, and Fate had made him
Wealthy in every way that she could aid him;
He lived in love's world, and he venerated
The heartfelt lyrics lovers had created.
The fame of Qais's plangent songs had grown
Until his tragic tale became well known,
And men of every sort and everywhere
Sang his sad plaints of love and love's despair,
And some who sang his songs tried to discover
The whereabouts of this composer-lover.
And so from town to town these poems had
Proceeded till at last they reached Baghdad,
Where connoisseurs of love and elegance
Would sing his songs as if within a trance.
Salam grew keen to meet the author of
Such sensitive accounts of desperate love—

He mounted a fast camel, loosed her reins,
And set off galloping across the plains,
Urging her onward, hoping he could question
The man whose tale was now his one obsession;
He asked if men had seen someone forlorn
And naked as the day that he was born,
Whom animals surrounded, as though they
Encircled him to keep mankind away.

From far away, Majnun saw him appear
And shouted to his beasts as he drew near,
That they should be prepared to fight the stranger,
And use their claws and jaws to ward off danger.
Salam saw that they thought he'd come to harm them
And quickly called out kindly to disarm them,
And when Majnun perceived his friendliness
He greeted him with heartfelt tenderness,
And welcomed him, and asked him why he'd come,
And where it was that he had ridden from.
He answered him, "It's you I've come to find,
When I set out it's you I had in mind,
I left Baghdad to reach this very place
Hoping that I could meet you face to face;
Baghdad's my home-town, I've been happy there,
Till now I've never traveled anywhere;
I'm here because of you, because I'm smitten
By all those marvelous poems that you've written.
Since God has given me this day, to see
You face to face, right here, in front of me,
My fervent hope is that you'll let me spend
The life that I have left, here as your friend.

I kiss the ground before you, hoping I
Can tend you faithfully until I die,
Not for an instant shall I cease to serve you,
With every breath I'll struggle to deserve you.
For every verse that you compose, my part
Will be to learn that sacred verse by heart,
And as I learn your poems I'm quite sure
My soul will grow more beautiful and pure.
I know this is presumptuous, but allow
Yourself to be acquainted with me now—
Give me your songs to sing, and think of me
As one of these wild animals you see.
I'll be your willing slave, I won't desert you,
You know a slave like me could never hurt you.
I too have been worn down by love; I too
Have known love's dreadful agonies, like you."

And when Salam had had his say, Majnun
Smiled at him like a slender crescent moon.
"You're used to comfort, I can see," he said.
"This road is hard, and dangers lie ahead;
Turn round, go back. Yes, you're a man, I know,
But not one who can go where I must go;
Of all the hundred sorrows I've been through
Not one of them has been endured by you.
My animals are all I have; how can
A wretch like me support another man?
Your coming to me here can only be
Like one more painful nail banged into me;
I can't endure myself—how can I share
My space with someone else whom I can't bear?
From my words even demons run away—
What use to you is anything I say?

All day I wander aimlessly, and then
Sleep on these stones till morning comes again;
Look, I'm a savage, outcast and despised,
Find someone like yourself who's civilized!
If you have iron's endurance, still you'll be
Worn out and sickened by the likes of me,
And if you're water, then I'm fire—in one
Night I'll evaporate you, you'll be gone!
I'm poor, I've nothing with me to detain you,
I haven't got the means to entertain you;
We can't get on, you like yourself, and I
Despise myself so much I want to die—
I've thrown my clothes off, whereas you feel best
Whenever you're well groomed and nicely dressed.
I need no friends, there's no one I feel free with,
You're on the lookout for new friends to be with;
For you to stay here'd be a bad mistake,
You love the idols that I love to break,
So leave this wasteland and leave me behind,
I'm not the kindly friend you'd hoped to find!
You had a hard time searching but you found me,
The life I live, the wild beasts that surround me—
You've seen I'm weird and sad, so simply say,
'God keep you, friend,' and then be on your way!
If kindness stops you going, then believe me
Life's harsh and cruel here, so you'd better leave me!"

Hopeful, Salam did not accept one word
Of all the counsel and advice he heard;
He said, "In God's name, don't try any more
To hide the water that I'm thirsty for;

You are my qebleh,[139] so allow me to
Bow down before you, and to worship you,
And if it's wrong to worship in this way
I'll seek forgiveness for it when I pray."

And so Majnun eventually acceded
To what he asked, touched by how hard he pleaded.
Immediately Salam produced a spread
Of halva, loaves, and little cakes, and said,
"Relax now, please sit down with me, and break
This bread with me, for our new friendship's sake;
And I admire your fasting, but these scraps
Are too small to be judged as a relapse,
We all need food, and that's to be expected,
The body's appetites must be respected."
Majnun said, "Not by me, my appetite
Has gone and I don't want a single bite;
Halva and bread's for those who are intent
On tending to their body's nourishment,
That's not my way, though; if food doesn't fill me
That's normal, fasting isn't going to kill me."
And when Salam saw that his grief had made
Him shun both food and sleep, and that he paid
No heed to anyone, and didn't care
If he was here or there or anywhere,
His heart went out to him, and all he felt.
He said, "It would be better if you dealt
With all this dreadful sorrow with much more
Patient forbearance than you've done before;
Your heart won't always grieve, the heavens never
Present one aspect to the earth forever,
And in the time it takes to blink your eyes
A hundred doors can open if you're wise;

Don't grieve for grief's sake, recognize your worth,
And don't let heaven make you like the earth!
Return from pain and mourning for a while—
As much as you have wept in sorrow, smile!
I too was once heartbroken, captive to
The misery I suffered, just like you,
But God's benevolence and favor freed me
As I allowed His love and grace to lead me—
And your complaints will end at last; tomorrow
You will forget the substance of your sorrow.
This flame of love burns fiercely, but in truth
It gets its heat and brightness from our youth,
This furnace fire that seems so uncontrolled
Becomes, as we grow older, calm and cold."

Majnun heard how this kindly man reproved him
And stood, but nothing that he'd heard had moved him.
He said, "So I'm just fanciful, you think?
Or I'm like this because of whims or drink?
I am love's emperor, and have no shame
In saying this, I glory in the name!
I have no earthly lust, I've been made pure
And chaste by all the sorrows I endure.
I have escaped from sensuality,
Such fancies have no value now for me—
My being is all love, and its chaste fire
Burns me like sandalwood with pure desire,
Love purifies my house, and all my heart
Is gathered now and ready to depart—
Who can describe my being, since I've none;
Only my friend exists—all else is gone.[140]
My love will last, secure and unbetrayed,
Until the glittering stars in heaven fade,

And from my faithful heart love will be sundered
When all the sand grains of the earth are numbered.
If you intend to talk to me, first learn
To hold your tongue, and don't talk out of turn;
Consider who you are, mind what you say,
And don't go taunting others in this way—
It's well said that the first and best defense
Is careful self-control and common sense."
Salam was chastened and dismayed, and heeded
The words of one who knew much more than he did.

You won't be disrespectful if you're wise
Since then you won't need to apologize:
A well-strung bow, or one that's slack, if it
Is badly aimed the target won't be hit—
And strong or weak, if you're impertinent
You will be hurt, whatever your intent,
Witty uncalled-for words will bring you shame
And weak ones will be ridiculed as lame,
To turn a key within a lock, make sure
That it's the right key you've been searching for,
A well requires a rope, and journeys need
Good feet for walking, then you can proceed.

Majnun and good Salam, for a few days,
Before the final parting of their ways,
Journeyed together; as Majnun would sing
Salam was keen to write down everything—
But soon Salam found that he couldn't keep
To never needing either food or sleep
And when he saw the cloth day after day
Empty of food, he knew he couldn't stay;

His weakness meant that finally he said
Goodbye to all the wild beasts there, and fled
Back to Baghdad; at least, though, now he brought
All of the perfect poems he'd been taught,
And everywhere he sang them men would stare
To hear such loveliness, and such despair.

ON THE GREATNESS OF MAJNUN

Don't think Majnun was one whose crazy ways
Were those of fools we meet with nowadays
Who never pray or fast, who've no respect
For manners, justice, or the intellect.
He knew each chapter, each obscurest verse,
Of laws that regulate the universe,
And by his knowledge could elucidate
The secrets of the processes of Fate.
His speech glowed like gold coins, his poetry
Glistened like pearls set out ingeniously
(It's common knowledge that a madman's heart
Could not produce such captivating art).
As drunkards do, he'd left the world, but stayed
Still cognizant of how it had been made,
And knew death's bitterness and had prepared
Provisions for the way on which he fared.
Since life was hard for him, his death appeared
As welcome, not a phantom to be feared—
It's hard to leave this world unless one knows
The secret ways by which the traveler goes,
And one who clings to this sad home will find
It's difficult to leave this place behind.
Majnun required no friends, and gradually
He loosened all earth's bonds till he was free,

Since he was anxious to be ready when
The lordly Hunter of the Souls of men
Asked for his soul from him, so that he could
Hand it to Him entirely, as he should.
Fear haunts the ship of life, and being there
Was what provoked in him such deep despair,
Food was like poison to him, and the sea
He sailed was like a long futility.
He'd calmed his nature and forgone its use
And his belovèd was a mere excuse;
He knew desire and readiness for sin
But kept them like a hidden sword within—
The love he sought from Layli's soul was one
They'd know eternally when life was done.

I asked a wise philosopher who knew
Love's nature, and the things that it can do,
To talk to me about the long delay
Some lovers know along love's endless way—
A man might search for thirty years before
He knows the love that he's been longing for!
He said, "After that moment he's enjoyed
All of love's bliss, his life becomes a void;
For thirty years he's searched for happiness
In something that is weak and substanceless.
I place one step beyond both worlds,[141] and wine
Unearthly and eternal there is mine."

ZAYD'S LOVE FOR ZAYNAB

At the same time, in the same place, they say
Another love-chained helpless lover lay
Incapable with wretchedness as though
Beneath a mountainside of heartfelt woe,
Sent wild by love, as if a demon had
Possessed his mind and made him wholly mad.
He was a fine young man, whose poetry
Mixed delicacy's charm with misery,
A man whom ardent love had captured, who
Was love's now utterly and through and through.
His name was Zayd, and he lived not far from
The place where Layli's household had their home.
It was his cousin that Zayd loved, and she
Returned his love with equal urgency;
Each felt the sign, and in an equal fashion,
That they'd been smitten by this lovesick passion:
Always, impatiently, she longed to stay
Beside her longed-for cousin, come what may,
While he was so in love, in such despair,
He felt his life was hanging by a hair.
She was so lively, beautiful, and smiling,
Her figure slim and prettily beguiling,
And she was tall, her waist as pliant, white
As quicksilver that seems composed of light;

Her cheeks were red-bud flowers, her lovely scent
Was like the breeze of dawn that's heaven-sent,
She was unique, bewitching . . . far and wide
Her praises spread throughout the countryside,
And men said she outdid the beauties of
Taraz[142] in qualities that lead to love,
In jokes and wiles, that seeing her would cure
The thousand sicknesses that men endure.
Her mouth was tiny as an ant, and where
Her waist was seemed as narrow as a hair,[143]
Her chin was like an apple that's more green
Than any senna Mecca's ever seen,[144]
Her kisses were like honeycomb, more sweet
Than sweetened syrups or a sugared treat,
And when she'd sugared kisses to bestow,
Her lips' sweet syllabub would overflow—
Then to her loving cousin she could seem
To be the source of life eternal's stream,
Or like a cypress tree whose curious crop
Of sugared rosewater would never stop.
Her face outshone the shining sun, her hair
Spread ambergris's fragrance everywhere—
Her name was Zaynab, and her loveliness
Was the continual cause of Zayd's distress
As he used all his cunning skill to find
How this unrivaled ruby could be mined.[145]
His one fault was that he was poor, whereas
His uncle had the wealth a rich man has.
Zayd asked him for some money—he refused him;
He asked him for his daughter—he abused him;
His uncle wouldn't see him, what could he
Contrive to do in this extremity,

A man who was so poor, a wretch who spent
His days and nights in one long love-lament,
Writing heart-rending songs, that hoped no one
Would ever grieve in love as he had done?
His uncle, meanwhile, was deliberately
Keeping his daughter under lock and key,
The suitor who was poor had been sent packing,
A suitable rich suitor was still lacking . . .
At last his headache ended when a man
Came forward who appeared to fit his plan,
A wealthy man whom he was satisfied
To give Zaynab to as his lawful bride.

Zayd gave up all his hopes of her, and knew
New depths of sorrow as his anguish grew,
He neither ate nor slept, and he became
A byword for his sorrow and his shame,
Bound hand and foot in hopeless love, he soon
Became as wild and crazy as Majnun—
His faithless friends all mocked him and departed,
Leaving him in love's furnace, brokenhearted.
Sparks from this fire reached Layli, and she learned
Of how love tortured him, and how he burned—
At times she'd summon him, and they would sit
And talk of love and never tire of it,
She would make much of him and ask him to
Describe the agonies that he'd been through
And as he told her of his love he'd sigh,
And hearing him she'd sympathize and cry,
And seeing all his faithfulness she'd dare
To tell him of her love and her despair,

Until she took him as her messenger
To take a letter to Majnun for her.

As soon as Majnun read her words, they made
Him dance with happiness in front of Zayd,
Who was content to help him and behave
Like one whose earring marks him as a slave,[146]
And seeing him so tractable and mild
Majnun's wild beasts forgot that they were wild.
The messenger became a friend, and soon
A proved amanuensis for Majnun
And all the lines of verse he improvised
Zayd carefully wrote down and organized,
And put them into Layli's hands, and then
With Layli's messages came back again;
So Zayd became their willing messenger
From her to him and then from him to her.

Majnun was singing something sad one day
But softly, in a semi-private way,
When suddenly, sarcastically, Zayd said,
"The heart that strings such jewels on such a thread,
Why does it choose to be so mad, when plainly
It would be better if it acted sanely?
Your words are noble and inspired, and yet
You're filled with self-contempt and with regret;
But this is how I am, so what makes you
Better than me when you do what I do?
I weep as much as you, my life is more
Unhappy than yours is, I'm much more poor;
I'm patient just like you, I think like you,
We eat the same things and I drink like you.

Give up this craziness, it's brought you shame,
Infatuation's ruined your good name."

Majnun, an earthly paragon, whose soul
Had conquered lust and mastered self-control,
Heard Zayd's impetuous and rash attack
And with his own impetuous rage struck back:
"Stop, stop! You've said enough! You're here to be
My messenger, no more. What's Zayd to me?
How long do you intend to tell me tales
About Zayd's life and all of his travails?
Why do you say I'm mad? A madman cares
For nothing but himself and his affairs
And I'm as innocent of all of this
As angels are who dwell in heavenly bliss.
God's made me so that I am not a creature
With anything demonic in my nature,
And this is why these animals you see
Are happy to associate with me—
My nature's to be sensitive and kind,
If you can't see this you've a wicked mind!
Since self-regard corrupts the soul, I pray
That when my eyes see me they look away—
Better the evil eye's fell influence
Should light on you with cruel malevolence,
Than that you ever come to idolize
Yourself with foolishly admiring eyes.
A madman's one who puts his trust and hopes
In earthly shelters tied with worldly ropes,
And I've tried hard to loose these ropes, to find
A way to leave earth's compass points behind.
I have a permit to depart, to leave

This village[147] where I waste away and grieve—
My ship is sinking and its sail has gone
And I have every reason to move on;
Before the waves engulf it I bestow
Upon the waters all I have, and go.
But now the dance of my long journey starts,
Hindrances block my soul as she departs,
Since it is hard to make the soul dispense
With all she's known of earthly elements.
Glorious the Friend whose voice demands your soul,
Glorious to place within His hands your soul!
You stand alone before Him, and your task
Is to present the soul for which He'll ask.

"You think I'll take the bait and step into
This worldly trap? That's what you think I'll do?
That I shall grab the hook that pulls me down
Into delusion's seas where I shall drown?
I struggle to escape this barren land,
This arid wilderness of thorns and sand,
And not as one who's perished but as one
Whose manliness is proved by what he's done.
You're trapped within a well, and to be freed
A rope to haul you out is what you need—
What man within this well, when sorrows seize him,
Escapes unless he grasps the rope that frees him?
That rope is the belovèd's hair, each strand
Of which is held within another's hand.

"The state I'm in is wise and sensible
Although fools think it's reprehensible,
It's licit, there's no reason to reproach it,

Safer than all, no evils can approach it.
The heavens rain down sorrows on my head
As if to prove that I were better dead,
As if to bring my soul into the light
And blanch it like an almond that turns white;
My soul, that is a black child I must save
And resurrect from its terrestrial grave.
And since God's given me this task, my role
Is to embrace these hardships heart and soul—
The man who sold sour grapes was right to say
To someone who sold figs, 'What better way
Of living could there be than ours, my brother,
And who would ever wish for any other?'
And men who won't accept their roles will be
Just as morose with others they might see.

"I aim my arrow as I should, I know,
But something falters as I draw my bow,
The treasury's before me, but alas,
My key to it is made of fragile glass,
In fear there's always hope, and hope is rare
Without fear's shadow also being there.
I'm in this ruined place[148] as one who lives
Cut off from all my friends and relatives;
I don't indulge in gossip or devise
Ways to live carelessly by telling lies,
And long before death cries, 'Rise up, move on,
The fatal caravan will soon be gone!'
I'm manumitted and no more a slave,
I leave this grave by going to my grave;[149]

This is the only madness I can see—
If this is truly madness—that's in me."

He scattered words like jewels, like a bequest
That's scattered from an opened treasure chest,
And Zayd sat listening there, bewildered, dazed,
Reduced to wondering silence and amazed;
He saw his sprigs were an impertinence
Beside this springtime of such eloquence—
He would be civil, to himself he swore
His lips were bolted shut for evermore.
Again he was the lovers' go-between,
Silent and faithful, as he once had been,
Their messenger, whose business was to go
To one, then to the other, to and fro,
Majnun to Layli, Layli to Majnun,
As Venus goes between the sun and moon.

THE DEATH OF LAYLI'S HUSBAND, EBN SALAM

Whatever happens in the world possesses
A necessary purpose it addresses,
All that exists is subject to control,
Leading it on to its predestined goal.
A piece of paper has two separate sides,
When one is visible the other hides;
On this side are the plans we contemplate,
On that side are the reckonings of Fate;
Few writing on one side have any guide
To what is written on the other side—
You count so many roses, how they charm you,
But pick them and their hidden thorns will harm you;
Going by just their colors and their shapes,
Who can distinguish sweet from bitter grapes?
Many are hungry, and they think that when
They eat a great deal they'll be well again,
Although the opposite is also true
Since overeating can be bad for you,
And moderate fasting's often preferable
To wolfing victuals down until you're full;
To sum up, then, just as the proverbs say,
Appearances can lead us all astray—
What looks like sherbet can be vinegar
And often things aren't what we think they are.

*

Layli, whose radiant grace and loveliness
Brought joy to others, to herself distress,
A treasure with a serpent coiled around her[150]
To keep off any predators who found her,
Lived like a ruby that remains unknown
Sequestered in the darkness of a stone,
A jewel that's like the moon in an eclipse
Confined within the dragon's slavering lips,[151]
Her watching husband glad that he controlled her
And sad that he could do no more than hold her.
She was a fairy being in her speech
But locked in iron walls he couldn't breach;
She was resourceful, patient, the deceiver
Of one who once had thought he could deceive her—
When he's not there, complaining, full of tears,
Rubbing her eyes whenever he appears,
Lamenting her virginity, grief-stricken
By him whose painful presence made her sicken,
Wanting to share her grief but well aware
No friend was there to share in her despair;
And sorrow hidden from the light of day
Weakens the soul until it slinks away.

Shame mixed with pride, the grief she had to bear,
Had made her thoughts as tangled as her hair;
Like a lost stranger wandering round and round,
A fallen tent-pole prone upon the ground,
So vehemently, so copiously, she wept
She fainted and lay still, as if she slept,
And though shouts reached her ears she didn't stir,
But wept and moaned and nothing shifted her.

Or sometimes she would sit and mask her tears
As candles do when dripping wax appears,
And then the flickering flame starts up and leaps
Like laughter hiding tears the candle weeps.
Her life seemed tasteless, saltless, but then heaven
Rubbed salt into the wounds she had been given
Until the skies' relentless turning made her
Show outwardly how heaven had betrayed her.

They stayed apart, and banished from her side
Her husband longed to see his absent bride,
Till Ebn Salam grew weak, then weaker still
And it was clear that he had fallen ill.
A fever gripped him and began to gain
A gradual hold upon his ailing brain—
The equilibrium in his body failed
As bit by bit the malady prevailed.
A doctor took his wavering pulse and checked
His urine for some sign he could detect
Of what was wrong, and by a wholesome diet,
A regimen of self-control and quiet,
Removed the weakness from his body till
The rallied patient was no longer ill.
But when his health revived at such a rate
That his thin flesh began to put on weight,
He broke his doctor's rules and started to
Do things his doctor said he shouldn't do.
(In sickness and in health, practice restraint,
It isn't good for only one complaint—
In health it is your body's firm foundation,
In sickness it's your cure and your salvation,

A herb from which a thousand remedies
Can be procured for mankind's maladies,
A village where a thousand walls protect
The treasure of our health and self-respect.)
While Ebn Salam was not yet well, he ended
The treatment that the doctor'd recommended
And cast restraint aside . . . his malady
Returned, but with increased intensity,
All of his sickly symptoms were renewed
And strengthened by the course that he pursued.
Water'd revived the rose, but now it made
The flower rotten and its petals fade;
An earthquake had occurred beneath the town
And right and left high walls had tumbled down,
And when the shaking started to redouble
The shockwave buried him beneath the rubble.[152]
For two or three more days the young man's breath
Came slowly, painfully, and presaged death,
Until the wheezing tightened to a groan
And broke like glass that's shattered by a stone,
And then it was as though his soul had waved
The world farewell, and flown up, and was saved.
He went, as all must go; the world's brief loan
Of life to us, it takes back as its own.
Try to discharge this loan as capably
As you are able to, and then fly free,
Don't sit and loiter in this mortal snare
As if your body's flesh were fastened there,
But with your spirit break the cage and fly
Like homing pigeons that traverse the sky.
All of creation, and the world of men,
Falls at death's hand, never to rise again:

Each morning fire falls from the heavenly hearth
To burn the teeming harvest of the earth,
Each night this muddy pit assails the dark
With smoke that rises up to heaven's arc;
All of the world, a wise man realizes,
Is a fire-temple,[153] from which smoke arises.

Like a wild onager when it leaps free
From where it's languished in captivity,
So Layli's fractious heart leaped when she heard
Her husband's death had finally occurred.
But though she was relieved that he was gone,
He'd been her husband when all's said and done
And so she mourned for him, while secretly
Her friend filled all her mind and memory.
Cries for her husband's death assailed the skies,
Tears for her lover's sorrows filled her eyes—
She wept for his long absence while she mourned
The passing of her husband whom she'd scorned.
She named her husband in her wild lament
But inwardly it was her friend she meant,
And though she mourned her husband who had died,
It was her friend for whom she moaned and cried—
The shell bewailed her husband's wretched end,
The kernel grieved for her still-absent friend.
The Arab custom was, a widow's face
Should not be seen in any public place—
For two years she should stay at home, confined,
Unseen, unseeing, cut off from mankind,
And grieving spend her time secluded there,
Repeating elegies or rapt in prayer.

Layli made use of this excuse, and she
Emptied her tent of guests and company
To mourn her husband's passing, as men thought.
A different grief, though, made her wild, distraught—
All patience left her, and her anguished cries
Filled in their vehemence the seven skies,[154]
She beat herself about the head as though
Disdaining fear and danger with each blow.

ZAYD TELLS MAJNUN OF
LAYLI'S HUSBAND'S DEATH

The bones of this beguiling tale contain
Marrow its teller hastens to explain:

Although the two of them had had to part,
Zayd longed for Zaynab still with all his heart,
Though now he lived as far from her as he
Earnestly hoped the evil eye would be.
In place of water now he drank down sadness,
Impatient with all patience, close to madness . . .
His friends and relatives who knew his plight
Longed to relieve him and to set things right,
Thinking him worthy of his love who'd been
Given to one whom she had never seen.
Hoping they could undo the knot that hurt him
Once Zaynab had no choice but to desert him,
They found a way both secret and discreet
To bring him to her, so that they could meet,
And so he went to her and cleansed the rust
Staining the mirror of their mutual trust.[155]
Breathless he breathed in silence to unclose
The petals of this chaste unopened rose,
And kindly, gently, then, her sweet lips kissed
Zayd's lips as they began their secret tryst,

Questioning, talking, and content to be
Simply in one another's company,
Careful to keep their talk and their desires
Within the limits chastity requires.

Zayd was preoccupied, but still he'd find
Thoughts of Majnun recurring in his mind—
A hundred ways, a hundred times, he tried
To help his friend the world had cast aside,
And was so faithful in this role that he
Became a byword for his loyalty.
When Ebn Salam died, and his soul had flown
Up from the earthly cage that it had known,
Zayd set off like the wind to tell his friend
All that he knew of Ebn Salam's sad end,
Of how death, like a servant at his side,
Had handed him the draught from which he'd died.
He said, "That bandit, that cruel highwayman
Who raided and despoiled your caravan
Of all you hoped for, is now dead and gone,
And can't obstruct the road you travel on;
He's dead, his life is yours, and may you live
Blessed by these added years the heavens give!"[156]
Majnun devoured this morsel, then he gazed
In wonder at the heavens, as if amazed,
And suddenly gave vent to deafening cries
That stridently re-echoed in the skies.
Death made him dance for joy, since death had brought
The longed-for happiness for which he'd sought,
And in his rival's grave he thought he knew
How all that he had dreamed of could come true.

His heart rejoiced to think his rose would be
Without a thorn, and set at liberty,
But thinking of her state he soon perceived
That she must grieve, as he too had once grieved—
His nature bade him laugh, his intellect
Commanded tears of sorrow and respect.
And when he'd wept a while, he turned to Zayd
As if to scold him for the part he'd played.
He said, "Dear friend, you've sympathized with me,
And suffered as you've shared my agony,
But in my heart are words I have to say
(I can't suppress them, they won't go away):
This message that you gave, there's something wrong
    there,
You said a phrase that oughtn't to belong there.
You said that when that man you spoke of died,
His life was mine, or that's what you implied,
But given that we're friends you should have said
His life was Layli's life, once he was dead;
In acting as our faithful messenger
You gave to me what should belong to her."
Zayd said, "Do you remember when you found
A piece of paper lying on the ground
With both your names on it? And that you tore
The paper in two equal halves and swore
That when it came to Layli and to you
You two were one and only one, not two?
That was my meaning—if I went astray,
Repentant, on bare feet, I'll crawl away!"
Majnun sprang up and clasped him to his chest
And cried, "Of all my friends you are the best,

Long may you live! Your kindly eloquence
Is like a breeze that's laden with sweet scents!
You spoke well and you meant well, and I see
You answered wisely and appropriately—
Only a soul-mate speaks so aptly, none
But you know all my secrets one by one
And everything a soul-mate says, I swear
Is licit in my heart and welcome there,
And while I live I promise you I'll want
No man but you to be my confidant;
Till death removes me, I won't tug away
My stubborn head from anything you say,
Your words will nourish me, and I will view
As blasphemy the thoughts I hide from you."
They lived together for a while, but then
After a week, Zayd set off home again;
Majnun sought out his old retreat, and stayed
Within the mountain eyrie he had made.

LAYLI PRAYS TO GOD

When jewelry made of pearls adorned the night,
Making the darkness glitter with their light,
Layli, the loveliest pearl, wept copious seas
Of pearls as numerous as the Pleiades.[157]
Companionless but for her torch's light,
Layli was there, with sorrow and the night;
A fluttering moth left sleepless, she inveighed
Against the night that never seemed to fade:
"Why is this night so endless," she demanded,
"As though the forehead of the sky were branded?
What boundless night is this, that it should be
Both fated for me, and the death of me?
How in this constant darkness can I strive
For ways to keep my wretched soul alive?
You'd say its anguish makes me faint with fear,
Or that God's final Judgment Day was here—
I'm stranded in this dayless night, oh may
This night at last convert itself to day!
I'm like a gardener who can't see the wall
Around her garden has begun to fall,
Or that the flowers she grew have disappeared
Or that her precious orchard has been cleared.
The rooster might be dead, but still the skies
Must lighten when the sun begins to rise;

And if the rooster's dead, as we suggested,
And if the street's mu'ezzin's been arrested,
But still we ought to hear the morning drum
Announcing that at last the dawn has come![158]
O God, bring me that torch whose blazing fire[159]
Has branded me with sigils of desire;
He lightens all the world, but tell him he
Must drive this smothering darkness back from me."
She did not cease this prayer until dawn's light
Began to glimmer and dispel the night.

LAYLI AND MAJNUN COME TOGETHER AGAIN

As daybreak's noble sovereign sat alone
And splendid on the morning's gleaming throne,
His shining presence made the heavens bright
And touched the far horizons with his light,
So that the day seemed more resplendent than
A thousand celebrations known to man;
The heavens promised joy throughout the day
And sounds of grief and sorrow died away.
But Layli, filled with longing for Majnun
And moving slowly like the heavenly moon,
Wandered at will, and did not try to hide
The yearning sorrow that she felt inside.
She'd always followed where her husband went,
Now she no longer needed his assent;
There'd been a watchman watching at her door
But no one watched her doorway any more.
Her heart all fire that nothing could assuage,
She had no fear now of her parents' rage,
Her eyes all tears, she walked through many places,
Mountains and streets and valleys and oases,
Seeking her heart, giving her message to
Strangers she met whose hearts she never knew,
Acting with constant kindness everywhere,
Her fragrant scent diffusing in the air,

Always, in every place, and without end,
She sought, in all the world, her one true friend.

After her husband's funeral, she'd returned
To where her father lived, with all she'd learned.
The glass was shattered and the wine was gone,
The rose had withered now, and she moved on—
Her love was something she'd no longer hide,
And casting all her modesty aside,
She locked the door of her old life as she
Opened the unlocked door that set her free,
And didn't rest but thought up clever schemes
To give her strength to realize all her dreams,
And soon she asked for Zayd to visit her
And once more be her trusted messenger.
She said, "Today is not a day for hiding,
It is a day for finding and deciding,
A day for being with that friend whose love
I'll always want and never weary of.
Go now, the world is sweet, bring sugar here,
Mix it with roses as love's elixir,
Have that tall cypress tree lie down beside
This humble grass, abandoning his pride,
Bring whitest jasmine here, so that it may
Be mixed with tulips to make one bouquet.
Capture for me that gracious deer and see
You bring his musky fragrance here to me;
His hide will be my silk, dust on his hooves
Will be the only scent I'll ever use.
A kindly friend is someone whom I've never
Shared sighs with, but we'll sigh our sighs together—

Before death sets his ambush, let me see
The longed-for friend's face here, in front of me."

And saying this she handed gifts to Zayd,
Sables, and clothes of silk and fine brocade,
As generous as a queen, she passed on all
The presents she considered suitable.
Zayd was so pleased to take them, filled with pride,
He seemed to rear up like a mountainside,
And set off for the doorless cavern where
That wingless bird Majnun had made his lair;
He gave Majnun her message, then displayed
The gifts he'd brought, the silks and fine brocade.
Majnun for joy jumped up and whirled around,
Then sat down suddenly upon the ground—
He did this seven times, each time as though
A compass showed him how and where to go,
And in his turning joy it seemed he whirled
Beyond the seven heavens of the world,[160]
Then bowed so low as if he sought to trace
The contours of the earth's elusive face.
As for the clothes Zayd brought, he thanked him
    for them,
And reverently he kissed them then and wore them,
But as he gently handled them, he caught
The scent of Layli in the gifts Zayd brought,
Which touched his troubled, wondering heart, and then
He grieved they were so far apart again.
Once more he set off singing, and the sound
Was like sweet sugar scattered on the ground;
Behind him like a motley regiment
His animals went everywhere he went,

And when he sat, they sat down too, and made
A circle round him like a barricade,
Attentive as respectful watching warders,
Or army officers awaiting orders.
This army, whose fierce armaments were claws
As sharp as sword blades, and devouring jaws,
Came close to Layli's home. To speak to her
Zayd was sent forward as a messenger.
He said, "Your friend, Majnun, is at your door
As lowly as the dust he bows before,
Prostrate, he pleads now for permission to
Enter your home and humbly speak to you."
Layli sprang up, no longer bowed and bent
But straight as is the pole that holds a tent;
As tense now with imaginings and hopes
As are a tent's securely tightened ropes,
She ran out from her tent, like someone drink
Had undermined so much she cannot think,
And neither horrified nor petrified
By all the animals she saw outside,
She fell before her traveler's feet, as meek
As grass before a box tree,[161] and as weak.
Majnun saw that his very soul was there
Bowed down before his feet as if in prayer,
And split the heavens with an anguished yell
As on the earth beside her he too fell;
She'd given up her soul and lived, while he
Had gained his soul and died there instantly—
Both lovers had lost consciousness, and they
Were deaf to all the world might sing or say.
The animals came forward to defend
With sharpened claws their master and their friend,

And round them, like a mountain chain, they kept
The lovers safe while all their senses slept;
There were so many guardians gathered there
No passer-by could see the shielded pair,
And one or two of those who ventured near
Were killed, while others fled away in fear.

Unconscious, side by side, these lovers lay
Unmoving on the earth until midday.
Zayd came, and sprinkled rosewater to make them
Stir to a semi-conscious state then wake them,
At last they woke, exchanging wondering looks
As silent as the pictures are in books.

Then Layli with a thousand hesitations,
A thousand silent, shame-faced, protestations,
Reached for his hand, and hand in hand they went
Into the dark seclusion of her tent
Where with a hundred gestures she caressed him
And as her soul's sole longed-for lover blessed him.
Now the belovèd sat beside her lover,
Zayd's function as a go-between was over—
He sat among the animals who made
Around the tent a sheltering palisade,
Which was so closely wrought that if a fly
Alighted there or simply flew nearby,
One of the animals was sure to catch it
And then another'd speedily dispatch it,
And fearing certain death no man would dare
To be caught passing by or loitering there.

*

Their love was true and real, untouched by lust,
By worldly provocations and mistrust,
And its perfection was what rendered all
Majnun's wild animals so tractable;
There was no animal in him, no taint
Of what's unclean, no bestial constraint,
And conquered by his uncorrupted soul
His animals acknowledged his control—
There was no doubt these lovers' probity
Sought only chastity and purity.
Only today I heard their lovelorn cries
And gazed myself into their loving eyes—
One goblet held the wine that neither drank[162]
(Tipsy, one fell: and drunk, the other sank),
When they embraced she fell back in a swoon
As consciousness departed from Majnun.
Their love was not a cursory concern
But something rare from which the world should learn,
A paradigm sad lovers everywhere
Should emulate to drive away despair.
Majnun, her lover, was her treasurer
Who'd safeguard her virginity for her,
While Layli's gifts to him were portions of
Herself to show the nature of her love;
Her curls to be his kerchief, and her arm
To be his necklace keeping him from harm,
She fashioned from the ringlets of her hair
A garment for her silent slave to wear,
And in the court he ruled, her heart became
The chamberlain safeguarding his good name,
While for a baldric she clung close and pressed
Her pliant arm across his naked chest,

So tightly clasping him that seeing them
You'd say they were two roses on one stem.
Her glances bound him to her, but a chain
Like this will make no wounds and cause no pain;
Likewise she made him drunk, although she gave him
No heady wine or kisses to enslave him.
They were two semicircles that defined
A single circle[163] when they were aligned:
Birds have two wings and scales two pans, there's no
Perplexing mystery that this is so,
Two candles melt into a single bowl
And so become one body and one soul,
One source can fill two flasks, two strands are spun—
Then in a rope they're twisted into one,
A head has two deep sockets, where we find
Two eyes that see, or are closed up and blind;
Earth has two poles, two mirrors can display
The single source that brings the break of day,
And these two lovers were entwined as light
And dark produced alternate day and night
While self-regard, that savage bird of prey,
From these two selfless souls had flown away;
Now they were one, that like a falcon flew,
A single entity that had been two.

Then like a sultan and his queen, the pair
Came from her tent into the open air.
The king had left his castle and his throne,
Ready to set out once again alone,
And in the empty streets he saw no one
(Since in his eyes all other sights had gone)

But Layli, and as if he could devise
Some way of drawing her into his eyes,
He seemed to be a sentinel whose stare
Would silently forever hold her there,
As if she'd be the queen within his heart
So that the two of them should never part.
In silence their lips met; it was as though
A heart-delighting wind began to blow
From Eram's garden,[164] and to fan the fire
That flared up with intensified desire,
And everywhere love's gratifying scent
Of burning rue[165] filled all the firmament.
They stood stock still, and made no sound at all,
Like painted frescoes on a palace wall,
Their hearts were full, but they said not a word,
Like nightingales whose song cannot be heard
(The world re-echoed with their love, but scorn
Had made it silent, hidden, and forlorn).
They stood till night, then till the morning came,
A candle burning with its steady flame
(Chatter is useless, it's mere verbal violence,
And knowledge's true signature is silence;
When it contains no gold, a treasury
Can stay unlocked for everyone to see,
But when gold's there, the owner wants to hide it,
He locks it then, and no one sees inside it).
Teasingly Layli said, "My love, why is it
Your tongue can't make your love for me explicit?
A songbird like a nightingale stays dumb
Until it sees the summer's roses come,
And then it sings its songs of lovesick praise
And shows its love a thousand different ways—

You are this garden's nightingale, and I'm
The rose you sang to once upon a time;
Today we are as one, what's gone amiss
That you should seal your jewel-case up like this?"[166]

Majnun replied, "Your lips are sugar-cane,
Sealing my lips like an unyielding chain;
Think that I have no tongue, that its despair
Has shrunk it to the thickness of a hair,
That seeing your dear face has made it moan
As if it had no language of its own—
These moans cut off my speech, they're my excuse
For why my tongue-tied tongue is of no use,
And I belong to you, it would be wrong
For me to stand and chatter all day long!
Tongues wound . . . better to offer silent balm
That makes uneasy hearts grow soothed and calm.
A speaker is a man who's drowned in seeking,
And when the goal is reached what use is speaking?
You're what I've found, and finding you I fell,
And now I'm lost in love's unfathomed well.
You are my being now, and I have none,
You are my strength, and I'm not anyone.
Who am I in myself? Men know me as
The lowly shadow lovely Layli has—
I think of me as nothing; I compare
Myself with no one, since there's no one there,
And you should understand that all you see
In me's a trace of you, it isn't me.
When as a falcon I flew high above
The world to hunt for that sweet partridge love,

I never saw a single trace of it;
Now that my wings are broken and unfit
For soaring flight, I see that partridge fly
Before me in the vastness of the sky.
While my small sparrow-hawk is flying round,
The peacock that is you cannot be found;
The king's dog went to hunt for deer, instead
It was the deer that left the king for dead.
Ah, how I longed for you, and now we've met
It is the self I was that I forget.
If someone's heart's entirely yours, when you
Depart this life, he has to do so too;
My soul is something that I gladly give
Into your hands since it's for you I live,
And all the time that I'm without you, I
Renounce my body and prepare to die,
And as your friend I'll teach you how to make
Your soul a sacrifice for friendship's sake.
As seas are to a fish, you are to me,
Burn me, and still I shan't desert this sea,
You're both my eyes, and how can eyes be far
From someone whose two watchful eyes they are?
How can I leave you then? O God forfend
That I should ever have to leave my friend!
For us, there is no me, there is no you,
In our religion there can be no 'two,'
We are one cloth that makes two shifts, one soul
In two parts that together make a whole,
Or I've no being, and I'm your creation,
A shadow thrown by your imagination;
Since I am you, why should two forms appear,
And who's to be the judge of who is here?

We're like two separate letters that are bound
Together and so make a single sound;
I'm here, you're there, yet we are one, and all
That isn't you is dusty and contemptible,
And we're so mixed and mingled we belong
Together like two voices in one song,
And if we're ripped apart the song will be
A tuneless chaos, a cacophony—
We're two sides of a shell, within us lies
A single pearl that's hidden from men's eyes.
Would that we were one body now, one whole,
A single body with a single soul—
Two edges on one sword, two kernels in
An almond underneath its second skin,
A duck egg with two yolks, a single letter
Repeated, making one sound, as in 'better,'
Two letters in one name, two drops of wine
Within a glass that flawlessly combine."

Majnun then wept a thousand tears that poured
Like tribute scattered from a hidden hoard,
While Layli wept an agate necklace of
Tears of intemperate, devoted love—
Her mouth as tiny as a perfume jar
That scented musky curls as black as tar;
The perfume jar spilled sugar, while her face
Mingled a rose's and a full moon's grace.
As though it were sweet scent and sugar she
Poured on her lover's head perpetually,
She wept such sweetness and such fragrances
It seemed all Egypt's fabled storehouses

And all of Africa's must have been taxed,
And every last provider been ransacked,
To bring the scents and sugar for her sighs
And all the tears that overflowed her eyes.

From watching her Majnun grew sick at heart
And in his anguish tore his clothes apart,
Losing all self-control, he couldn't think
But fell, like someone overcome by drink—
Regret had purified his soul, but still
He felt torn open by his restless will
That cut him to the bone, as if a knife
Would strike into his soul and take his life.
He howled, and ran across the plains as though
Snatching his head back from an axman's blow,
And with his animals around him sought
For refuge, though still weeping and distraught.
His love had taught another way to him,
That was as yet uncertain still, and dim,
Within her curls he had forgotten who
His self was as he'd felt himself renew,
And seen that "I'm her lover" must be wrong
In love where thoughts of self do not belong.
He'd torn himself away, as if to tear
A page from one with which it made a pair,
While Layli was the facing page that stayed
Unblemished by the tear that he had made.

Seeing such springtime made Majnun far more
Filled with desire than he had been before,
And he proclaimed her presence in each song
Praising love's tryst, for which he'd longed so long.

He sang of loyal love, of a fruit's skin
That peeled away reveals the pith within,
And Zayd was like an eager slave who heard
And noted down his master's every word,
And cried, "Bravo! Your poems are so clever
That you and they deserve to live forever!
How wonderfully you venerate pure love—
Your poems are like prayers to God above!"

Love without chastity and abstinence
Is not love, it's licentious violence;
Love is the mirror of celestial light
And is untouched by sensual appetite,
Love that is sensual craving cannot last,
It's fleeting, in a moment it has passed.
To love is to be pure, forsaking lust
And resurrected from our earthly dust,
This is what true love is, this is the Way,
And love that's not this leads mankind astray;
When love is real and true, it's like a name
Stamped on the noble currency of fame.
So Nezami has spoken, and this sentence
Contains the substance of his own repentance.

A Description of Autumn;
the Death of Layli

When autumn leaves are falling, it's as though
Blood drips in droplets on the earth below,
The blood within each branch swells up until
Through scented apertures it starts to spill;
Or leaves are urine that's grown cold and sallow
So that the garden's face turns golden yellow—[167]
Cracked blisters on each branch's bark abound
And leaves drift slowly to the golden ground.
Narcissi pack their clothes up now they're leaving,
The box tree droops its head as if it's grieving,
The jasmine tarnishes, each rose's heart
Drops blood-red petals as it falls apart,
Vine tendrils dry into a twisted mass
As if Zahhak's snakes writhed across the grass.[168]
When hostile winds blow, and the leaves are driven
Across the garden's breadth, their fall's forgiven—
They're bales of cloth thrown overboard to save
A ship that's threatened by a massive wave.
The grass grows dark with dust, bright flowers turn pale
And sickly-sallow in the dusty gale.
Quinces and grapes are picked, ripe apples greet
Red pomegranates when their branches meet—

The pomegranates split and drip bright red
As if their injured vital organs bled,
And red dates enviously eye the shade
That red pistachios' opening shells have made,
While oranges and citron fruits compete
As to whose musky spheres are more complete.
The gardener's drunk when he goes home, a sign
That he's been tending vats of Magian wine—[169]
And gradually the weary garden shows
The wounds that it's received from autumn's blows.

As if she'd stepped down from a splendid throne,
Layli now grieved in darkness and alone,
Her springtime was laid waste, her torch's light
Flickered and failed in autumn's windy night,
The golden scarf she'd worn about her head
Became the shroud with which men clothe the dead.
She was a linen thread, who'd been a rose
Clothed in the loveliest of linen clothes,
The full moon was the new moon, hardly there,
The cypress like a mirage in the air.[170]
Grief and confusion filled her heart and head,
As one began, the other grew and spread;
Summer had dried the dew, now autumn squalls
Ensure each petal of each tulip falls.
The day Majnun had left, the cypress dried
And withered like a barren tree that's died,
But all the love that she had felt before
Only increased a hundredfold and more;
Seeing Majnun held by a hundred chains,
A hundred agonies and burning pains,

She felt all that he felt . . . and ten times over
Now that she'd been abandoned by her lover.
As all this misery usurped her mind,
Moment by moment her frail health declined;
Fever sapped all her beauty, fever bit
Into her sweetest self and swallowed it.
The cypress lay alone and brokenhearted,
While from her boughs the pheasant had departed;[171]
As if she were a fallen seed, she lay
Quite still, and hid her wasted face away.

She called her mother to her, to confide
In her the secrets that she'd sought to hide.
She said: "How is it that a suckling doe
Drinks poison in her milk, and doesn't know?
I lie here, waiting to depart; don't speak
Too harshly to me, I'm worn out and weak.
This is not love but grief, this is not life
But agony and soul-destroying strife;
I've suffered secretly so much that I
Know that my heart is ready now to die.
If as my soul is leaving me, I say
Secrets that I've kept hidden till today,
If I draw back that final veil, you'll know
I'm setting out for where I have to go.
Now place your hand upon my neck, and bless
My parting as I wish you happiness;
Know as my soul's released that I depart
Because my friend and I've been forced apart.
Dress me in death: prepare me kohl from earth
He's trodden on, for it's of unmatched worth,

Mine all his woe, and sprinkle on my head
As rosewater the copious tears he's shed,
And scatter fragrant camphor, with cold sighs,
Where that poor yellow flower,[172] my body, lies;
See that my shroud is soaked in blood since I've
Died as a martyr while I was alive—
Adorn me as a bride, my veil will be
My grave's earth as it's scattered over me.

"And when my wanderer knows the details of
How I have wandered from this earth for love,
He'll come, I know, to where my body lies
To greet me, and to mourn with tears and sighs.
He'll sit beside my grave and, unresigned,
He'll seek the moon but earth is all he'll find;
Beside my earth that lonely earth will mourn,
Filled with regret now, wretched and forlorn,
My love, who is so strange, and who will be
A strange memento for your heart of me.
By God, I pray you, see you treat him kindly,
Don't rush to blame him, don't condemn him blindly—
There's no one like him; seek him out, relate
My story to him, and my final fate.
I loved him well, I cherished him, may you
Like me, for my sake, love my lover too;
Tell him, 'As Layli broke free from the chain
That tethers us to this brief world of pain,
Your love was all she thought of as she gave
Her soul to heaven, her body to the grave.
She said her love for you was pure and true,
Her soul sought love, and love was all she knew.

What should we say? Love for you filled her mind
As she set out, and left this world behind;
While she was in the world her thoughts were all
Of you, and you were all she could recall,
And as she died, it was those thoughts she bore
To be her heavenly food for evermore,
And even now, within the earth, she longs
To be with you again, where she belongs.
Like men who watch the road, she waits for when
She'll see you as you come to her again,
She waits and turns and paces and looks back
To see you coming on that heavenly track.'
And tell him that I said with my last breath,
'O you who are my soul and my soul's death,
From now on look at no one else, unless
It's with God's unalloyed kindheartedness;
Look at how wrong you were to think of you,
Your self, so that this "you" was all you knew!
So that for all your shrewdness you became
Mad in yourself, your life, and in your name!"

Tears wet her eyes now, and she turned her face
To start her journey to another place;[173]
She'd told the secrets that she'd tried to hide—
She'd sought her soul, and gave her soul, and died.
Her mother saw the bride depart, and she
Knew Judgment Day then, and eternity.
She tore her head-scarf off, and let her hair,
As white as jasmine, stream out in the air;
Grieving, she held her child in her embrace
And wept above her lovely hair and face,

And in the agony of her despair
Defaced her own face and tore out her hair.
Age soaked youth's pillow with her desperate cries,
Against her head she placed her weeping eyes,
So much she wept, her tears became a flood
(They were no longer tears but drops of blood),
So much she groaned that, hearing her, the sky
Groaned in response a thunderous reply.
Agates were formed with every blood-soaked tear
And starry pearls were formed when they were clear,
And as they fell they made a necklace for
The lovely moon that would arise no more,
Whose coffin was her mother's aching heart,
The catafalque in which she would depart.
Then she arrayed her child as custom said
Was fitting for the burial of the dead,
Sprinkling her rose with fragrance redolent
Of ambergris and rosewater's sweet scent;
She did not fear to place her in the ground
Knowing that only there can peace be found.
This princess was despoiled of all she had,
All that could worry her, or make her sad,
Her life was at an end now; on this date
The world had signed the firman of her fate.

Majnun Learns of Layli's Death

This famous story's earliest author's pen
Recorded word by word what happened then:

When brokenhearted Zayd became aware
Layli had died, he gave way to despair—
How long he wept (and is there anyone
Who's never had to mourn those dead and gone?);
He dressed in black, and like a man who's bowed
Beneath oppression's yoke he wailed aloud.
He visited her grave, and roared in pain,
Weeping like thunderous clouds of springtime rain—
Don't ask me how he fared, as like a wave
Of suffering he broke upon her grave.
Men fled away from his heart-rending cries
And from the tears that flooded from his eyes;
He wept and wailed with such intensity
It seemed the world turned black in sympathy,
And burning still with grief he set out over
The barren waste to visit Layli's lover.
He reached that lost soul as his torch's light
Succumbed to darkness in the dead of night,
And sat down wearily beside his friend,
Weeping as though his tears would never end.
Sobs choked his voice, he looked down, and then tried
To speak again, and still he wept and sighed;

Majnun perceived how pallid and distraught
Zayd was, how tongue-tied and how overwrought,
And said, "My brother, tell me, why these sighs,
This smoke beneath which fire assuredly lies?
Why is your face in such a state? What's made
You wear these clothes of such a dismal shade?"
He said: "Because Fate's turned its back, because
Nothing is as we used to think it was:
Up from the earth itself black water pours
And death has broken through its iron doors,
On our enchanted garden hail storms rained
Till on our rosebush not a leaf remained;
The brightest moon has fallen from the sky,
The cypress fell, and lies where she must lie.
Layli has gone, she's cast this world aside,
Grieving she lived for you, and grieving died."

As though he saw an earthquake, or as though
His shoulder felt a sword's decisive blow,
Majnun stood still, unmoving and in silence,
And then the thunderbolt's tremendous violence
Hurled him against the ground as if it spurned him,
And as it threw him headlong, lightning burned him.
He lay a moment, turned his head aside,
And started up, and to the heavens cried,
"O faithless bringer of a bitter fate,
How clumsy are the outcomes you create!
A thunderbolt against a little plant?
Such anger hurled against a tiny ant?
When, with a little spark, the wretch expires,
Why should an ant deserve hell's thousand fires!

Wine's poured according to the goblet's measure
And just proportions are what give us pleasure.
You've made me like a sputtering torch, a breath
Of wind's sufficient to ensure my death;
Why did you strike me with your sword like that?
I'm not a dragon, I'm a tiny gnat!
This is how savage beasts act, beasts that roam
The empty wastelands and who have no home."

His animals approached, and saw him tear
His clothes to tattered rags in his despair,
His flowing tears proclaimed his misery
While they shed tears of silent sympathy.
Zayd like his shadow followed him, and sought
To free him from the shadow that he'd brought,[174]
And thinking it might help him, and be just,
Proposed a pilgrimage to Layli's dust.
Majnun said he'd be like a plant that dries
Within that dust and withers till it dies,
And asked Zayd how to reach the hallowed ground
Where Layli's dusty graveside could be found,
Then ran from hill to hill, from plain to plain,
Weeping with inextinguishable pain,
And never rested but dashed on and on
Like a disheveled drunk whose reason's gone,
Sadder than anything that could be said,
More shameless than whatever should be said,
His head and heart worn out with countless fears,
His hair torn out, his faced besmeared with tears,
Stumbling and reeling, but with wild persistence
Still going forward till, there in the distance,

He saw her grave, and at this longed-for sight
He fell, as shadows fall before the light.

He reached the grave, writhing as serpents do,
Or like a thorn-pierced worm that's slashed in two,
And on the grave itself he was the snake
That writhed there for the hidden treasure's sake.[175]
He wept such bloodshot tears it seemed as though
The grave became a spot where tulips grow,
His tears dripped like a candle's wax, his cries
Were like its flickering flame that flares and dies.
"What can I do?" he cried. "My agony
Has made a melting candle out of me;
She was the one who held my heart, above
All kings and queens she was my sovereign love,
And now the wizened king that rules the world[176]
Has snatched her from me with this spear he's hurled.
She was the rose I held, till winds made all
Her lovely petals loosen and then fall,
She was the cypress sapling whom I chose
Till death brought all her growing to a close,
She was my springtime blossom—would that Fate
Had guarded her before it was too late!
I held fresh violets in my hand, so bright
And sweet they seemed to be my heart's delight,
Injustice snatched them from my hand, and I
Grow ever weaker now and long to die;
I chose a rose-red wine, no other wine
In all the world could be compared to mine,
A thieving ruffian spilled the wine, and dashed
My glass against the roadside where it smashed."
He paused, over the grave his head was bowed,
In agony he wept, and cried aloud:

"O new-blown rose that autumn's winds have taken,
You never saw the world that you've forsaken,
O ruined garden, torn up root by root,
O fruit tree destined never to bear fruit,
How do you fare, my love, now you lie there
Coerced into this pit, how do you fare?
How is that musky mole? How are those eyes,
Wide as a doe's are when she turns and flies?
How are your agate lips, how is your hair
Whose fragrance sweetened the surrounding air?
What colors paint your portrait now, what flame
Now melts the candle of your beauty's fame?
What splendid sights are your sweet eyes now viewing,
What musk do you imagine that you're strewing?
What stream does your tall cypress grow beside,
Safe in what gardens do you play and hide?
How do you fare, wounded within this grave,
How pass your time, within this cheerless cave?
Caves always harbor snakes, they're not a place
For someone such as you to show her face;
I grieve you're there, though I would willingly
Befriend you there and keep you company.
And you're a treasure now you're underground—
Where treasures are, a snake is always found,
And if a treasure's in a cave, beside it
There's sure to be a snake to guard and hide it;[177]
Now I'm that guardian snake, who from my nest
Of sorrow's come here as a watchful guest
To be the sentinel that seeks to save
The treasure that lies hidden in your grave.
You lived like sand, whose grains disperse and spill,
Like water in a well now, you lie still;

You're like the moon itself, and so I see
Why it's not strange you're far away from me.
Your face is hidden from me now, it's true,
But inwardly my soul stays close to you,
And in the twinkling of an eye, although
My eyes can't see you where you've had to go,
No distance now can keep my lovelorn heart
And all you are and have been far apart,
And if your outward form has gone from me
My grieving for you lives eternally.
I set my heart on you for good, so how
Could I desert you or forget you now?
I've always longed for you, whether you're here
Or not, my longing cannot disappear,
But then your horse rode on, and to my shame
I'm hobbling after you, inept and lame;
You've left this ruin, in the gardens of
Eram[178] you feast in everlasting love,
But when I've slipped these chains, in just a few
Short days I'll reach that heavenly garden too;
My loyalty won't fail before I meet you
And cry out in delighted joy to greet you,
But till then may your shroud be purified
By all the tears of sorrow that I've cried.
May heaven be the everlasting place
Where you abide surrounded by God's grace,
And may your gentle soul forever be
A lamp whose light shines there eternally."
He spoke, and briefly wrung his hands, and then
Turned round and set off on his way again.

*

He headed home, accompanied by a few
Wild beasts from his attendant retinue;
And as he went he sang of loyalty
And love, of lovers' long fidelity,
Beating against the wayside stones his head
That were already red with tears he'd shed.
But then within his heart he couldn't bear
To leave his love alone without him there—
Swift as a mountain flood he sought once more
The grave of Layli where he'd wept before,
And laid his head upon the earth, and kissed it
A thousand times to show how much he'd missed it,
Protesting that his love was unabated
While all his animals kept watch and waited,
And as he wept and murmured prayers, they made
Around him a protective barricade,
Watching the road, and giving no one leave
To see their weeping master mourn and grieve,
Ensuring that he wouldn't be disturbed,
Not even by an ant, or passing bird.
Majnun's days were a black page, with each breath
He longed to end his life and welcome death;
His life was like a dog's, and death would be
Far preferable to this long misery.
At times he'd keep watch by her grave and pray,
At times he'd run distractedly away—
The world grew small for him, he was alone,
Living between his love's grave and his own,
Until he saw no way ahead but one,
To sing his life's farewell, and so be done.

SALAM BAGHDADI COMES TO VISIT MAJNUN
FOR THE SECOND TIME

Faithful to the Arabian tale he'd read
The teller of this lovers' story said:

Salam Baghdadi had resolved to find
This man who'd lost his heart and lost his mind;
Across plains, over mountain passes, he
Searched for a month for him assiduously,
But everywhere he rode he could discover
No sign at all of this notorious lover,
Till in a valley he caught sight of him
Seated on stones, with blisters on each limb,
His body scratched by thorns, his color gone,
His bony torso pallid now and wan,
A bird that's injured, that no longer sings,
But lies upon the ground with broken wings.

Majnun soon saw Salam and hailed him: "Hey,
You there, young man, what's brought you here today?"
He answered, "I'm Salam, I've come to greet you,
From far away I've traveled here to meet you."
Majnun made all his animals retire
As day drives night away and water fire,

And then, as soon as he had recognized him,
Fondly embraced this guest who had surprised him,
And said, "Why take this trouble when you know
That I insulted you once, long ago?
You're innocent, I'm the sad guilty one,
Surely I'm someone you'd prefer to shun?
Given our past, what's made you want to be
Associated with a wretch like me?
But now you've come here I can hardly say,
'Be off with you, young man, be on your way!'
So tell me why you've come, and if I can
Be of some use to you, then I'm your man!"
Salam replied, "You acted well to me,
With graciousness, and magnanimity,
Your kindnesses are my most valued treasure,
Remembering how you were's my dearest pleasure,
And still your poems' priceless pearls console
The emptiness within my heart and soul.
I thought I'd come to ask if I might take
One more fruit from your tree, for old times' sake,
I mean forgiveness for what's gone before . . .
If you refuse, I'll trouble you no more.
But I'm amazed to see you in this state,
A flightless bird, alone and desolate.
You've suffered in this past year, I can see,
You're not at all the man you used to be,
Your wings of joy are broken, and you sit
Groaning and grieving here because of it.
Tell me what's happened, and what's hurting you,
And how you are, and how your friend is too."

*

And at the mention of his friend, Majnun
Lost consciousness and fell into a swoon;
When he revived, he thought of her and cried
A little while, and then he sorely sighed
And said, "Never mind me! Who do you mean?
What friend of mine? Who do you think I've seen?
My only friend lies in the earth. And why
Should you ask this? Do you want me to lie?
She is a houri made of loyalty
And lives in heaven for eternity;
She's dead, her lamp's flame is alive, and I
Live as though dead and wish that I could die."
He talked at length like this about his friend
As though he read a book that had no end;
He took Salam's hand then and gently led
Him to the grave where Layli lay, and said,
"Here is my angel-love, and here is where
My soul succumbed to death and to despair."
And when Salam saw all of his distress
At being friendless now, and comfortless,
He suffered grief's contagion and his eyes
Grew wet as unsought tears began to rise,
And he too wept a rosy flowing flood
Of falling tear drops mingled with his blood.
He answered kindly, since he recognized
Majnun's just feelings and he sympathized;
He said, "Hearing she's gone, I feel my heart
Quake like a ship's deck as it splits apart,
I follow you in grief—this thunderbolt
Struck heavily and hard from heaven's vault;

Your face glows with your grief, and I too feel
A burning sorrow that will never heal."
But all his eloquence was salt applied
To open wounds that were still raw inside.

Salam stayed with him for a month or two,
Writing down any poem that was new;
Ghazals and couplets, fragments, he would jot
On scraps of paper and preserve the lot.
And when he'd gathered all that could be had,
He took them as a wonder to Baghdad.

Majnun Dies on Layli's Grave

The teller of this tale of lovers chose
These lines of verse to bring it to its close:

What tears he'd reaped! How small the heavens ground
His being as their mill-wheels turned around!
How he had wept, but now he wept far more
And was far weaker, sicklier, than before;
As day gives way to night, his soul was on
The brink of parting, and would soon be gone.
As though he were a storm-tossed sinking boat
On pitch-black seas, that could not stay afloat,
Weeping and wailing now he made his way
To where the dusty grave of Layli lay,
And in the dust began to writhe and quake
As if he were an injured ant or snake.
He sang a wistful line or two, and shed
A bitter tear or two, then raised his head
And gestured with his fingers to the skies
And as he did so covered his sad eyes,
And cried: "O Lord, Creator of this earth,
Great Guarantor of everything of worth,
Free me from all my sorrow and convey me
Into the presence of my true friend, Layli,

Release my grieving soul and speedily
Bring me to her for all eternity."
He sprawled then in the dust, and clutched, and
    grasped it,
And in his arms, against his chest, he clasped it,
And feeling it against his skin he cried,
"O friend . . ."[179] and rendered up his soul, and died.
He too had left this world, and who is there
Who doesn't have to tread this thoroughfare?

No one avoids the horror that attends
The moment when oblivion's highway ends,
And who is there who can escape the way
Time moves forever onward day by day?
The world is like a fire that grills its meat
And salts the wounds before it deigns to eat—
No life's not answerable to sorrow's laws,
No face remains unscratched by cruelty's claws.
You're like a lame ass toiling in a mill
That turns the mill-stone and is never still,
So quit the mill! But this will happen when
You quit the world itself, and only then.
Why linger in this flooded house?[180] Don't wait,
The flood's here, leave before it is too late,
And leave before the heavens have destroyed
The bridge that carries you across the void.
There blows, within the navel of the world,
The wind of nothingness, in which we're hurled—
Don't boast of what you are, since all your life
Is nothing but that tumult's windy strife,
So leave this world, make haste now, don't delay,
The caravan's already on its way.

This seven-headed dragon[181] twists around you
Till all its writing, crushing coils, surround you—
If any part of you should hesitate
Don't think you'll get away now, it's too late!
This ancient crone displays her dragon nature,
She's all in all this savage dragon's creature,
Leave this false world, this foul, notorious thief,
Light-fingered and unworthy of belief;
Don't act unrighteously, you'll be the one
Who suffers for the evil things you've done,
Commit your heart to truth, and never fear
Whatever threats or dangers might appear.
Get off your high horse, modestly confess
Your inability, your powerlessness—
Act humbly, and the lion of death will be
Your comforter and not your enemy.

Majnun had left the world, and was now free
Of others' ridicule and mockery,
His eyes were closed now as he slept beside
The cradled body of his sleeping bride,
And sleep was like a recompense that cured
The worldly sorrows that he had endured;
He lay like this a month at least, I'm sure,
And some have said it was a year or more.
His animals had gathered all around him
And formed a guardian phalanx to surround him,
As if they were the guards who watch and wait
Beside a dead king as he lies in state,
Making his catafalque a place of rest,
A house of comfort and a kindly nest.

These guards made passers-by retreat in fear
Of what might happen if they came too near,
So that they'd hover round and then hold back
As if afraid that hornets might attack,
Thinking the stranger they could see lay there
For some strange reason that he didn't share—
A king perhaps, with posted guards to see
No one intruded on his privacy . . .
Not knowing that this stranger "king" was dead.
Time's wind had blown his diadem from his head,
His corpse was drained of blood, and all his bones
Were scattered pearls dispersed in dust and stones—
Haphazard bones were all that could be seen
Of his sad life, and what he once had been.
No wolf had gnawed these bones, no man could touch
Majnun's corpse while his animals kept watch.

But then a year went by, and one by one
The watchful guardians of the grave were gone;
Time passed, as though a lock that had been there
Was slowly worn away with wear and tear,
And gradually audacious souls intruded
And found the grave its guardians had secluded;
They saw that bones lay there, bones that retained
No flesh, only the skeleton remained.
His faithful family came, and they were sure
This was their son whom they'd been searching for;
They and his well-wishers, all those bereaved
By his sad death, approached, and mourned and grieved.
With aching hearts they tore their clothes and sighed
For one whom love had harried till he died;

Their tears rained down like pearls and precious stones
Upon the white shell of his sun-bleached bones,
And with their tears they laid within the ground
The scattered earthly remnants they had found;
Through Arab lands, his story and his name
Became love's emblem and ensured his fame.
Men made a tomb for him, and at his side
They laid his Layli as his longed-for bride;
She was the lovely cup-bearer who brought
Her king the wine of love that he had sought.
They were no longer blamed or scorned, but lay
In peace, and side by side, till Judgment Day;
They'd kept one vow on earth, now they were given
One cradle to be shared by them in heaven.

A lovely garden was laid out around
Their earthly resting place and burial ground,
Unrivaled in its beauty and its fame,
A garden where the world's sad pilgrims came;
And there these votaries of love would find
Joy was restored to them, and peace of mind,
No one would leave this garden willingly,
Only when forced to by necessity.

O God, since those two left the world still pure
And chaste, despite their earthly selves, ensure
They dwell in peace, safe in each other's love,
Welcomed with mercy in the world above.

ZAYD DREAMS THAT HE SEES
LAYLI AND MAJNUN IN HEAVEN

Zayd lived for generosity and truth—
May God look kindly on this noble youth.

He lingered at the lovers' grave to grieve
For those two streams of light, and could not leave,
But murmured to himself Majnun's sweet lines,
Each shining as a splendid ruby shines,
And eagerly endeavored to discover
All of the verses written by this lover,
And in so doing he became the cause
Of their renown, and well-deserved applause—
It was through him this lovers' tale became
So loved and widespread and achieved such fame.

Thinking of them one day, he wondered how,
Beyond the veil, these two were faring now—
Was the dark earth their home? Had they been given
A place beside God's shining throne in heaven?
Just before dawn, when breezes stir, one night
As darkness yields to musky morning light,
Zayd dreamed an angel came and showed him where
A garden glittered in the lambent air;

It was a scene whose tall trees' slender grace
Made it a happy and enchanted place,
New gardens could be glimpsed within the roses,
Each petal could provide a wealth of posies,
The grass there glowed, to a discerning eye,
Celestial blue, like heaven's cloudless sky.
The garden's green outshone an emerald's green,
No lovelier shade could anywhere be seen.
Roses seemed bowls of wine, and nightingales
Sang to them lovelorn and lamenting tales,
Musicians plucked sweet strings and doves were there
Cooing what seemed a Zoroastrian prayer.[182]
A throne was set up near a stream that played
Gently beneath the overarching shade,
Brocades so lovely that they would suffice
To decorate the halls of paradise
Adorned the throne, and on these splendid covers
Sat the transfigured and contented lovers;
From head to foot they were a dazzling sight
Adorned like houris with celestial light,
Wine in their hands, lost in their shared, sweet story,
Surrounded by the spring's voluptuous glory—
At times they'd drink their wine in little sips,
At times they'd gently kiss each other's lips,
At times they'd talk of all they'd been denied,
At times they'd lean together, side by side.
Next to the throne an old man stood, and he
Poured offerings on them intermittently;[183]
Zayd asked, "Who are these two who seem divine,
Who sit in Eram's garden[184] drinking wine,
Whose wishes are fulfilled in this new home—
How is it that they're here? Where are they from?"

The old man answered him, but silently,
"These are two friends for all eternity,
He is the world's just king, she is the best
Of women, their full moon, the loveliest,
And she belongs to night,[185] since she's the moon,
And he, the king, is always called Majnun;
They were two unpierced rubies, prisoners of
Fidelity's sweet casket, sealed by love.
Thwarted when in the world, they knew no peace,
It seemed their sorrows there would never cease;
Here they see no such grief, and they will be
As now you see them, everlastingly.
Those disillusioned in that world are given
The reparations that you see in heaven;
In that world they knew sorrow, and in this
For all eternity they live in bliss."

When morning's candle lit the flame that burned
The harvest of the night, and day returned,
Zayd woke up from his dream-state and revealed
Secrets that hitherto had been concealed.
He said, "Whoever knows that world will tread
On this world's joys and leave them here for dead;
This world is fleeting, empty, and unsure,
That world is everlasting, safe, and pure—
Better to choose eternity than be
Consigned to dust and vain futility;
Beware, see that the rose for which you're born
Does not transmogrify into a thorn,
Don't seek for jewels here that you'll never find,
It's not in this world that such jewels are mined.

Commit yourself to love, and so renew
Your spirit, and escape from what was you—
If love is like an arrow, see you hit
The longed-for target, don't fall short of it.
Love will undo the tangled knot of being,
Love saves us from the whirlpool of self-seeing,
Love's sorrows are a medicine that will give
Health to the soul, not harm, and help it live;
Love makes life's bitter draughts taste sweet when she
Urges them on us so appealingly,
And though they disconcert a man, he takes them,
Knowing they're good, since it is love that makes them."

This sea of words is done, my boat is beached,
Eden, my destination, has been reached.
And now thanks be to God, O Nezami,
Your poem's reached its end and you are free!
May reading it be like a key that brings
Solutions to obscure and stubborn things.
It was a joy to start, may you commend
The way that I have brought it to its end.

NOTES

1. *Hear what the teller . . . verse's thread:* Throughout his poem Nezami frequently opens a new section by referring either to himself as the poem's author or to a previous teller of the tale (sometimes it's not wholly clear which is meant and the ambiguity is perhaps deliberate). Gorgani opens his romance *Vis and Ramin* in a similar way, but after this initial mention of himself he refrains from such remarks as he begins new sections of his poem. Nezami's more frequent interpolations that draw our attention to the poem's composition seem of a piece with his insistence that we are reading something composed, elaborated, a work of art, rather than simply the recounting of an old tale.

2. *Lord of the Amir tribe:* The Banu Amir were an ancient tribe that lived in Najd, in what is now Saudi Arabia.

3. *Wealthy as Korah:* Korah is the Qarun of the Qor'an, a contemporary of Musa (Moses) known for his fabulous wealth. Nezami opens his poem by describing the great wealth of the king who is the nearest male relative of his hero (Majnun), and comparing him to Korah/Qarun. Gorgani's *Vis and Ramin* opens in exactly the same way, by describing the great wealth of the king who is the nearest male relative of the tale's hero, and comparing him to Korah / Qarun.

4. *A dark blue dye:* applied to a new born child to protect it from the evil eye.

5. *Like tulips held in violets' dark embrace:* Violets are a common metaphor for thick, glossy, black hair.

6. *a few girls shared:* Gorgani's hero and heroine in *Vis and Ramin* are also classmates as children. The motif of young girls and boys being educated together will probably have been strange to both Gorgani and Nezami, and it's not clear where it comes from; it is likely to be pre-Islamic, and perhaps Parthian as Gorgani's romance had a Parthian origin. It doesn't seem to have been a Greek motif, as Greek girls were not normally educated with boys, and it does not crop up in any of the Hellenistic novels that show striking similarities to medieval Persian romances.

7. *yet a Turk / In stealing hearts and suchlike handiwork:* Turks had a reputation for beauty, but also as formidable opponents in both love and war.

8. *a charm against disaster:* literally a Qor'anic verse placed in an amulet to give protection.

9. *her name / was Layli:* The Arabic word for "night" is *layl*, and Nezami is punning on his heroine's name, which could be read in Persian as "of the night."

10. *basil's green to gold:* The color of the sky just before dawn is quite often referred to in Persian poetry as "green." One of Hafez's best-known ghazals begins: "I saw the green fields of the sky / And there a sickle moon . . ." For basil, see note 95.

11. *As beautiful as Joseph . . . and like Zuleikha's maids / Who cut their careless hands with sharpened blades:* The story of Joseph (Yusuf) and Zuleikha is told in the Qor'an (although there the female protagonist, who came to be called Zuleikha in later commentaries, is unnamed). Zuleikha is the woman known in the Bible as Potiphar's wife; Joseph is a servant in her household with whom she falls in love, and whom she attempts to seduce. In Islamic literature Joseph/Yusuf is the pattern of male beauty, and Layli is being compared to him as his female equivalent.

At one point in the Qor'anic story Zuleikha's maids are peeling oranges when Yusuf enters the room; the maids are so overcome by his beauty that their knives slip and they cut their hands. The story as a whole was much loved by Sufi writers, who gave it a mystical interpretation: Zuleikha is the human soul "married" to the world, but in love with the beauty of God (Yusuf). As Nezami's *Layli and Majnun* proceeds, it contains an increasing number of references to or suggestions of Sufism, which has led to its being seen by many of its interpreters (though not all) as primarily a Sufi tale; this is the poem's first such reference. For more on this, see the Introduction, pp. xxxii–xxxiv.

12. *sallow . . . golden yellow:* A sallow or yellow color was associated with sickness and misery.

13. *the scent / Of musk stays richly strong and redolent:* It became conventional in Persian poetry that all deer (not only musk deer) smell of musk.

14. *The sack ripped open and the donkey fell:* a proverb based on a load carried by a donkey bursting open and thus meaning "everything fell apart." Here the "everything" is Qais's (Majnun's) self-control.

15. *the bright / New moon:* that is, Layli.

16. *Layli's street . . . her door:* The door and the street imply that Layli is living in a house; elsewhere in the poem she lives in a tent. In Nezami's Arabic source her home would certainly have been a tent; Nezami has taken Layli's "house" (later on she goes up on its roof) from Persian romances, based on pre-Islamic Persian tales (not ones that are Arabic in origin, as *Layli and Majnun* is) that preceded him, especially Gorgani's *Vis and Ramin*. See also the Introduction, p. xxii.

17. *Kay Khosrow:* a legendary pre-Islamic king who is one of the noblest heroes of the Persian epic the *Shahnameh*.

18. *Majnun whose earring marked him as a slave:* An earring, indicating to whom he or she belonged, was worn by slaves.

19. *burned rue:* Rue is still burnt in present-day Iran as a prophylactic against misfortune.

20. *cleanse his rose of grime and dust:* that is, put things right for his son.

21. *Seyed Amiri:* Qais's (Majnun's) father.

22. *Had left both this world and the next behind:* a hint of the poem's possibly Sufi implications.

23. *Vameq whose search for Ozra: Vameq* and *Ozra* (sometimes transliterated as "Azra"; "Ozra" is the modern pronunciation) was the name of a romance by the poet Onsori, (*c.*961–*c.*1039) of which only a few hundred lines have survived, describing the love between Vameq (the young man) and Ozra (his beloved). The story is a version of the Greek story *Metiochus and Parthenope,* and in most cases retains recognizable variants of the Greek names of characters and places.

24. *to kill himself:* again a phrase that can be taken to have a Sufi meaning, as "killing the (animal) self" is one of Sufism's fundamental concerns. As is often the case in Nezami's poetry, the phrase can be interpreted literally, or figuratively (which implies the Sufi meaning), or both.

25. *the evening star in Yemen's night:* Stars were said to have an exceptional brilliance and beauty in the night sky over Yemen.

26. *and chain me:* a reference to the fact that lunatics were often chained up, especially if they were considered to be dangerous.

27. *Why is your neck encircled with such chains:* The "chains" around Layli's neck are her curls; Majnun's speech means: "Why are you chained up (as a madman is)? I am the madman and the chains should be around my neck, not yours."

28. *in the ka'bah's shade:* The ka'bah is the black stone that marks the geographical center of Islam, and around which pilgrims perambulate.

29. *knocker on a door . . . love's bright earring:* The moment merges two metaphors commonly used to describe a lover: Majnun is like a ring-shaped knocker, in that he stays as close as possible to the beloved's door but can never get past it, and he is like a slave who wears an earring denoting that he belongs to his beloved (see note 18).

30. *and give / Them all to her as added years to live:* This is a traditional rhetorical request, that God take the years one has left to live and assign them to someone one loves, implying that this person is loved more than one's own life. Perhaps the most famous instance of this occurred when the first Moghul emperor, Babur, circled the bed of his sick son, Homayun, offering to die in his place—that is, to "give" his remaining years of life to his son.

31. *murmured sound . . . like Zoroastrians when they're praying:* Zoroastrian prayer is commonly described in medieval Persian poetry as "murmured"; the invocation of Zoroastrianism at this moment implies that Majnun is in some sense forsaking his religion. It also ties what is essentially an Arab story to Nezami's Persian cultural milieu.

32. *the page he'd read there:* a metaphor for the enlightenment Majnun's father hoped his son would receive from visiting the ka'bah.

33. *hoping to see dust rise . . . and clouds the skies:* Dust rising from the road would mean someone, possibly Majnun, was approaching.

34. *better to be a fox . . . wolf that's vulnerable:* Both Layli and Majnun are being compared to hungry animals: Majnun's hunger is literal, Layli's is metaphorical (her hunger to be with Majnun). As is often the case, Nezami then expands this moment in his tale to make a general observation (here about hunger and its opposite).

35. *Freed from his self:* a phrase that suggests a Sufi interpretation.

36. *And fall as quickly as his fortunes fell:* Nezami often employs syllepsis, the rhetorical device of using a word with both a metaphorical and a literal meaning, as he does here with the verb "fall." Only occasionally, as in this instance, is it possible to reproduce this in English.

37. *Be drunk, but not from wine, seek something higher, / And love desire while feeling no desire:* the sentiments of Sufism.

38. *I slap my thighs:* that is, in exasperation.

39. *It's drinking celery for a scorpion's sting:* A concoction made from celery was a folk remedy for various ailments, but it was believed to be fatal if drunk after the patient was stung by a scorpion (See Aliakbar Dehkhoda, *Loghatnameh* ed. M. Mo'in and J. Shahidi (Tehran: Tehran University Publications, 1372/1993), 11:16017).

40. *When I'm a bird that's famous for my laughter:* A partridge's "laughter" and misplaced confidence in itself were proverbial. Hafez ends a ghazal with a similar reference: "Hafez, you've seen a strutting partridge / Whose cry sounds like a laugh—/ He's careless of the hawk's sharp claws / By which he'll be undone."

41. *Najd:* that is, Layli's home.

42. *the seven climes:* that is, the whole inhabited earth.

43. *Roses and honey mixed in one confection:* Rosewater and honey are still ingredients in Middle Eastern confectionery.

44. *A pheasant perched there in its topmost place:* Pheasants were thought of as particularly beautiful birds and for this reason were sometimes invoked as a metaphor for a beautiful person, or a beautiful face. This is an example of how Persian imagery tends to be more abstract, and less "concrete," than its English equivalent. The face and the pheasant share the quality of beauty and so one can stand in for the other; the fact that they don't actually *look* similar, which would seem necessary in an equivalent English metaphor, is irrelevant.

45. *She went up on the roof... Hoping to see Majnun:* This implies that Layli is living in a house or palace, rather than in a tent; see note 16. The source of this scene is probably the palace in which Gorgani's heroine Vis (in *Vis and Ramin*) lives; Vis frequently goes up on the palace roof hoping to glimpse her lover Ramin. Similarly in Ferdowsi's *Shahnameh*, the princess Rudabeh waits for her future husband Zal while watching from her parents' palace roof.

46. *While fire and water:* Fire is her suffering (compared a few lines previously to "A trembling candle flame"), water is her tears.

47. *An arrow... a spindle spinning round and round:* A spindle moves round and round in one place; an arrow goes from one place to another. As an emblem of a woman's traditional role in the cultures from which the poem comes, the spindle implies that a woman stays in one place (at home), repetitively doing the same things. Layli decides she will be like an arrow (that is, in her culture's terms, like a man) and make active efforts to reach, or at least get in touch with, Majnun, and so change her situation.

48. *And virgin as herself, and as demure:* Layli's virginity while she is unmarried (and after she is married) is much insisted upon throughout the poem. It might be thought that this is simply typical of narratives from the Middle Ages, but it is hardly a matter of interest to Nezami's Persian-speaking predecessors (except for Ayyuqi), and neither Ferdowsi nor Gorgani make much, if any, fuss about it (in their poems it matters only that the woman's "true" love be the first and only person to sleep with her; whether this happens in or outside of marriage seems hardly relevant). The insistence on virginity is a feature of the Arab story from which Nezami's poem derives, and it is significant that Ayyuqi's poem *Varqeh and Golshah*, in which virginity is also a matter of concern, also had an Arab origin. See the Introduction, p. xi.

49. *wrote / In blood:* As is quite often the case in Nezami's poetry, it's not wholly clear whether this is meant literally or as a metaphor (as a metaphor, "blood" can mean "suffering," hence "she wrote / In blood" could mean "she suffered as she wrote").

50. *The lowly violet's . . . glossy curls:* See note 5.

51. *The box tree's leaves:* The box tree (*shemshad*) is quite frequently mentioned in Persian poetry as a metaphor for a tall, slim, beautiful young person of either sex. Left untrimmed, it can grow up to thirty feet (ten meters) high.

52. *She seemed a Turk:* referring to the Turks' reputation for beauty; see note 7.

53. *This houri:* Houris are the beautiful angels who welcome the faithful into the Islamic paradise.

54. *Eram's enchanting paths and trees:* Eram was a legendary pre-Islamic garden of great beauty. Nezami often uses the word as a synonym for paradise.

55. *Tall box tree:* See note 51.

56. *the pearl sought out her shell:* that is, Layli went to her room (to be alone), which again suggests she is living in a building rather than a tent.

57. *Provide more livestock than they'd ever need:* Livestock as a form of wealth, and especially as a bride price, is an indication of the story's pastoral origin.

58. *sugar will be sprinkled as you're wed:* Ground sugar is sprinkled over the bride and groom during a traditional Persian marriage ceremony.

59. *Pleased with the promise Layli's father'd made:* The line implies that Ebn Salam had accompanied the go-between on the visit to Layli's parents, even though he wasn't present during the actual conversation. Etiquette required that a proposal of marriage should be made and discussed by third parties (here a parent and a go-between).

60. *Zahhak:* a demonic king, from whose shoulders snakes grew; here, a metaphor for night.

61. *Bu Qubays:* a mountain to the west of Mecca.

62. *And bit his finger in astonishment:* This is a traditional gesture in Persian poetry and painting; in Persian miniatures that depict something extraordinary, at least one observer of the scene is often shown biting his finger.

63. *His shout was sharp:* an example of syllepsis (see note 36). It's typical of the often complex convolutions of Nezami's rhetoric that he takes an element in a real situation (the knife about to cut the deer's throat) and makes a metaphor from it (the doctor cutting a lesion to make it bleed), which is used to illustrate metaphorically the "sharpness" of the next real event (Majnun's shout).

64. *If you're afraid . . . ascend the skies:* that is, God will hear the sighs of the "wretched sufferers" and move to exact retribution.

65. *the copious tears he cried:* It's not quite clear whether the tears are those of the deer (later on it is described as weeping) or Majnun himself.

66. *Your scent evokes her fragrance:* See note 13.

67. *Like Joseph's face within his darksome well:* referring to the Qor'anic (and biblical) story of Joseph being hidden in a well by his brothers before they sell him into slavery. Because of his beauty, Joseph is often compared to the full moon.

68. *Kosar's stream:* a stream in paradise.

69. *he rested from his seeking / From hearing nothing and from always speaking:* again, a hint of Sufism, as getting rid of this inattentive self-absorption is one of the first requirements for setting out on the way of Sufism.

70. *A jet-black stone within a turquoise rim:* This can be read as an image of the black raven surrounded by the green leaves of the tree in which it is perched (although less valued than its blue counterpart, green turquoise is also used in Middle Eastern jewelry), or the turquoise could be the blue of the sky against which Majnun sees the raven.

71. *not a crazy madman . . . deserve a prison cell:* Madmen were often chained up (see note 26); the woman is saying the man is neither a madman nor a criminal.

72. *gladly sacrifice myself . . . I'll be like Esma'il, rather than be / A brute convicted of apostasy:* that is, rather than be an apostate from the religion of love; in the Qor'an, it is Esma'il (Ishmael) whom Abraham is commanded by God to sacrifice, rather than Isaac, as in the Hebrew Bible.

73. *narcissus eyes:* This is a common metaphor for eyes in medieval (and subsequent) Persian poetry; the comparison is to a narcissus with white petals surrounding a brown center.

74. *And seeing they were both lost equally:* "they" refers to Layli and Majnun.

75. *To shield her honor's glass from every stone:* In Nezami's day, glass was almost as valuable as the pearls and silver to which he has just compared Layli. Her "honor" here indicates her reputation and her virginity; the fact that they are compared to glass threatened by stones indicates that both can easily be lost/broken.

76. *He brought such gifts it seemed they'd never cease:* Luxurious and fabulously expensive and extensive marriage gifts are traditional in Persian romances, which have almost exclusively royal protagonists. In keeping with the Persian romance tradition, Nezami has given the Arab families of his *Layli and Majnun* quasi-royal status (when Layli dies he calls her "a princess"), and the wealth appropriate to such status. The specific model for Nezami here is probably the gifts given to Vis's family by King Mobad (who like Ebn Salam is the "rival" who marries the poem's heroine) in Gorgani's *Vis and Ramin*.

77. *Jesus's reviving breath . . . back from the point of death:* In Islamic lore Jesus's breath could bring the dead back to life.

78. *To place the moon within the dragon's jaws:* The moon is Layli, the dragon's jaws refer to Ebn Salam's possession of her, or more broadly to an unwelcome fate. The expression

is often used in poetry to describe an eclipse of the moon: usually the metaphor describes the moon escaping from the dragon's jaws, indicating the end of the eclipse; here, in describing the moon being placed in the dragon's jaws, the metaphor indicates that Layli's "eclipse" is just beginning.

79. *heaven's bride:* the sun.

80. *Jamshid's goblet:* Jamshid was a mythical pre-Islamic king whose story is recounted in Ferdowsi's *Shahnameh;* in his goblet the whole world could be seen.

81. *Sugar was ground and sprinkled:* See note 58.

82. *That lovely garden, and that lamp that glowed:* The garden and the lamp are both metaphors for Layli.

83. *whose liver smoldered . . . in passion's ardent flame:* The comparison of a lover's heart or liver to meat that is being grilled or roasted was conventional in medieval Persian poetry. Both the heart and the liver were associated with love and desire; in so far as there was a distinction, the heart was associated with affection and sentiment, the liver with animal vitality and physical longing.

84. *Majnun, proprietor of a little town . . . all tumbled down:* The "little town" is a metaphor for Majnun's wretched condition as someone whose "civilization" is in ruins.

85. *A sallow color:* See note 12.

86. *Women have more desire than men, for sure:* an Islamic cliché, as it was of ancient Greek civilization (summed up by the remark attributed to the blind prophet of Greek myth, Tiresias, who had been both a woman and a man: "Of ten parts of sexual pleasure a man enjoys only one").

87. *The bride's maidservant . . . to the world outside:* This refers to the woman who dresses and prepares a bride for her wedding. Nezami is comparing her to the poet (that is, himself) who "dresses and prepares" his story in verse, and leads it out into the world (as the maidservant leads Layli from her litter). The tenth - eleventh-century poet Ayyuqi uses this metaphor in his romance *Varqeh and Golshah,* which is probably where Nezami found it.

88. *China's wealth and Africa's are there:* Her black hair represents Africa and her pale face China.

89. *Washed Africans can't change to Turkomen:* that is, we cannot change how things are by their nature. Nezami is continuing the metaphorical juxtaposition of dark- and fair-skinned peoples (see note 88); this contrast is quite commonly used in the rhetoric of medieval Persian verse.

90. *Know death . . . Before the body's subsequent demise:* The necessity of dying before death comes—that is, to "kill" the self and its physical desires—is a tenet of Sufism.

91. *So what's this ghoul's behavior that I'm seeing:* Majnun is behaving like the ghouls that are believed to live in the wilderness.

92. *yellow sunset must appear:* Yellow is associated with weakness and illness in Persian poetry (see note 12), which is why Majnun's father refers to the sunset of his life as "yellow" (rather than as red or purple or any other color).

93. *I'll wear dark blue, I'll weep a Nile for you:* Dark blue was the color of mourning; the Persian word for "Nile" also means the color indigo.

94. *And bruised and blind:* bruised by grief, blinded by tears.

95. *Majnun, that basil in a barren land:* Basil is a herb that is particularly loved in Persian culture (and cuisine), and in poetry it is sometimes associated with love and so with a lover like Majnun. The word for "basil" in Persian is sometimes used to mean "wine," but it seems likely that the herb is the main association here.

96. *I ought to be her veil . . . I'm just the shell:* Majnun is saying that Layli and her reputation should be shielded by him, as the association of an unmarried girl's name with a lover would bring scandal to her and her family. But a Sufi meaning is also implied—Layli represents the hidden mystery, the reality behind the veil of earthly appearances (of which he is one).

97. *Rabe'eh:* The reference is to Rabe'eh Adawiya, an eighth-century female mystic from Basra, who was said to be the first important female Sufi (not to be confused with the tenth-century poet Rabe'eh of Balkh). Rabe'eh Adawiya was also revered as the first person to emphasize the central role of divine love in Sufism, and she was known as someone who for a time lived in the wilderness, surrounded by animals who had befriended her because of her vegetarian diet. Her biography is obviously relevant to Majnun's situation, and in the following few lines Nezami draws an implicit parallel between his protagonist and Rabe'eh by describing Majnun's life in the wilderness, his vegetarianism, and his retinue of friendly animals. The implication of the parallel is that Majnun is, in some sense, a male Rabe'eh, concerned with love as it was seen by Sufis like her, as much as with carnal love.

98. *And as their own King Solomon they crowned him:* In Islamic lore Solomon was able to converse with animals (ants and birds are mentioned specifically), and they had a special affection for him.

99. *A gift of foodstuffs for devotion's sake:* Because of the peace he has established among his animal companions, Majnun is seen by passers-by as a saint to whom it is appropriate to make charitable offerings.

100. *Beneath the sky's six vaults:* The universe is conceived of as in the Ptolemaic system, with spheres or vaults nesting inside one another like Russian dolls, at the center of which lies the earth.

101. *You'd say . . . missiles strike:* This couplet and the ten that follow it use the description of the night sky to praise the king who commissioned Nezami to write the poem, Shirvanshah Akhsetan I (r. 1160–97). (For more on this, see the Introduction, pp. xv–xvi).

102. *As pale as Joseph hidden in his well:* See note 67.

103. *the breeze / Was like the breath of Jesus in the trees:* See note 77.

104. *A dragon's jaws:* a metaphor for bad luck.

105. *I saw that serpent, and I fear a rope:* proverbial. The origin seems to be the Buddhist story of a monk who sees a rope and recoils in fear, thinking it is a snake. In a later version the person involved had previously been bitten by a snake, which is why he quickly assumes that anything resembling a snake is in fact a snake—a case of "Once bitten, twice shy."

106. *that bowl / That shows the world as an enchanted whole:* a mythical bowl or goblet mentioned in the *Shahnameh*, originally belonging to King Jamshid, in which the whole world and all that was happening in it could be seen. See also note 80.

107. *Her eyebrows met:* Eyebrows that met in the middle were considered especially attractive.

108. *as though / The sun were flooded with the moonlight's glow:* The sun is Layli's face, the moonlight's glow her tears.

109. *Dressed in dark blue:* the color worn in mourning (see note 93).

110. *O stream of Khezr:* Khezr is a figure from pre-Islamic Middle Eastern mythology whom Qor'anic commentators identified with a companion of Moses mentioned in the Qor'an. His name means "the green man" and his "stream" is the water of eternal life. From being a fertility figure associated with flowing water, in the Islamic world he became associated with Sufism and arcane mystical knowledge, as well as being a secret helper of those in distress. Some scholars have linked him to Utnapishtim in *The Epic of Gilgamesh*.

111. *The sacred water that Khezr guards for me:* See previous note.

112. *This inn:* that is, the world.

113. *I bear your burdens, toiling in despair—/ Whose is the earring that you humbly wear:* that is, "I am your slave; whose slave are you?" (for an earring as a mark of slavery, see note 18).

114. *You are a pearl dropped in a glass of wine:* A pearl dissolved in wine was said to have medicinal properties (although it is apparently very difficult to dissolve a pearl in wine). Nezami probably has Majnun use the phrase to describe Layli because of a metaphorical meaning for a pearl (a virgin) and another for wine (the pleasure associated with love making).

115. *You are a treasure . . . guarded by a snake:* Treasures were proverbially guarded by snakes (or dragons). The motif is common in Indo-European epic narratives; for instance in the Icelandic *Volsunga Saga* a treasure of gold is guarded by the dragon Fafnir.

116. *Eram's garden:* See note 54.

117. *Tell me the pale moon will break free at last / From the fell dragon that has held her fast:* For the moon and the dragon, see note 78. Layli is the moon and her husband the dragon.

118. *the treasure's guardian snake:* See note 115.

119. *guarded by / Your dragon will, your untouched treasures lie:* a metaphorical example of the topos of the dragon or snake guarding a treasure (see note 115).

120. *this fine young man:* Ebn Salam, Layli's husband.

121. *apple chin:* The comparison of a pretty chin to an apple is relatively common in Persian love poetry.

122. *Apologized for their poor quality:* It is still customary in Persian culture to apologize for the poor quality of a gift.

123. *A Tale:* It's clear from Majnun's reaction that this tale is told by Salim, although Nezami does not actually say that it is.

124. *My face is black:* that is, "I am ashamed."

125. *He would not leave the jewel without the mine:* The jewel is Majnun, the mine is his mother. The paradox of bringing the mine to the jewel is deliberate, as this kind of reversal of a metaphor's implications (one would expect the thing that had been contained to be brought to the container,

rather than vice versa, and how does one "bring" a mine anywhere?) is particularly valued by the more rhetorically elaborate writers of Persian poetry.

126. *The red rose had turned yellow, rust had shrouded / The mirror's brightness now grown dim and clouded*: that is, Majnun looked ill (for "yellow" see note 12); the metaphor is of a metal mirror tarnished by rust—a frequently used Sufi metaphor for the state of an unenlightened soul, though here the primary meaning is physical, that is, his body was in a dreadful state.

127. *My soul is like a trapped bird*: a common Sufi simile.

128. *those four elements*: earth, air, fire, and water.

129. *Like rosewater their tears revived Majnun*: Rosewater was used as a kind of smelling salts to revive those who had fainted.

130. *Mount Qaf*: a legendary mountain of fabulous height, sometimes identified with the Caucasus mountain range.

131. *like Khezr, a man both wise and holy*: See note 110. Khezr's association with Sufism seems relevant here, as he was said to appear to would-be Sufis who had no available teacher in order to instruct and lead them.

132. *Joseph in his well*: See note 67.

133. *Drink from your source like Khezr, like Alexander / Traverse love's world and be its sole commander*: For Khezr, see note 110. Alexander is Alexander the Great, the Macedonian king who conquered Iran in 334 BCE. Again there is a Sufi implication, as Alexander was seen in Islamic lore as a kind of proto-Sufi who traveled the world for spiritual enlightenment as much as for conquest (see also the Introduction, p. xx) and met Khezr during his travels.

134. *feeling he'd found / Life-giving water welling from the ground*: Again, the old man is being implicitly compared to Khezr (see note 110).

135. *I claim it's Rakhsh I ride upon*: the marvelous horse owned by the hero Rostam in the *Shahnameh*.

136. *heals me in the way that mummia heals:* Mummia is a medicinal substance—originally a kind of bituminous pitch, and later supposedly made from the flesh of mummified bodies—referred to in both European and Asian medieval texts.

137. *And like a harp:* that is, a small medieval harp that could be held on the knee.

138. *I grasp your apple chin:* See note 121.

139. *You are my qebleh:* A qebleh is the niche in a mosque that shows the direction of the ka'bah (see note 28) in Mecca and toward which Moslems pray.

140. *Only my friend exists—all else is gone:* Because God is often referred to by Sufis as "the friend," Majnun's utterances about Layli often sound like Sufi references to God, and this seems to be intentional on Nezami's part, especially toward the end of his poem.

141. *I place one step beyond both worlds:* that is, this world and the world to come. The "wise philosopher" is explicitly recommending divine love as greater than either earth or heaven, and as preferable to earthly love, which is gone in a moment.

142. *Taraz:* a town in what is now Kazakhstan that was famous for the beauty of its women.

143. *Her mouth was tiny as an ant, and where / Her waist was seemed as narrow as a hair:* In medieval Persian poetry (as also in some medieval European poetry), a very small mouth was considered beautiful, as was an exceptionally slim waist.

144. *Her chin was like an apple that's more green / Than any senna Mecca's ever seen:* The medicinal herb senna when grown in Mecca was said to be the most effective. The metaphor plays with two meanings of "green," one literal (for the herb), one metaphorical (for Zaynab's chin, as a descriptor of which it means "fresh, young, charming"). For the chin as an apple, see note 121.

145. *How this unrivaled ruby could be mined:* that is, how she could be separated from her family so that he could have access to her.

146. *Like one whose earring marks him as a slave:* See note 18.

147. *This village:* that is, the world.

148. *this ruined place:* that is, the world.

149. *I leave this grave by going to my grave:* "this grave" is the world, which Majnun says he leaves by dying; the line implies that by dying to the (physical) world he lives spiritually.

150. *A treasure with a serpent coiled around her:* for the treasure–serpent topos, see note 115; here the treasure is Layli and the serpent is her husband.

151. *Confined within the dragon's slavering lips:* See note 78.

152. *An earthquake . . . buried him beneath the rubble:* a metaphor for the ravages of Ebn Salam's last illness.

153. *All of the world . . . Is a fire-temple:* The world is compared to a Zoroastrian temple where a flame, which here represents man's suffering, burns perpetually.

154. *the sevens skies:* the seven heavens of the Ptolemaic system (elsewhere Nezami mentions six heavens; see note 100).

155. *the rust / Staining the mirror of their mutual trust:* For the mirror and rust topos, see note 126.

156. *Blessed by these added years the heavens give:* See note 30.

157. *When jewelry . . . as the Pleiades:* Nezami uses "pearl" metaphorically in three ways within four lines: in line one it means "stars," in line three "virgin," and in line four "tears." For more on Nezami's use of metaphor, see the Introduction, pp. xxvii–xxx.

158. *And if . . . the dawn has come:* one of the poem's few touches of humor; Layli is querying why she hasn't yet heard any of the three usual sounds of morning—a rooster's crowing, the local cleric's (mu'ezzin's) call to prayer, or the drum that was beaten to announce the dawn.

159. *that torch whose blazing fire*: that is, Majnun.

160. *Beyond the seven heavens of the world*: See note 154.

161. *As grass before a box tree*: See note 51.

162. *One goblet held the wine that neither drank*: The metaphor implies that they did not sleep with each other, and their "drunkenness" as mentioned in the next line is from their proximity to each other and the other-worldliness of their love.

163. *A single circle*: a symbol of perfection.

164. *Eram's garden*: See note 54.

165. *burning rue*: See note 19.

166. *That you should seal your jewel-case up like this*: alluding to the metaphor that the mouth is a jewel-case containing pearls (teeth).

167. *cold and sallow . . . golden yellow*: See note 12.

168. *As if Zahhak's snakes writhed across the grass*: see note 60.

169. *Magian wine*: that is, Zoroastrian wine. Since Moslems were not supposed to be involved in wine-making, this was often undertaken by members of minorities, including Zoroastrians. The pre-Islamic religion of Iran had been Zoroastrianism, and its rituals involved wine-drinking, which reinforced the association of Zoroastrianism with wine once Islam became the dominant religion in Iran.

170. *The full moon was the new moon, hardly there, / The cypress like a mirage in the air*: Nezami uses the traditional images for a beautiful face (the full moon) and a beautiful body (a cypress tree), but with a difference; the full moon has become as thin as a crescent moon, the cypress as insubstantial as a mirage, and both images indicate that Layli is physically wasting away.

171. *the pheasant had departed*: that is, her beauty was gone. For the pheasant as a metaphor for beauty, see note 44.

172. *that poor yellow flower*: For yellow as a color that indicates sickness (and here death), see note 12.

173. *To start her journey to another place:* "Another place" is a relatively common locution for death in medieval Persian narrative poetry.

174. *the shadow that he'd brought:* that is, the news of Layli's death.

175. *And on the grave itself he was the snake / That writhed there for the hidden treasure's sake:* See note 115.

176. *the wizened king that rules the world:* Fate, and here perhaps death.

177. *There's sure to be a snake to guard and hide it:* See note 115.

178. *this ruin . . . in the gardens of / Eram:* "this ruin" is the world; for Eram, see note 54.

179. *"O friend . . .":* Majnun's last words are ambiguous; the obvious meaning is that he is referring to Layli, but "the friend" is a common Sufi name for God, and the phrase could also be read as meaning "O God . . ."

180. *this flooded house:* that is, the world.

181. *This seven-headed dragon:* that is, the world.

182. *Cooing what seemed a Zoroastrian prayer:* that is, the doves' cooing was like a low murmur, as in Zoroastrian prayer (see note 31).

183. *Poured offerings on them intermittently:* as was traditionally done for a king at his coronation, or to welcome him to a town; the offerings could be petals, coins, or jewels, or anything small and valuable.

184. *Eram's garden:* See note 54.

185. *And she belongs to night:* See note 9.

THE MIRROR OF MY HEART

Translated with an Introduction and Notes by
Dick Davis

The Mirror of My Heart is a unique and captivating collection of eighty-three Persian women poets, many of whom wrote anonymously or were punished for their outspokenness. Touching on such universal topics as marriage, children, political climate, death, and emancipation, the collection reveals striking similarities to our lives today.

SHAHNAMEH

Abolqasem Ferdowsi

Translated by Dick Davis
Foreword by Azar Nafisi

This prodigious narrative tells the story of pre-Islamic Iran, beginning in the mythic time of creation and continuing forward to the Arab invasion in the seventh century. One of the greatest translators of Persian poetry, Dick Davis presents Ferdowsi's masterpiece in an elegant combination of prose and verse.

ROSTAM

Abolqasem Ferdowsi

Translated with an Introduction by Dick Davis

No understanding of world mythology is complete without *Rostam*, Iran's most celebrated mythological hero. This titan of magnificent strength bestrode Persia for five hundred years and owed allegiance only to his nation's greater good. Anyone interested in folklore, world literature, or Iranian culture will find *Rostam* both a rousing and an illuminating read.

FACES OF LOVE

Hafez, Jahan Khatun, Obayd-e Zakani

Translated by Dick Davis

Together, Hafez, a giant of world literature; Jahan Khatun, an eloquent princess; and Obayd-e Zakani, a dissolute satirist, represent one of the most remarkable literary flowerings of any era. Acclaimed translator Dick Davis breathes new life into the timeless works of these three masters of 14th-century Persian literature.

VIS AND RAMIN

Fakhraddin Gorgani

Translated with an Introduction by Dick Davis

Against a background of court intrigue and conflict, Vis finds herself escorted to her future husband, King Mobad, by his brother, Ramin, who falls in love with her and jeopardizes their fates. Considered the first Persian romance and the inspiration for *Tristan and Isolde*, this masterpiece is a timeless story of forbidden and dangerous love.

THE CONFERENCE OF THE BIRDS

Farid Attar

Translated by Afkham Darbandi and Dick Davis
Introduction by Dick Davis

Composed in the twelfth century, Farid Attar's great mystical poem describes the pilgrimage of the world's birds in search of their ideal king, the Simorgh bird. The most significant of all works of Persian literature, this masterly translation preserves the poem's rhymed couplet form and nuances of language.

PENGUIN CLASSICS